A FATED BOND

A FATED BOND

CHRONICLES OF AN URBAN DRUID™ BOOK 9

AUBURN TEMPEST

MICHAEL ANDERLE

DISRUPTIVE IMAGINATION

LMBPN Publishing
PMB 196, 2540 South Maryland Pkwy
Las Vegas, NV 89109

Version 1.01, December 2021
eBook ISBN: 978-1-64971-913-3
Print ISBN: 978-1-64971-914-0

THE A FATED BOND TEAM

Thanks to our JIT Team:

Dave Hicks
Rachel Beckford
Deb Mader
Dr. James Caplan
Diane L. Smith
Micky Cocker
John Ashmore
Paul Westman
Dorothy Lloyd
Larry Omans
Kelly O'Donnell

Editor
SkyHunter Editing Team

CHAPTER ONE

You are invited.
Clan Cumhaill, et al.
Housewarming party at Dionysus' new abode
Place: 11th floor of Nikky's Acropolis building
Date: Tonight - Dinner and drinks served
Attire: Clothing optional
Gifts: Greatly anticipated

I run a finger over the gold leaf lettering as I come in from the mailbox. Dumping the flyers and junk mail straight into the recycle box by the back door, I toe off my shoes and hang my jacket on my hook.

Male voices in the front of the house draw me toward the open concept kitchen and living room, and I smile up at the four guys I live with: my brothers, Calum and Emmet, Calum's fiancé, Kevin, and my partner of heart and adventure, Sloan.

"What have ye there, *a ghra?*" Sloan asks.

I hand him the invitation and grin. "Dionysus is joining the local scene and planting roots. He's having a housewarming party tonight, and we're all invited."

"Hells yeah we are." Emmet hustles over to look at the invitation and chuckles. "Clothing optional. You gotta love that guy."

Heaven help me, but I do. I absolutely adore him.

Sloan finishes reading the black, velvety invitation and passes it to Kevin and Calum at the breakfast bar. "Aye, there's somethin' to be said about people who live authentic lives. They put themselves out fer all to see and couldn't care less about what other people think."

I reach up to the top of the fridge to grab my cereal box. "He's one of a kind."

"Thank Zeus for that," Sloan says. "I don't know that the world could handle two of him."

Calum reads over the deets and frowns. "Gifts greatly anticipated. Shit. What do we get for the God of Wine and Ecstasy? Think fast because the party is tonight."

I check the microwave and frown at the time. "We have just over eight hours to figure that out."

Kevin grins. "I have an idea, but I'll need Nikon to make it happen."

"Oh? And what is that?" Calum asks.

Kevin cups his mouth and whispers into Calum's ear. My brother bursts out laughing and nods. "Yep. That's the one. Text Nikon and see if he has time to take you. I'd love to join the shopping spree, but I've gotta roll. I'm on duty at nine."

I grab a bowl and spoon from the cupboard and stand at the breakfast bar. "Are you two going to share your great idea?"

"Nope." Kevin takes out his phone and starts texting. "This one's all ours."

Calum finishes his coffee, takes his mug to the sink, and strides over to where he secures his sidearm in the small lockbox on the hallway wall.

Once he punches in the code, he retrieves his Glock and an extra magazine. "Duty calls, family. Laters."

"Safe home, bro," Emmet calls out. "Watch your six out there."

"Always. Text me if anything exciting happens."

"Promise."

"Wait!" Kevin jumps off his stool. "Fi? Can you do your thing please?"

Calum frowns. "Kev, I'm fine. I gotta book it or I'll be late."

"Please. It only takes a second. I feel better when we do the protection thingy."

I grab the container of sea salt out of the cupboard and wave at Sloan and Emmet to get up too. "We might as well all do it. Come on. It gives Kevin peace of mind, and you never can tell what's coming down the pipe."

Calum frowns. "I've been on the job for four years. I don't know why you're so nervous now."

Kevin blows me a kiss and tugs Calum into an open spot on the hardwood floor. "Because now it's not only bad guys out there stirring up trouble, there are dark wizards and vampires and zombie chihuahuas."

Emmet makes a wide-eyed face. "Have we come across zombie chihuahuas?"

Sloan chuckles. "Not yet, but knowin' yer sister and the magnet of mayhem branded on her back, I wouldn't discount the possibility entirely."

I shake the salt container and pour a quick circle on the floor, then set it on the counter. "All right, everyone in and assume the position."

Calum snorts. "Now you're getting weird. Ew. You're my sister."

I roll my eyes and hold out my hand. "Not that position. It's you who's weird, smartass."

"Better than a dumbass," he says.

"Or a pain in the ass," Emmet adds.

The five of us settle, and I stretch out my neck. After a deep breath, I release my intention to the world and recite the spell.

Earth to Sky and Land to Sea,

The power of nature protects me.
Keep my mind alert in work and play,
Keep my spirit free and danger at bay.
Mother Goddess and Fae Powers
Protect me in the coming hours.

When I finish, Kevin exhales and steps out of the circle. "Thanks, Fi."

"Anytime, sweetie."

Calum kisses my cheek and moves to his fiancé. "Now I *really* have to hustle. Go shopping with Nikon and try not to worry. I love you, big time."

"Love you too."

When the door clicks shut, I grab the broom and head toward the path of the granule ring left behind.

Kevin confiscates the broom. "I've got this. My idea. My mess. You've got to get rolling too. Aren't you expected at the bookstore?"

I check the time, kiss Sloan goodbye, and put the cereal box back onto the fridge unopened. Tim Horton's drive-thru it is. "Yeah, and I want to drop in and chat with Dora this afternoon. If the day goes my way, I'll swing by STOA after that and check in."

Sloan wraps his arm around the small of my back and keeps me from zipping off. Slowing me down, he claims my mouth in a proper kiss goodbye.

When he eases back, a smug smile warms his impossibly handsome face. "If I think of the perfect gift fer Dionysus, I'll text ye. Otherwise, I'll be there, tinkerin' with my treasures."

"Fair enough. Have a great one, hotness."

"You too. Give Myra my best."

Fifteen minutes later, I pull out of the Queen Street traffic, park along the curb, and turn off the engine to my SUV. Myra's Mystic

Emporium is visible from the street, but only for the empowered members of Toronto's citizens, and only if they have needs to be fulfilled by visiting the magical bookstore.

After grabbing my take-out tray off the passenger's seat, I lock things up and head toward the line of storefronts. The brass bell chimes over my head as I enter and—

I screech as a book comes flying at my head.

"Don't let him out!"

I wave a hand to block the escaping tome and turn to grab the door handle to make sure it shuts tight behind me. The disgruntled hardcover swoops, cracking me in the back of the head before flying up to the painted beams near the ceiling to sulk.

Rubbing the point of contact, I stride down the main aisle toward where Myra is finishing with a client at the cash register.

"Mr. Simchas," I say, recognizing the tightly wound little man gathering his purchases. A personal aide to some wealthy and empowered man in the city, Mr. Simchas is always well dressed and never has a hair out of place. Except for today.

It looks like he went a round with the disgruntled book too. Good.

I hope his goose egg is bigger than mine.

I used to think the man was a sweet old guy with questionably macabre tastes in literature. Then Liam and I were kidnapped by vampire thugs, and I found out firsthand that he's a spineless douche-canoe who panders to the whims of a psychopath.

I never met the man, but his boss tried to have Myra kidnapped and ended up with me and my bestie as a consolation prize.

When he learned of the switch and realized I was useless in getting him the book he wanted, he threw us away, and the hobgoblins took their shot at us...literally.

Fool me once; shame on you. Get my bestie shot, and you're a stinky smear on the bottom of my shoe forever.

"You look a little ruffled today, Mr. Simchas. Having troubles navigating shit's creek? Did the virgin escape before the sacrifice? Are you in need of someone's intestines to tie your boss's loose ends?"

He turns a cool eye on me. "Ms. Cumhaill, always a pleasure."

"Except when getting sold to hobgoblins and shot at. There ends the pleasure."

He lifts his bag and turns for the door. "I'm sure I don't know what you're referring to."

I snort. "I'm sure you do."

Myra widens her cat's eyes at me and grins. "I'll walk you out, Mattius."

While they make small talk on the way to the door, I pull my fruit explosion muffin out of the bag and prop my ass on my stool.

Myra makes it quick at the door—likely to keep the book from mounting another attack—and is back in a flash. "Well, you're in a mood." She joins me, pointing at the two cardboard teacups in the carrier. "Is one of these for me?"

"Yep. Either. They're both the same."

Myra takes one of the peppermint teas out of the drink carrier and removes the plastic lid to pour it into her mug. "Mattius Simchas is a very good customer and has been for over a century. I realize you dislike him, but perhaps you could tone it down a bit. He spends a lot of money here."

"Sorry. I get hangry when I meet up with past kidnappers on an empty stomach."

Myra arches a brow and blows across the top of her tea. "We can't prove he was involved in my kidnapping or yours, so I choose to take the 'keep friends close and enemies closer' approach with him."

"You do that. I'll take the 'if you fuck with me, I'll shove Birga so far up your ass you'll be a unicorn' approach."

Myra laughs and chokes on her tea. "Eat your muffin. You *are* cranky today."

I rip the top off my breakfast and try not to let that beady-eyed little fucker ruin my morning. "Speaking of unicorns, how is Contessa McSparkles these days?"

Myra grins. "She's learning to dance."

"A dancing unicorn. Fun. Is Imari teaching her?"

"Oh, no. Garnet hired a dressage trainer and flew him in from Germany. He is legitimately having our daughter's unicorn taught how to dance."

I bend forward, laughing. "That's awesome. Let me know when it's time for her first recital. I'm so there."

Myra sips her tea, her gaze locked on the hardcover attacking text perched up near the ceiling.

"What's with the berserker book?" I ask. "Has it lost its mate or something?"

My blue suede spellbook, Beauty, fell in love with Sloan's brown leather spellbook and the two have been a match made in Myra's hutch drawer ever since.

Myra shakes her head. "He has no mate that I know of. He just started acting up a couple of days ago. Today he's downright aggressive."

"I noticed." I run my fingers over the back of my head. "He cracked me a good one."

"Not as good as he got Simchas. The text took a definite disliking to that man."

"Smart book." I sip my tea and let the sugary warmth of my breakfast wash away my disdain for the beady-eyed little creep. "That's why he looked like he just had a wild wall-banger in the coatroom?"

Myra busts up laughing. "I don't suppose Simchas is the wild wall-banger kind, but yes. He got dive-bombed quite spectacularly."

"And you have no idea why Mr. Book is suddenly so annoyed?"

"None."

"Have you tried asking him?"

"I have, yes, but either he's not interested in telling me, or I don't speak his language."

Huh. "As a Fae Historian of the written word, I find that hard to believe."

"And yet, here we are…and there he is."

I think about that while I dig into the second half of my muffin, then I give it a try. "Hello? Angry book? Why don't you come down here and tell us what's wrong? We'd like to help."

When nothing happens, I shrug. "I'm out of ideas."

Myra giggles. "Well, thanks for the effort. I asked Dora to come by. She's going to have a go at it."

"Noice. I haven't seen her for a few weeks. Not since she located Emmet and Ciara for us in the South Pacific."

Myra's eyes widen. "So, how is that going? Are they still hot and heavy?"

I swallow another bite of fruity goodness and sigh. "Honestly, it's more than a little weird. My brother had this Dionysus-induced sexploitation with Sloan's ex-lover, and the two of them are acting like the experience bound them as fated mates or something."

"So, they're long-distance dating?"

"Dating? They've skipped the dating part of things. It's like they're married, bought the house, and are building their life together. It's crazy."

"Crazy in your perspective." Myra sobers. "There are many fae races where mates recognize one another on sight. Shifters can be scent-struck, and their animal sides are locked. Vampires can see colors more brightly and taste the spice of a mating bond in their mate's blood. Elves can meet the gaze of a stranger, and their soul name can unlock in their minds. If you believe in magic, you can't discount a fated bond simply because it's happening to your brother."

"Yeah no, I don't think that's what's happening. They were

spell-induced and got carried away. They are nothing alike. He's a fun-loving, sweet goofball who buys takeout and sits with homeless people for hours shooting the shit. She's a rude, haughty, snood who thinks herself above the rest. The two of them as star-struck soul mates is crazy. Don't you think?"

Myra lifts her chin and meets my gaze. "It's not my place to form an opinion. I don't belong in their love affair any more than they belong in mine."

I get the not-so-subtle hint and eat my muffin. "Okay. Consider me told. I'll butt out and keep my concerns to myself. I tend to be a little protective when it comes to my family and friends."

Myra laughs and strikes off toward where the rabid book is hiding up in the mechanics of the exposed ceiling. "You don't say. I hadn't noticed."

CHAPTER TWO

Dora joins us after she's tended to the lunch rush at her soup kitchen and brings a selection of wrapped sandwiches and cookies for dessert. The three of us share a lovely meal and get caught up on all the things girlfriends miss when busy lives take over.

"I spoke to Davin and Darcy last night, and your name came up." Dora taps a sparkly purple nail in front of me. "They are concerned, girlfriend."

I blink and finish chewing. "I'm sorry, who are Davin and Darcy? And concerned about what?"

"Davin and Darcy Perry?" she clarifies. "The young men you encouraged me to train in dragon care."

I laugh and sip my ginger ale. "Right, the twins. I don't know what it is about those two. I can never remember their names. What are they concerned about? Don't tell me Dart's being difficult again."

She brushes back a curl of her purple wig and sits back in her chair. Dora is tall and broad-shouldered, and whether she's decked herself out in glitz and glam or is in a conservative fuchsia blouse and navy slacks like today, the power of her presence sucks the air out of the room.

You can't hide amazing.

"The boys asked me about the dangers of a dragon's fated bond. It seems you're running out of time. Young Dartamont is exhibiting all the aggressive tendencies of a dragonborn denied his complement. He's getting snappy with his siblings and baying at all hours. Apparently, even the Dragon Queen is losing patience with him.

The news hurts my heart. "My plans are underway. Wallace is coming this weekend to help with the expansion of the grove. We'll make a place for Dart there and bring him over early next week."

Dora frowns. "And what else?"

"What do you mean?"

"You plan to make him a spot to nest in the grove but what about a place to train and fly and practice his magic? Where are you thinking of sourcing him out fresh meat? There's a great deal more to bringing a dragon into your life than where he sleeps."

The slightly pitchy tone to Dora's deep voice doesn't bode well. I guess I hadn't thought about it thoroughly enough. I'll need to do more and get my ass in gear. "All right. Help me make a list, and I'll expand my thinking. I have a dinner party tonight. Then I'll spend the whole weekend working on it."

Dora brushes cookie crumbs off her fingers and glances at Myra. "Do you have the *Sheatzo Guide of Dragons?*"

Myra nods. "Second floor at the back. There's a section on care of mythicals in general and a few good books on dragons specifically. I started sourcing them out and stocking them when Fi told me twenty-three dragonborn hatched in Ireland."

Dora stands. "Good thinking. Eventually, some of them will end up in North America. Ireland's not big enough to support that many as they grow into adulthood. Come along, girlfriend. There is much for you to learn in a very short amount of time."

I get up and follow without question. When someone of Dora's power and expertise offers to school you on something, anyone with half a brain nods and smiles.

I have at least half a brain.

"Cooleroo. Mold me. Shape me. Show me how woefully inadequate I am."

Dora snorts. "Dramatic. I love it."

Dora and I spend the next two hours combing through texts and reading ancient tomes. Some of them, Dora says, are shite. Others she stacks in a pile for me to purchase and study. Well, mostly it will be Sloan who studies and me who asks for the highlight version.

I like reading as much as any other normal person, which means a sexy romance novel on a winter's night or a menu at dinner.

TTGFS—Thank the Goddess for Sloan.

"Hey, Dora, can I ask you something?"

She lifts her gaze from scanning through a hugely heavy book. "Sure, cookie. What is it?"

"Dionysus is having a housewarming party tonight, and I'm stuck on what to give him. What do you get an immortal Greek god with virtually unlimited powers?"

"Something he can't get himself."

I close the book in my lap and set it onto the take-home pile. Good gravy, even with my staff discount, this collection of books will cost a fortune. It's a good thing Garnet pays me a fortune to represent as the Guild Governor of Toronto Druids.

Thinking about Dora's answer to my gifting issue, I consider what Dionysus can't get himself. "Give me a hint. If you were having us over and made a point to mention presents, what would you be fishing for?"

Dora winks at me. "Let me answer your question by asking you another."

"If you think that will help."

She chuckles. "It's better than simply giving you the answer —trust me."

"Always."

She winks a gold-glittered eye at me and smiles. "Why do you think, of all the places in the world, and in all the times in the past, present, and future, Dionysus chose to move to Toronto now?"

I think past my kneejerk answers and give that careful consideration. "He finds us entertaining and enjoys Nikon's company. They talk a lot about the good ole days of ancient Greece."

"Do you think Dionysus does that for himself? As a god, he can be back in those times with a mere thought. If he's nostalgic, why not just zip back?"

At first, I don't have an answer. Then I remember what Nikon said about Dionysus's childhood. He was hidden from the world to keep him safe from Hera and then tormented, ridiculed, and outcast by his peers in the pantheon for being only a half-god.

His father is Zeus, so even his half-god status still holds more magical mojo than most full-gods.

So, if his childhood sucked ass, why spend so much time with Nikon chatting about it?

Why did he choose Toronto? What is it he—

"Ohhhh, I understand. He never had a family or friends who loved him before he became who he became. We're more than an amusement. *We* are what he seeks."

Dora nods. "Clan Cumhaill is a mighty example of what unconditional love and support can accomplish. I would guess that him including you in his life is his hope to be included in yours."

I make fireworks fingers beside my head with both hands. "Mind blown. Damn, Dora. Wisdom of the ages. Thanks."

She winks and shrugs. "Or I could be completely off base, and he wants a Chia-pet. What do I know of mice and men?"

I'm still mulling that over when my phone rings and the Lion King song announces Garnet's call. "Hello, boss man. How's things at the top of the food chain?"

"Good morning, Lady Druid. About as much fun as usual... which is to say, not at all." The growl in Garnet's voice is unmistakable, and for once, I don't think he's directing it toward me.

"Trouble?"

"I need you at a crime scene. I'm texting you the location now."

"All right. How quickly? I drove, but if you need me to portal?"

"Where are you now?"

"At the emporium."

"I'm sending Anyx."

I hang up and stand, gathering the stack of books Dora and I have amassed. "Gotta run. There's trouble, right here in River City. The Grand Governor has growled for me."

Dora chuckles and helps me carry the books to the cash desk. "As far as autocratic leaders go, Garnet is a gem. He may be brusque and brutal, but he genuinely cares for his people."

I set the stack of books on the desk and head back to grab my jacket out of the little staff area in the back. "Myra, can you ring me out? Your hubby has beckoned and is sending—" I jog back, and Garnet has Myra bent backward over his arm claiming her kiss— "Never mind. He's here."

When he straightens, Myra looks at me with flushed cheeks. "Well, that was a lovely good morning."

I hold out my arms and pucker up. "Where's mine? Is that how we're rolling these days?"

Garnet arches an ebony brow at me and tilts his head toward

his second in command. "Not touching that one. Maybe Anyx is game."

In my mind, I liken the two of them to Scar and Mufasa from *The Lion King*. Garnet has the dark, ebony mane of his lion form and Anyx is all golden hair and eyes like his.

I used to think Garnet was incredibly dark and intimidating. Not anymore.

Don't get me wrong. The guy is ruthless and lethal. Part of him is more predator than human, but I don't fear for myself or those around me anymore. Now that we're part of the "in crowd" s'all good.

Still, I like to poke the lion's paw now and then, just to keep things interesting.

"I better pass," Anyx says, steel-faced. "Zuzanna has been known to gut females for less."

"Ooo, I respect a possessive female. She must really lurve you, puss."

He frowns, a growl rolling like thunder in the air. "I thought we discussed you calling me that."

He's all hiss and no bite. My shield isn't even a little warm and tingly. "Yep. Sorry. It slipped out. Now, if Garnet has finished macking on Myra should we go?"

Garnet grunts. "I wasn't macking on Myra. I was called out of bed early this morning on yet another matter of consequence and didn't have the opportunity to wish my mate a good day."

Dora chuckles. "I wish I had a guy that wished me a good day like that."

"Right?" I waggle my brows at Dora, and the three of us girls laugh.

Garnet and Anyx, however, do not. Garnet is waiting. "Are you finished?"

Fine. Grown-up time. I sober and straighten. "All right, sorry. What's up?"

"You mentioned you have your SUV and I'm not sure how

long this will take. Anyx will drive your truck home and join us at the crime scene or Guild Headquarters later."

"Guild Headquarters? Why do I get the feeling this is more than a standard crime scene?"

Garnet gives me a tight grin. "Because you're an incredibly intuitive female. Now, if you're ready?"

I sling my purse over my head and take out my credit card. After placing the card into the hand machine and a charge slip over the top, I drag the press across the digits and back. "Ring me up for these books and Anyx can leave them in the truck for me for later. As Dora says, I have a lot to learn and little time to do it."

Myra rolls her amazing cat-slit eyes and waves that away. "You're a natural. Dart is in good hands."

I appreciate the compliment, but Dora doesn't look convinced, so I give her the benefit of the doubt and keep my self-confidence low. Holding out my hand, I turn to Garnet and smile. "One disaster at a time. First murder and mayhem, then chaos and calamity."

Garnet chuckles, his deep voice a rumble in my chest. "As long as you've got things prioritized."

Garnet flashes me to a large wooded area surrounded by buildings in the distance on all sides. As the magic of his glamor dissolves, I survey the land. The architecture beyond the parkland is both centuries-old as well as modern. There are buildings as small as Victorian houses and as large as stone castles of old. Lifting my gaze and turning to orient myself, I find the bulb and spire of the CN Tower due south.

"We're on the U of T campus."

"You got it in one," Garnet says. "This way. Oh, and prepare yourself. It's a bit grisly."

I check my current state of digestion and am pleased to find my roast beef and Swiss secure and settled. Let's hope it stays that way.

Garnet places a gentle hand against the small of my back and leads me past a bronze statue of a guy on horseback. He's perched on an oval base, and I read the plaque as we walk by. "King Edward the seventh. He's been up there riding that horse since 1919. Good for him."

Garnet smiles indulgently at me and points at a spot where the air is shimmering with the wavy mirage of a hastily set glamor. "We haven't moved the body, so tell me what you see. I always appreciate your insights."

I snort. "Your pants are on fire, Lion King."

He rolls his stunning amethyst eyes. "I may not appreciate what your insights are, but I always appreciate the fact that they are unique and unfiltered."

I can live with that.

We walk together through the magical veil keeping whatever happened here out of human mainstream and—

"Holy crapamoly. Yikers, would you look at that." I shuffle closer to the body and bend to get a closer look. "It's like something out of a horror movie."

"And here I worried you'd be squeamish."

I look at the iridescent campus club stamp on his hand and frown. "It is upsetting. Last night he was partying his way through student life at one of the top twenty universities in the world, and today he's been gnawed hollow and sucked dry. From a crime scene standpoint, though, it's fascinating. Look how shrively he is."

Garnet looks at the medical examiner from the Guild lab and shrugs. "Like I said, unique and unfiltered."

I snag a stick from the forest floor and lift the flap of his spring jacket to see into his body cavity. "I don't think I'll be eating barbequed ribs for a while. Where are his missing innies?"

"Undetermined."

"And there's next to no blood."

"We noticed that too."

"When I saw the desiccation, my first thought was necromancers and Barghest, but the lack of blood makes me think vampires. What other empowered species feed on blood?"

"Feed? There are several species of monsters referred to as vampires, which in truth, are based solely on them being undead blood-suckers, but that's a stereotype and unfair to true vampires. Aside from empowered creatures like Xavier and his seethe, there are strigoi, chupacabra, succubae, wendigo, baobhan sith, kappa, lamia, some lycanthropes."

"Huh. That many, eh?"

"Then there are the creatures who use blood in spell work or ritual."

"Okay, so I assume you did a sniff test and know what kind of creature it is, and you're testing me?"

He smiles. "Not testing. I want your first impressions. Once I tell you everything, you'll know why. Finish running the scene for me, and I'll tell you what I know."

Before I do anything, I pat the fluttering pressure in my sternum and reach out to Bruin. *Hey, buddy. Do you want to explore the area in spirit mode and see if you come up with anything Garnet and his crime scene team missed?*

Happy to.

I release my bear and study the body again before I look around. "He was coming through here, likely headed to meet a group of buddies for drinks before heading to the Scotia Centre for a Raptors game."

"How'd you get there?"

"Because it's Friday afternoon and the game start times are seven or seven-thirty. No college kid who wears a Sinn Series watch and Brioni jeans would wear a purple poly-mesh basketball jersey unless he's headed to the game. Trust me. I live with a fashion whore. Sloan is a beautiful man and has incredible taste in clothes, but what he spends on clothing could feed a small village."

Garnet nods. "Very, well, I appreciate your logic so far. Carry on."

"So, it wasn't a robbery of anything other than organs and blood. Otherwise, they would've taken the watch and hocked it. That sucker's worth at least four grand."

I check the ground around the scene but don't find anything interesting so I go back to the body.

"His lips are blue. Is that a blood-oxygen thing or something else?" I ask the examiner.

The guy looks at Garnet, and he nods. "Answer her."

"The color isn't his lips. It's on his lips. We believe it's a drug of some sort and have taken a sample. Toxicology will tell us more."

"Well, if he's lucky, the drug had him high enough he didn't realize he was getting eaten alive by an empowered predator."

I can't help but notice that this guy is my age and is likely someone's brother. I can't imagine the horror of losing one of my brothers to something like this. Brendon getting shot was horrible, but he died for a reason. He is forever a hero.

"What will his parents be told?"

"There will be a car accident resulting in catastrophic damage. Closed casket, of course."

I nod. "Mention that he died instantly and didn't suffer. That will help."

"Of course."

"Was there a backpack or anything?"

"Not that we found."

I walk around, studying the ground, my instincts telling me there isn't much more. "Unlucky. Someone caught him off-guard on his way to meet his buddies... maybe someone enhanced with stealth or super speed or maybe someone he recognized from around campus."

"What makes you say that?"

"There's no sign of struggle. His clothes are ruined at the points of attack but not ripped like there was a fight. There are also no defensive wounds. Whatever happened, it happened extremely quickly."

I straighten and step back with him. "The attacker made quick work out of doing whatever this is and likely took off toward Spadina... which, we both know takes us a few blocks north to Casa Loma. If it was a vampire, that is handy and close to home for Xavier's crew. That's all I'm getting—

"Let me out! I'm stuck in your pocket."

"What the fuck is that?" Garnet snaps.

I laugh and retrieve the victim's phone from his jacket. "Emmet had this silly ringtone for a while." I check the screen and glance at Garnet. "Obed is calling. Shall I answer it?"

He nods. "See what you can find out."

"Elliot! Where the hell are you, dude? You're late."

I swallow, my chest tightening up. Between time spent with Da and our Team Trouble liaison, John Maxwell, I'm familiar with procedure and protocols, but this is still going to suck ass.

"Hey, Obed, this is Fiona Cumhaill of the SITFO task force. I'm sorry to inform you, Elliot has been involved in an accident. Where are you now? I need a few moments of your time."

"An accident? Is he okay?"

"No. I'm afraid it's quite serious. Where are you?"

As Obed rattles off the address, I repeat it, and Garnet jots it down.

"My supervisor and I will be there shortly." I hang up and hand Garnet the phone. "Well, that sucked."

"You handled it well."

Anyx joins us. He dangles my keys and hands them over. "Your truck is parked in the lane behind your house. Kevin was home, so I gave him your books rather than leave them in the front seat to be seen and possibly stolen."

"Thanks. That's awesome."

Garnet hands Anyx a wallet and Elliot's phone. "Elliot VanClay. Find the parents and deliver the news. Be sure to mention it was quick, and he didn't suffer. Fiona says that will help."

Anyx nods and is off again. "Lady Druid."

"Laters."

When Anyx flashes out, Garnet shows me a Google map and points across the treed land. "If you don't mind walking, I'll fill you in on what I know en route."

I fall into step, and we stride off. "You're the boss. Bruin? Are you coming?"

I'm here, Red. I'm with ye.

CHAPTER THREE

Garnet and I cross the U of T grounds, which cover an incredible amount of downtown landscape. Over the years, the institution has acquired and built on almost every lot from Spadina to Bay and College to Bloor. That works out to be one hundred and forty-six acres, which houses more than two hundred and ten buildings.

That's just the St. George Campus.

"First of all, I know what you're going to say, and as you told the male on the phone, I *am* your supervisor on two fronts of your life."

"All right." I'm guessing by that intro that I'm not going to like what's coming next.

"While you were in Ireland last month, Andromeda received an anonymous tip about a body found near the varsity stadium of the university."

I crank my head on a swivel and blink up at him. "Last month? Now we have a second body? Is this going to be a serial killer kinda thing?"

"The body found today marks the third student killed, but no, it's not a serial killer."

"The third? In a month? We are solidly in serial killer territory. Why are you saying we're not?"

He lowers his chin. "Because in each of the three cases, we know the killer. What we don't know is why they're killing."

I capture my hair in the breeze and move it out of my face. "If you know who Elliot's killer is, why did you have me work the scene for half an hour?"

"Because there's no logic to it."

"It's the vampires, right? Xavier's family of undead are feeding off-menu, and you're what…making excuses for them?"

The growl of his lion vibrates in my chest. "Not excuses, Lady Druid. Look beyond the killings. Think in broader terms of what's going on here."

"All right. Three victims were drained of blood and gored hollow in some gruesome fashion to eat or harvest their organs. You know who did it…and I'm hoping they are in custody?"

"They are. And according to vampire law, they are to be destroyed."

"That's a bad thing why?"

"Because I've spoken to Xavier. He vouches for the three. We aren't talking about young, newly made vampires who lost control. They are long-term, established members of his seethe."

"What do they say about what happened? I assume you've interrogated them."

He grips my elbow and pulls me to a stop as we come to the end of the greenspace. "They are understandably distraught but can offer no explanation as to why they did it. They say they were simply overcome."

"Why do we think that's anything more than vampires do what vampires do?"

He frowns. "That's very closed-minded. It's your job to investigate not determine guilt."

"But guilt has been established. You have your killers in

custody." I know I'm pissing him off, but I don't understand what's crawled up his ass crack.

Students dead.

Vampire killers caught.

What more does he want?

"How about this," he says, "until I'm satisfied we have a complete understanding of what happened with these killings and why, we continue to look into it."

I drop my gaze and gesture at the pathway. "Then, by all means, let's continue to look into it."

Obed lives on the edge of campus along with seven other students. From the outside, the house reminds me a lot of the house I grew up in. From the inside, even more so. The mishmash of bags and belongings and beer cases is home to me.

I'd bet these guys get into similar hijinks and shenanigans as me and my five brothers always did. And once you add in Liam, Kevin, and their other friends, I doubt college life has anything on us.

"You said an accident," Obed says as he ushers us into the main common area.

There are a bunch of sober faces sitting around the room, all of them looking like someone just nut-punched them hard, all of them wearing the purple and black jerseys of Toronto's basketball team.

"That's right," Garnet says. "A hit-and-run car accident off Wellesley West."

"You said it's bad? What hospital is he in?"

"I'm sorry, son. There's no hospital for you to visit. Your friend didn't survive the accident. He's gone."

The students in the room reel and it sucks the air from my lungs. It hasn't even been a year yet since Gran told me about

Brendan's death. Moments like this bring it all back with gut-wrenching force.

Obed wipes his hands over his face and drops to the arm of one of the couches. "Shit. I had a feeling you were going to say that."

I draw a deep breath. "I'm sorry. I couldn't say so on the phone because we hadn't notified his parents. I'm so sorry for your loss."

"But they know now?" Another guy asks. "El's parents? They've been told?"

Garnet nods. "Yes, son. They are being informed now by a colleague of ours."

"I can't believe this." A blonde girl launches off another couch and rushes from the room, followed by a crying brunette.

Garnet steps aside to let the girls pass. They run up the stairs, and a moment later a door slams shut above our heads. "Did Elliot live here?" Garnet asks.

Obed shakes his head. "No. El's parents rented him a private apartment. They have money and wanted him to be able to leave the partying behind and get sleep and study when he needed to."

"We're going to need the address of that apartment."

Obed's face pinches. "Why? You said it was a hit-and-run. Why do you need to go through his apartment?"

Garnet frowns. "Because we don't know who was driving. Elliot was likely a victim of a random accident, but we wouldn't be doing anyone any favors if we didn't look into every possibility of what happened."

That bit was not-so-subtly aimed at me.

I notice the back of Obed's hand. "Elliot had the same stamp. Were you guys out last night?"

Obed nods. "Yeah, me, Elliot, Stoner, Duncan, Bryant, and Chris."

He points at a couple of the guys in the room when he says their name and looks at his hand. "I can't believe this."

I swallow. "I know. It won't sink in for a long while either. It's good that you're all close. That will help."

"On the off chance that it wasn't a random accident," Garnet says. "Can you think of anyone who might want to harm Elliot?"

Obed frowns and looks at the others.

Cue the shaking heads around the room. "Elliot was a solid guy. Funny as fuck. Smart. He knew when to have fun and when to dial it back."

Xavier's seethe is known to be made up of criminals and thugs. I wonder if maybe Garnet's right and the murders are about something else other than vampires not being able to control themselves.

"What about drugs? Could Elliot have gotten mixed up with a wrong crowd, pissed someone off, or maybe stopped off to meet someone on his way here?"

All the heads start shaking as Obed waves me off. "No way. Elliot was high on life, not substances. He was a 'my body is a temple' kinda guy, you know? I think I saw him drunk maybe half a dozen times and smoke weed less than that in the three years I knew him. Even now that it's legal, he doesn't touch it."

"He was a great guy," one of the others says. "Life of the party, you know?"

"I know the type," I say, thinking about Brenny. "So nothing weird or out of the ordinary in the last few days? No fights. No crazy ex. Nothing that had him edgy or worried?"

They all shake their heads, then the guy Obed called Stoner cracks a smile.

"Would you care to share with the class?" I ask.

He shrugs. "You said weird and out of the ordinary. I was thinking about last night at the club. This uber-sexy goth woman in black leather—like Underworld kinda leather—comes up to El last night out of nowhere and face plants on him."

"How did he respond?"

"He went with it and enjoyed the moment." Stoner smiles. "He laughed it off later and said she was a med-school chick checking if he still had his tonsils."

Obed chuckles, pulls out his phone, and shows me the pictures. They're dark, but with the strobes of the club lighting you can make out what's happening.

"That solves the mystery of his blue lips." I hold out the phone for Garnet to see.

Calling the Kate Beckinsale wannabe an uber-sexy goth woman is damn accurate.

If I went for girls, she'd be my type.

"Had you ever seen her before? Does she have a boyfriend or someone who didn't appreciate the PDA?"

Obed shakes his head. "No, but we don't go to that club much."

"Do you mind if I forward this picture to myself?"

He shrugs. "No. That's fine. If you think it'll help."

I tap in my details and forward the image to my email. "I don't think it means anything, but like Agent Grant said, it doesn't do anyone justice to not look at things thoroughly."

I hand him back his phone and tap on the screen. "You have my email now. Can you please send me Elliot's address and the name of the club last night?"

He does as I ask and when it *pings* my inbox, I check it and pull out a couple of cards. "This is me. If you think of anything else or need anything, let me know. Again, I'm super sorry you lost your friend. It sounds like Elliot was a great guy."

"He was. He really was."

Garnet flashes us into his office at the Guild Headquarters, and I wait to see where he's going to sit. When he's annoyed with me, he generally sits at his desk, and I have to sit opposite him in one of the smaller chairs. Today, he heads straight over to his wet bar and points at the leather couch and club chairs. "Have a seat. Would you like a dram?"

"Sure. Thanks."

He pours us each a drink, hands me mine, and sets his down on his coffee table. Then he strides over to his desk and returns with a beige folder. "Have a look and see what jumps out at you."

I set the folder down on the table and open the file. Sifting past the lab reports, I find the crime scene photos of the two other victims. I guess we're past the part where he warns me things are grisly because yeah, wow, vampires are messy eaters.

"All three were U of T students?"

He nods and sips from his tumbler.

The first was a guy, the second a girl. "Did they both live on campus?"

He nods again.

I find the headshots of the other two and frown. "And they both have blue lips like Elliot."

He nods a third time. "I thought much the same as you did at first glance, that it was something to do with a lack of oxygen in the blood or something, but the lab work didn't support that."

"It can't be a coincidence that all three of them ended up with blue lipstick for their morgue shots."

"Agreed."

"So, who's the blue-lipped seductress?"

"I suppose that's what we have to find out."

"What does Xavier think happened? If the three killers are senior members of his seethe, he should have a fairly good read on them, shouldn't he?"

"He's at a loss. These are people he trusts and respects. They are his family."

I swallow. "His family is known to be high-handed and dangerous. He's a criminal who surrounds himself with opportunistic thugs and killers. The student kills are gruesome, yes, but really, how is it any different than his business-related kills?"

"The hierarchy of power in the empowered world isn't the same as it is in the human world, Fiona. I thought you were grasping that better by now."

I sit back and stare at the whiskey swirling in my glass. "I do. Good guys kill bad guys in this world to keep the innocents safe. I get that and can get behind it. But when bad guys kill good guys or the innocents, why do you not want justice for the victims?"

"What is just? These kills offer the consumption of blood and the harvest of organs, but the inevitable exposure isn't worth that, is it?"

I take another sip and frown. "You're assuming that during blood lust they can make that decision."

Garnet nods. "They can. Especially vampires of the age and experience of the ones who committed these crimes."

"So maybe it was intentional, and he's playing us. Maybe Xavier ordered them to make the kills. Maybe their parents pissed him off or something and killing their kids is retribution."

Garnet shifts his butt back and sits deeper in his chair. The leather creaks under the change of position, and he takes another long drink. "It's not Xavier. He's too smart to be this sloppy. He runs this city and has the vampire community locked down. If he wants people dead, they disappear. If his people needed blood, he has his flock of feeders eager to offer them a vein."

Ew. "I still think that's demeaning and exploitive and a million other offensive things but as a supporter of people making their own life choices, I respect their right to choose that life even if I think it's disgusting."

"Tell me how you really feel."

The words are more growled than spoken, and I send Garnet an ocular fuck you for allowing me to rant my way under the bus. I swivel in my seat and turn to meet Xavier's cold caramel-colored gaze.

The head of the Toronto seethe is a stern-looking Korean man with an unassuming build. Nothing about him flashes "Danger! Vampire!" but that doesn't mean I'm safe by any stretch of the imagination.

"You always sneak up behind me from the shadows. It's a bit cringy." Well, more than a bit. Especially when my shield is tingling hot against my back. "Someone needs to put a bell on you."

"Try it. It'll be interesting to see how far you get."

When I first got educated on Xavier and the vampires of Toronto, Myra, Zxata, and Suede all warned me they are far worse than they seem. Considering how my skin crawls and my shield flares being in the same room with him, I truly don't want to find out what "far worse" looks like.

"I apologize for my blunt comment but not for what I said. I'm not a fan of women supplicating themselves for a taste of danger or to brush immortality at the hands of death and violence."

Xavier steps around me and sits in the middle of the couch, reaching his arms out onto the backrest left and right. "If I cared what you think I'd speak to my defense and point out how ignorant of our customs you are. Our feeding system saves thousands of lives over each century a vampire lives, but I *don't* care so I won't explain."

Garnet sighs. "Hostilities aside, Fi's question was valid. Yes, I considered Xavier a suspect. I interrogated the three vampires in question and had not only my Moon Called sense of smell but also a wizard empath to discern lies from truth. Xavier had nothing to do with these kills."

Xavier offers me a cool smile. "Nice try, though."

"I didn't try anything. I'm genuinely glad to hear it."

Xavier casts me a look and brushes a hand over his trim beard and mustache. "You sound sincere, Lady Druid."

I finish my drink and reach beside my chair to set the tumbler down. "I *am* sincere. You're a fellow governor of an organization I value. What you do reflects not only on you and yours but on how the empowered community looks at all of us. If we're working to convince members of the magical and supernatural world to trust us as a governing body, it looks bad if one of us is chewing up university students and sucking them dry."

Xavier seems to agree...or, at least not disagree.

"Okay, so all the victims were killed by one of Xavier's seethe. Is that by nature or design?"

"A good question," Garnet says. "The only other connection we have between the victims is that they were students living on St. George Campus."

"And kissed by a hot woman with blue lipstick."

Xavier's brow pinches tight. "Who? What's that about blue lipstick?"

I pull out my phone and call up Obed's club picture of the hottie in black leather. "Do you know her? We believe she had contact with each of the victims hours before someone in your seethe killed them. That's hard to swallow as a coincidence."

Xavier examines the photo for only a brief moment and remains as stone-faced as ever. "How would this woman be involved?"

"No idea. So far it's just an odd coincidence. If you know her or can give us insight, maybe we can upgrade that to a working theory."

He looks at the picture again and shakes his head. "I can't help you. I wish I knew how someone like her could manipulate members of my bloodline into the frenzied killing of innocents, but I don't."

I sigh. "So, assuming it's not a breakdown in your feeding system at the root cause—"

"It's not."

"Then who would want to take down your seethe and ruin you in the process?"

Xavier grins. "Every vampire from every other seethe around the world."

"Awesomesauce. So, what's that...a couple of thousand suspects to go through in two weeks before she strikes again? No biggie."

Garnet makes a face at me. "As much as I wanted to keep a low profile on this and protect Xavier's reputation from insult, it's time we have an emergency meeting and bring the Guild Governors up to speed."

"All right. When's that?"

He stands and gestures toward the door. "Shall we?"

CHAPTER FOUR

The first time I attended a governor's meeting, I was a guest at a luncheon on a riverboat cruise. I'm not sure what I thought the guild was all about, but at the time they seemed odd and mysterious: Malachi's mossy green skin, Suede's silver hair and fetish for hippy clothes and fringe, and the drippy face of the supreme witch bitch at the head table.

We were seated according to power rankings. Those of us who call and command magic ranked higher on the power scale and sat closer to the head of the table. Those who were simply magical because of who they were born, like nymphs and elves, or who became members of the "other" society, like vampires, were farther down the table.

That doesn't mean they're not dangerous or powerful... just not as highly charged on the magic scale.

That first day, my seat was fourth from the end of one of the tables between a rugaru and a troll. I had just established myself as a druid, and our sacred grove was brand new.

Everything about my powers was new, and I only had a half-dozen mastered spells inked into my skin.

I glance down at the twining fretwork covering my arms and

smile. Much of my arms and back are covered now, and more when I activate my armor.

At first, I thought the inking was ugly.

Now that I'm accustomed to what it means and offers me, I think it's rather beautiful—at least the way Dora does it. She's a wonder on many fronts.

Plus, it's not like it's visible to humans. The magic in the ink means that only members of the empowered community can see the real me anyway.

The rest of the world sees nothing.

"Take your seats." Garnet gestures at the table as we stride in.

With the chaos of my life over the past six months, I've missed as many meetings as I've attended and I'm not exactly sure where my seat is anymore.

Suede waves from the far end of the room, so I take the long way around. Hustling down the tables, I stop to hug her. "Hey. I miss you. We need to catch up."

"Are you and Sloan going to Dionysus' party tonight?"

"Yeah, you?"

Suede grins. "Wouldn't miss it. So, see you there?"

"Definitely. Looking forward to it." I continue around the room to Zxata. "How's things in the land of you?" I ease back from our hug and kiss his cheek.

"Peaceful and fulfilling these days."

"Well, that sounds lovely. I'm glad."

"My sister says your adventures have kept you busy on several continents." Myra's older brother is as sweet as they come. I'm not sure if it's an ash nymph thing or if it's just them, but Myra and Zxata are two of my favorite people in the world.

"Busy, yes. I wish I could say peaceful, like you. Be thankful for that."

Garnet clears his throat, and I widen my eyes at Zxata and hustle around the table looking for my seat.

Over here, Red, Nikon says into my mind. *You're no longer at the kid's table.*

Seriously?

Congrats, babe. You deserve the recognition. Own it...work it...work it...

I laugh as I stride up the window wall of the meeting chamber and sit beside him at the head table. My new position bumps Queen Drippy-Face one seat down the row and onto one of the side tables. She doesn't seem at all happy about that.

Sorry not sorry.

As Garnet starts from the top and relays an edited version of what he shared with me all afternoon, my mind wanders to the most pressing problem in my life at the moment.

What are you getting Dionysus for his party tonight?

Nikon doesn't turn to look at me but his mouth curls at the corner in that cute smirk of his. *Shouldn't we be paying attention?*

I was at the crime scene. I'll fill you in with all the gories later. So, Dionysus?

I took over an amphora of Papu's wine after lunch and helped him set up...and, who are we kidding, he's squatting on the top of my build-ing. I did my part.

I cover my mouth to clear my throat to hide my laughter. *When I read the address on the invitation, I laughed. He added an entire floor to your building.*

Yeah. Honestly, I don't care. He's a good guy, and for what he did helping us take on Hecate and getting home, we owe him big.

True story.

So, what are you and Irish getting him?

Undetermined.

Nikon checks his watch. *Tick-tock, Red.*

Oh, I'm aware. What did Kev and Calum get? They mentioned roping you in for the logistics of getting their gift sorted.

He chuckles. *Can't tell you. I'm sworn to secrecy.*

Hey, you were my partner in crime first. What happened to us being the magic marauders managing mischief? Whatever they offered you, I'll match it.

He barks out a laugh and holds up his hand to fend off Garnet's glare.

"Something funny, Greek?"

"No. Sorry. As you were." When the room settles, Nikon casts me a sideways glance. *I would love for you to match it, but there's no way you would. You're a one-man woman, and I respect that.*

Seriously? They bribed your sworn secrecy with sexual favors?

He waggles his brow at me. *What can I say? I'm a simple guy with simple needs.*

I roll my eyes. *Fine. Don't tell me. I'll think of something great without your help.*

He slides his hand across the surface of the table and laces our fingers. *I never said I wouldn't help you...only that I can't tell you what Kev and Calum have planned. Whatever you need, I'm your guy.*

I squeeze his fingers and notice the arched eyebrows focused on us instead of Garnet. Releasing Nikon's hand, I roll my eyes. *These people need to get a life. Do they honestly think we're having an affair?*

Well, we have been leading them on.

I think about the time Nikon kissed me in one of our meetings, then I snotted all over him and poured my heart out to him after I speared him and thought I killed him at another. *Ha! I suppose we have.*

Ignore them. Tell me what you're thinking about for your gift, and I'll help make it happen.

I reclaim his hand despite the looks. *Thanks, Greek. You rock.*

I'm not sure how I envisioned a house party hosted by Dionysus starting, but when the doorbell rings at nightfall, and I open it to find a footman in tails, I'm surprised. When I look past him to the glistening carriage on the back lawn with two white, winged horses, I realize I didn't think big enough.

Dillan, Aiden, and Kinu come out from next door, and I meet their dazzled gazes. "Our chariot awaits."

"Oh, Mommy," Jackson says. "You goes to the ball. I wants to go too."

Kinu chuckles. "Not tonight, monkey. Uncle Anyx and Aunt Zuzanna are taking you to a sleepover with Imari, remember? You don't want to miss that by going to a ball with a bunch of silly adults."

"No. But I wants to ride in the carriage with the flying horsies."

"Hey, monster." Anyx appears on the back lawn. "Contessa McSparkles is waiting to show you her new dance. She's been practicing all week. Let's get your bag and your sister and get going."

The poor kid looks torn.

Imagine being five years old and having to choose between an enchanted carriage with winged horses or flashing to the African savanna to play with your bestie and her pet unicorn. Decisions. Decisions.

Empowered life is crazy fun.

"If you're ready." The footman gestures at the carriage.

Sloan steps out and holds my jacket for me and then I duck back inside and grab my gift and our contributions to the bar. A bottle of Redbreast and a jug of Gran's famous blackberry pear wine.

"After you, sir."

Sloan winks and takes possession of the jug. "Ye look lovely tonight, *a ghra.*"

"It's a hit to a woman's ego to stand next to you, hotness. I gotta do my part."

"Yer ridiculous."

Kinu waddles over to join us while Aiden gets Anyx sorted

with the kids and their overnight bag. "This is likely the last moment we have before the babies come. Might as well make a night of it."

"Might as well."

The seven of us pile into the carriage, and it's magically roomy within. Sloan sets the jug of wine between his feet, takes the gift, and sets it on his lap.

Once Aiden gets Kinu settled, we're good to go.

"Emmet and Da are missing out," Dillan says, taking the window seat.

"Is Emmet picking up Ciara?" Kinu asks.

I nod. "Yeah. Nikon is bringing the heirs."

"All of them? I didn't know he knew them."

"He met them at our house party a few months ago and invited them to join."

"So, other than us and the guests he met through us, who else is coming?" Dillan asks.

"No idea. Maybe some of his pantheon friends."

The shrill whinny of the horses signals our departure, and we take to the air like Santa's sleigh behind his reindeer. The quick lurch over our fence unleashes a wave of butterflies in my tummy, and I lean to see out the little portal window.

"Jackson's not wrong." I giggle. "This reminds me a lot of Cinderella's magic carriage."

"Except for the flying part." Aiden looks a little stricken. "You don't suppose anything could go wrong, do you?"

"Do I think Dionysus, Zeus's son, would allow anything he does to harm us? No. I don't. We're as much family to him as friends. I think that's what this party is really all about."

Dillan snorts. "And here I thought it was about wine, sex, and casting aside the expectations of society."

I laugh. "That's you projecting what you *hope* it's going to be. Dionysus is more than the hedonistic gigolo image he portrays."

"Now who's projecting?" Dillan asks.

All too soon, the Pegasuses… Pegasae… Pegasi?

All too soon, the pretty winged horses land atop the Acropolis, and we pile out of our magical carriage.

The last time I saw the rooftop of Nikon's building was a month ago when we were battling Mingin and trying to keep him from merging his dark entity with Melanippe of Scythia. Between them and Droghun's Barghest bastards, they did a real number on the Team Trouble Batcave and the top floor of the Acropolis.

With that damage repaired and a new floor added, the rooftop has transformed into a lovely outdoor retreat. The pergola's wooden slats vanished among the growth of grapevines, which promise a bounty of fruit and fragrance this summer.

A hot tub, an outdoor seating area, and a stone grilling station set the stage for gatherings to come.

And strings of tiny white lights crisscross overhead like a million stars against the night sky.

I haven't the heart to tell him this won't go well come winter weather. Then again, maybe he can use his godly powers to counteract the cold.

"Welcome, Clan Cumhaill." Dionysus opens the door to the penthouse stairs and greets us with open arms. He's barefoot and dressed in a navy tunic with gold banding and a gold braided rope. A vine laurel crowns his brown curls, and I can't help but notice how attractive happiness makes him.

"Thanks for the invite." I step in to kiss his cheek. "I'm so happy you're gracing our city with your presence. Toronto is lucky to have you."

"Thanks, Red. Come. There's much to show you." He holds out his hands to Kinu and me, and the two of us get the royal escort downstairs.

We step into the open floorplan and yep, he has the entire floor of a building for his playground. "This is it. Mi casa es su casa. For those of you who'd like the tour, come with me. Anyone who doesn't give a shit spread out and have fun. In my home, everything is a touch station. No rules. No judgment."

Kinu giggles. "All I need is the closest powder room. These babies are sitting on my bladder."

Dionysus starts the tour there, and we drop her off to pee. "Wow." Aiden checks things out. "This place is off the hook. Is that an arcade? Is that MotoGP side-by-side racing?"

"It is. And that door to the side of the arcade is the VR room where you can upload any number of possible virtual scenarios and adventures to act out. There's an occupied light attached to the lock on the door, so if you want privacy, just flip that."

Dillan snorts. "What kind of VR scenarios do you have in there, dude?"

Dionysus grins. "Spend time in there and find out."

I laugh, my attention catching on a dozen other fun stations for adults who never grew up...which is pretty much everyone I know. "Well, you have quite a party in store for us, don't you?"

Dionysus grins, continuing to point as we go. "We also have sumo suits for those who want to get physical but not sexual. Raptor suits and costumes for no reason at all. The Segway races will start after we have a few drinks. I have the track mapped out on the floor. Just watch out for the bumper cars on the far wall. And for those who don't like racing or bumping, I have four sets of trampoline boots over by the climbing wall."

"Dude!" Calum says, smacking Kevin's arm. "Hells to the yeah. Game on."

Sloan checks his phone. "Yer father says Shannon and Liam are ready. I'll pop over and pick them up. Try not to break your neck before I get back."

I give him my cheek. "No promises. This is like Cumhaill heaven. You might never pry me away."

Dionysus claps his hands together. "Then my evil plan is working, and we're one step closer to me claiming you as my own."

I burst out laughing. For a flash of a moment, it looks like Sloan's considering if he's serious. He's not. He just doesn't know Dionysus that well yet. "You go, my love. Da already missed out on the chariot. I don't want him to miss anything else."

When Sloan *poofs* off, Dionysus bursts into a fit of giggles. "Did you see his face?"

I laugh. "I don't think he believed you'd steal me away, but after the past months, I can't blame him for being cautious about maybe misplacing me."

Dionysus grins. "Wishes and dreams are hard to capture. They often slip through our fingers. I don't blame him for worrying. He's a lucky man."

I slide my arm around his waist and raise my hand toward the apartment. "Show me everything. I want to see it all."

"This is quite a party," Liam says a few hours later. He's sitting on one of the tasting couches, and I'm lounging on the cushioned rugs.

I dip another square of bread into the olive oil and roasted garlic bulbs, and even though I'm pretty sure I'm about to split open, I can't stop myself from putting it into my mouth. "It's wonderful. It's much like Jackson's fourth birthday party. I saw Dionysus in his natural element while we were in ancient Greece and this is much more G-rated than I anticipated."

Liam tips back his beer and finishes it. "That's going to end soon. I heard Niall talking to him when we first arrived. The deal is G-rated while he and Shannon and Aiden and Kinu are here. Then, once they make their exit, Dionysus is free to take off the gloves...or whatever it is he's planning to take off."

"Good to know. There are far too many people here who I consider family to stay for the late-night performances."

"You and me both." He sets down his empty bottle, and another appears in his hand. "That's been happening all night.

Thanks, but I gotta slow down." He sets that one down and another chilled bottle appears in his hand.

I giggle. "You're magical."

"If only I were twenty-one again. This party would've been the best thing to ever happen to me."

I think about Liam back then and smile. "You and Brenny were bad enough as it was. Remember the time the two of you got drunk and high at that party over by the Catholic school, and I had to pick you up?"

He laughs. "Yeah, I'm not sure what was in that pot, but we were both fried and looping bad. To this day I swear vengeful squirrels were chasing us."

"So why hide in the bushes?" I chuckle. "You scared the piss out of me when you jumped out."

His chest is bouncing now. "Brendan wanted to make sure it was really you, so he said we needed to stay hidden until we were sure."

"Yeah. There I am trolling the school parking lot at two in the morning, and you two eejits jump out of the bushes and bang on the hood of my car."

Liam's smile grows soft and nostalgic. "Brendan used to tell me the saying was wrong. You don't only live once. You only *die* once. If you're smart, you live every single minute of every single day."

I pick up one of the beers he set down and lift it toward him. "To Brenny and living every single minute."

Liam clinks the neck of his bottle with mine. "*Slainte mhath.*"

"Presents! Presents." Dionysus is waving everyone into the gaming area. When we first arrived, it seemed that he'd decked out the entire floor of the building like an adult amusement park. When we explored further, we found an adult side too with furnished vignettes and lovely furniture, and some stunning pieces of art.

Liam and I took a time-out from the festivities to enjoy a quiet moment in a massive living area. Behind us is an open kitchen, a library wall, an area with a beautiful candy apple red piano, and the lounge area that reminds me of our time in ancient Greece.

The two of us get up, pass a life-sized game of Jenga between Dillan, Suede, and Tad, and head over to join the group gathering for the unwrapping of the greatly anticipated gifts.

"Were we supposed to bring gifts?" Tad asks, locking horror-struck.

"It was on the invitation," Dillan says.

Tad pulls his out of his pocket and shakes his head. "Not on my invitation. Mine says come as you are for an evening with friends."

Suede pulls out hers and laughs. "Mine says, 'your flexibility is requested. Drink. Kiss. And be merry.'"

My mouth drops open. "Seriously?"

Suede laughs. "Don't look so shocked. I'm an elf. He and I hit it off at your party. I'm not the only one who's flexible. He's a freaking gymnast. Having sex with him should be called Cirque du So-laid."

Even drunk I can't go there. "Then I guess you're off the hook for gifts. The Cumhaill invite said to bring presents."

Nikon waves away the confusion. "Dionysus is a man of whimsy. It's best not to try to understand him. Just go with it."

Emmet chuckles and wraps an arm around Ciara. "I've got us covered, babe. D and I got him the best gift *evah!*"

"I don't doubt that for a second." When Ciara leans in, and the two of them start kissing, I turn and head off to get our gift.

Nikon's gaze narrows, and he lifts his chin. *Why the hasty retreat, Red? You okay?*

Is it weird I can't even look at Ciara and my brother like that?

You mean is it weird that you're not on board with your brother sleeping with Sloan's ex-workout partner?

I wince. *Yeah, that. I mean, I'm not weird about Kady with Liam after she was with Dillan and I crushed on Liam off and on for my whole life. Why does Ciara set me off?*

This is a convo better had between you and Irish.

I meet Sloan's gaze across the room as he brings me the wrapped package I put together for Dionysus.

You're probably right.

I usually am. Wisdom comes from centuries of observing life and not participating.

Catchy. You should put that on a Hallmark card.

"Everything all right, *a ghra?*" Sloan leans in to kiss my cheek. "Ye look odd and a little ill."

There's no way I'm getting into things at Dionysus's party when I'm three-quarters drunk. "Fine. Are you having fun?"

He nods. "Sure. Although, yer father and Aiden are takin' the ladies home right after presents. If tonight is anything like our party, that's when things will take a hedonistic turn. We might want to think about when we're makin' our exit."

"Yep. Presents, then we'll wrap things up."

"Wrap up before the unwrapping," Nikon says. "You should put that on a Hallmark card."

The two of us join the huddle as Dionysus rips open Kevin's and Calum's gift. He tosses the wrapping paper in the air and grins. "You remembered."

He holds up a painted enameled wind chime, and I burst out laughing. "Penis wind chimes? That's your super-secret perfect gift?"

Kevin nods. "It's more than functional. It's sentimental. When we were trapped in ancient Greece, waiting hours while you and Calum faced the trials of Hecate's torture, Dionysus, Nikon, and I toured the market one day for a few hours. Several merchants were selling these and Dionysus said no home should be without one. Now his home won't be without one."

Dionysus holds his up higher and shakes his hand to rattle the penises together. "It's perfect. I'll think of you both every time the wind blows. Thank you."

Next, he accepts the wrapped box from Da, and his eyes widen. "It's heavy."

"From Shannon, Liam, Aiden, Kinu, and me." When he opens it, Da leans in and points to the contents. "It's a traditional Celtic home kit. The horseshoe is fer luck, and since ye don't have a plaid, I took the liberty to wrap it in the pattern of the Fianna— our heritage fabric."

"I'm honored."

"Fi and Sloan will help ye hang it over yer entrance properly. Then ye have a piece of coal so that ye'll always have fire in your hearth. The wee roll of bread is so ye always have food on yer table. The silver coin brings ye the wish fer money to ever fill yer purse. The box of matches is so ye'll always have light in yer life. And the swatch of cloth is so ye always have clothes on yer back —" he laughs. "Och, well, so ye always have the *option* to have clothes on yer back. Ye tend to be naked more than most."

Dionysus smiles, examining every item in his box as if each one was a treasure. "You forgot the shot glass."

He shakes his head and reaches his drink over to pour some into the little shot glass. "Now, from one friend to another, we share a wee dram to warm our hearts and seal the luck."

"*Slainte mhath.*" Sloan raises his drink.

"*Slainte mhath,*" the rest of us say in response.

Dionysus empties his shot glass and sets it back in the box. "An excellent gift well received. Thank you."

I look at Dillan and then Emmet, but they laugh and wave me away. "Our gift is to be opened privately."

Dionysus laughs. "Perfect. I look forward to it."

I shrug. "I guess that leaves us. I hope you like it."

Dionysus settles our gift on his lap, opens the box, and finds it's similar to Da's and Aiden's. Great minds and all that.

I lean forward and point things out to explain. "The key is to our home so you know you're always welcome. You gave me your pendant a few months ago, and now I give you ours. That pendant allows you entrance to the Batcave downstairs and if you ever need us, press it. It will send out a tracking signal so we can find you. You need it because you're part of Team Trouble now. You proved that when you helped us face off against Minginippe and the darkness."

"With a rocket launcher!" Dillan says.

"Classic." Emmet laughs. "I'm still so bummed I missed that."

Dionysus grins. "It was quite spectacular."

I point at the box. "There's more."

He flips back the tissue and picks up the first of three collage picture frames.

"I've already filled them, but you can swap out pictures if you want."

He looks at the candid shots of us drinking at our party a few months ago. Of him with the boys laughing. Of him in his Tarzan outfit in the treehouse hugging me and making me blush. Snapshots of moments of him being part of our family.

"Every home needs pictures of family. So, if it's all right with you, we'd like to consider you part of our family. Welcome to Clan Cumhaill."

When he looks up at me, I tear up. His bright, beautiful eyes are glassy and brimming. He blinks fast, but there's no stopping it. A few tears escape, and he swipes under his eyes. "Thank you."

"I mean it. You've proven yourself to us time and again. We love you. You're more than a fun guy, more than a god, and a good time. You're brave and honest and worthy to be considered part of Clan Cumhaill."

"To Dionysus." Da holds up his drink. "We're honored to have ye, son."

CHAPTER FIVE

Leaving Dionysus's party at a decent hour is a good idea, but it doesn't completely spare me from the morning-after hangover. Still, I prepare a batch of Gran's cure-all for the boys and drink some myself.

By noon, I'm up, dressed, and passing a broom over my floors to keep things quiet for those suffering upstairs. "What time are we expecting your father?"

Sloan looks up from polishing the sink faucets and checks the time lit up on the stove. "Half-twelve, so, not long now."

It's cute how intent he is on everything being perfect, but honestly, he lived in a home with house staff. I'm quite sure Wallace doesn't care if there are water spots on our sink. "I asked Myra to join us for the expansion of the grove and Dora's coming to help me get Dart's nest sorted out."

"That's a fine idea." He's only half-listening. "Did yer brothers come home last night?"

"They were in their beds this morning when I checked in on them."

"Tad *poofed* them into the man cave around five," Bruin says, lumbering up the hall. My bear isn't a morning person by nature, but noon is within his wheelhouse, so I'm not sure why he seems so cranky. "And Goldilocks is still there."

I chuckle. "That's what the sofa bed is for. Friends and guests are welcome to claim it."

"That frat boy snores."

I catch Sloan's look and smile. "No one snores like you do, buddy. I'm surprised you even noticed."

He lifts his black nose and snuffs at me. "Sure, pick on the bear."

Sloan's phone buzzes on the counter, and he checks the message. He responds immediately and continues to buzz around like a crazy person.

"Relax, hotness. Your dad's been here before. He's seen our lives in progress. He's coming to see you, not judge how we keep our home."

He bites his lip and makes a face. "Ye say that now, but I think I maybe should've told ye somethin' which I didn't. Now I might be in hot water."

"Uh-huh. What should you have told me?"

His face scrunches up, and I know I'm not going to like what he says. "Yer not the only one who invited a couple of extra bodies for the expansion of the grove. Lugh and Laura are comin' fer the day as well."

The squeak of panic that escapes my throat is nothing I can control. "Here? Gran is coming here? In—" I check my Fitbit. "—*twelve* minutes?"

Sloan hisses. "I wanted ye to be surprised, but in hindsight, maybe that was a mistake."

"You *think*?" I kick it into high gear, finishing with the floor and racing around straightening pillows and grabbing the cleaner to polish the table.

"What about the speech ye just gave me? She's coming to see you, not judge how we keep our home."

I spray the table quickly and wax on/wax off until it's

gleaming with a shine. *"Ha!* Gran is a superhero housewife. Oh, gawd. I should've baked something. We should have flowers for the table."

Sloan grabs my arms and pulls me to a stop. "Yer losin' yer mind. I've been extra diligent on cleanin' and tidyin' up. Lara isn't coming to examine yer silverware. She's comin' to work in yer grove, see our home, and spend some time with her grandkids."

I exhale a deep breath and yeah, I know he's right. Still, this will be her first impression of my home life with Sloan.

The back door opens, and Dillan shuffles in looking like road-kill. "Coffee and cure-all."

I point at the stove, and suddenly I don't feel so bad. If first impressions of our home life are what we're in store for, Sloan and I won't even register a second glance. "Since you're wearing last night's outfit, I take it this is your walk of shame?"

He pours himself a fifty-fifty mug of hangover pick-me-up. "Shame? Hells no. Other people might call it a walk of shame. I call it the got laid parade. I'm on a high…celebrating a great night with an amazing female. I'm the man. You should've stuck around. Andromeda stopped in with a few friends, and things got interesting."

"I don't want interesting. I'm happy with Sloan."

Sloan frowns at me, and I burst out laughing.

"That totes came out wrong. I love our kind of interesting. I don't need the Dionysus free love kind."

"Nice save, loser." Dillan sips his coffee.

I chuckle and pick up my phone, calling up my camera. When I'm ready and have the video running, I get him centered in the frame. "Loser, eh? Huh, what do you think Gran will say when she gets a look at you?"

Dillan scratches the scruff at the side of his jaw with his middle finger. "You wouldn't dare. I have so much damming footage of you locked away that I'd bury you."

"Oh, I'm not sending her anything. We're expecting Gran to snap in here any moment for a visit."

The glare he pegs me with is epic. "Fuck off. Not even a little funny."

I laugh, patting myself on the back for capturing this on video. "Not even a little joking. She's coming with Granda and Wallace for the grove expansion. Surprise!"

He lowers the mug from his lips and glares, gauging my expression. "You're fucking with me, right?"

"Nope. Pinky swear." I hold out my hand.

He extends his hand, waiting for me to withdraw and crack up. When I don't, and our pinky fingers lock, he curses, drops the mug to the counter, and runs for the back door. "You suck, sista."

"You're the man, bro. Lead that got laid parade."

Sloan and I are still laughing about that when Nikon snaps into the living room with Wallace, Gran, and Granda a few moments later.

"Hello, the house." Granda comes to hug me.

I wrap my arms around him, excited that Sloan included them. When I ease back, the pure joy in his expression says he feels the same. "Hey, Granda. Howeyah?"

"I'm not dead so they could be worse."

I laugh and hug Gran. "True story. Welcome to our home. I'm so thrilled you're here."

"Och, luv. We're thrilled to be here."

When I step back from Gran, I move to Wallace. Sloan's father isn't much of a hugger, but he's not as rigid with me as he once was.

Cumhaills are huggers.

There's not much to be done about that.

"It's good to have you back, Wallace. We're looking forward to the weekend."

"As am I, Fi. Thank you."

Before things get awkward, Sloan steps in and holds out his

hand. "Da, let me take yer bag up to Emmet's room and tell the boys ye've all arrived."

Wallace surrenders his overnight bag and Sloan jogs up the stairs to rouse the troops. Which—if it were anyone other than our grandparents—would never work.

Gran surveys the lay of the land and smiles at the pot on the stove. "Have we caught ye at a bad time, luv? Sloan said he was keepin' our visit a surprise, but maybe it wasn't good to spring it on ye."

I wave that away. "Nonsense. Dionysus had a housewarming party last night. Sloan and I came home when Da and Aiden left around midnight. We're all up for the day. I can't say the same for the rest of the boys. How are you doing, Greek?"

He offers me a weak wink. "I'm upright."

"But that's all you've got?"

"At the moment, yeah."

I laugh and put him out of his misery. "Do you need to go crash now?"

He nods. "Yeah, so badly."

Gran pours him a mug of coffee cure-all and hands it to him. "Then off ye go, sweet boy. Drink this, get yer rest, and if ye fancy a family dinner later, make yer way back."

Nikon smiles. "Thanks, Gran."

When Nikon snaps out, I chuckle. "Dionysus throws quite a party. It might take a bit to whip the boys into shape for a visit."

"But whip them into shape we shall," Da says, striding in from the back door. "Dillan said Fi was expectin' ye and I could scarcely believe it. Welcome to our lives."

When Da hugs Gran and nods at Granda, I realize how monumental this visit is.

They spent thirty-five years estranged. Gran and Granda never got the chance to meet Mam or see the life Da built for us here. Having them here now is about more than us accepting druid life and building our grove. It's a new beginning.

And, of course, Sloan's right.

That is *much* more important than whether or not I had time to bake or get flowers for the table.

"So, let me give you a quick tour of the main floor," I say, well aware that we have drunk and hungover boys on the floors above and below. "Then we'll take you next door to gather the monkeys, and we'll show you the grove. Once everyone is alive and recovered from our night out, we'll give you the presidential tour of the whole place."

Gran hugs me again. "That sounds lovely."

By mid-afternoon Myra, Dora, Gran, and I are working on expanding the greenery of the grove while Sloan, Wallace, Da, Granda, and Aiden tear down the fence dividing the properties. We managed to get two sections down in December, but that was it.

Now that the ground thaw has taken hold, we can remove the posts entirely. We'll reuse what wood we can and build one extended back deck, connecting the back of our house to the house next door.

"Yer trees are doing very well," Gran says, getting to know each one. "And yer fae are happy and excited about the expansion too."

"I'm glad." I reach into my pocket and take out the teal, bronze, and navy blue rabbit poop that the original Ostara hare pooped for me. It was warm and squishy when first gifted to me, but now it's as hard as stone, and its power tingles in my fingers.

I roll it in my palm, assessing its contained fae energy. "Will it work again? I mean, it helped us expand the first time, but is it a single-use kinda turd or is it good for more than that?"

"It's an enchanted charm stone," Gran says. "It holds the blessing of Ostara's familiar. That is very powerful indeed."

"That's her pretty poop," Jackson says, pointing at my hand. "A bunny pooped that out, and Auntie Fi picked it up. Mommy says not to pick up the Ostara poop, but Auntie Fi puts hers in her pocket."

I chuckle. "He's not wrong." I hold up the multi-colored rabbit turd between my thumb and index finger and try to remember how it worked last summer.

Intention and need.

Kneeling at the edge of the original grove, I pull Jackson into my lap, and we face the backyard of our home. "You and I are going to do some magic. Ready?"

"Ready."

Sunlight warms our skin, and I wrap my arms around my nephew to hold my charm stone in front of us. "Imagine the grove with more trees. The Ostara rabbits and spriggans have more space to fly, and Pip, Nilm, and the deer have more forest. Wouldn't that be nice?"

"Yeah."

"Focus on that, and we're going to try to magic it."

Intention and need. I focus on connecting with its power and setting it free. "Are you picturing it, buddy?"

Jackson has his eyes pinched shut. "More grove. More trees. More fae friends."

Intention and need.

As we kneel and focus, the earth rumbles below my shins, and my skin tingles with power. "Jackson, look. It's working."

The depth and width of the treed area in the yard of my childhood home expand before us, stretching to cover the ground in mine and Sloan's backyard.

We stay very still until things take hold, then I hug him tightly and get up. "Great job, buddy."

"We did it," Jackson says, running toward the men. "Daddy! We did it. We magicked it!"

Thankfully, Sloan and Granda already glamored the backyard for sight and sound.

"That's awesome, buddy." Aiden stacks posts between our houses. "Why don't you go tell Mommy and Meggie to come out and see."

Jackson takes off like a shot, and I brush off the shins of my jeans.

"Well done, luv." Gran wraps her arm around my back as we take our first steps into the expanded woods. "You have a lovely ambient power here. I can feel it responding to your workings already."

"Is lovely, miss," the purple spriggan with the lacy white wings says. "Is more green."

"Yep. Definitely is more green," Myra says. "Twice as much at least."

Pip raises her hands, and I pick her up and sit her on my hip as I do with the kids when I carry them. She places both of her tiny hands gently on my cheek and chitters, her huge, round eyes shining bright.

"I'm not sure what you're saying, sweet girl, but I'm sure it's lovely."

"She's thanking you for more trees," Dora says. "And asking if we can make her and her mate a proper home. She's nesting and needs things she can't get here."

"Nesting?" I look from Pip to Dora and back again. "Does that mean she's pregnant?"

Gran nods. "It does indeed. Spring is a magical time in the groves. Yer about to have yer first generation of Canadian-born fae arrive."

"Congratulations, baby girl." I hug her, careful not to squish her. "Dora, please tell her we'll get her whatever she needs."

Dora lists off a few things and Myra nods. "I told Fi back in December that I'd introduce a few ground plants in the spring to feed the soil. I have a couple of hours tomorrow before I open the store. I'll gather the plants and a few things for your expectant brownie too."

"Thanks, Myra, that's awesome."

"Daddy!" Jackson shouts, running outside. "Mommy doesn't feel good. She falls on the floor crying."

For a split second, the world freezes…then we all bolt for the house.

"Have we heard anything yet?" Daisy asks.

I look up from skimming the pages of my latest "How to Train Your Dragon" book and shake my head. My eyes are bleary and burning, but I can't stand the idea of going to bed when we don't know what's happening.

"Nothing yet, baby girl." Setting the book down, I scoop up Calum's skunk and snuggle her onto the couch with me. "Gran and Wallace fixed what they could, and Da drove behind the ambulance to sit with Aiden at the hospital."

"Do you think the babies will be okay?"

"Och, the babies are strong, little one." Sloan brings me a chamomile tea. He moves the stack of books onto the coffee table and slides in tight to hug us both. "My Da said the problem isn't with the babies. It's the strain the pregnancy is takin' on Kinu's body. Lara said much the same thing. Don't worry. I'm sure we'll hear something soon."

I sip my tea and lay my head on his chest. "I love you, Mackenzie."

"Right back at ye, *a ghra.*" We sit like that for a little while, me sipping my tea and him holding me and stroking Daisy's fur.

Eventually, Emmet and Ciara come up from the man cave. "Anything?" Emmet asks.

"No. Nothing yet."

He heads to the fridge and stares inside. "I'm glad Wallace and Gran were able to help Kinu until the ambulance got here."

Ciara steps in behind him, wraps her hands around his waist, and hugs his back. "Wallace is one helluva healer, and yer Gran is tops in nature magic. Nothing is more natural than babies. Kinu couldn't have been in better hands."

Emmet lets the fridge fall closed and turns to pull Ciara into a hug. "I'm glad you're here, *mo nighean donn*. Thanks for staying."

Doc scampers up the steps and bounds over to check his bowl. "Sorry. The boys and I were wondering about dinner. We know there's a family emergency, but it's almost nine and...."

"No need to explain, dude," Emmet says. "Sorry, I guess we could all use a bite to eat."

Sloan extricates himself from me, and I miss him immediately. "Let's see what we can pull together, shall we, Em? I bought a bunch of sausages and burgers for the barbeque. If you start the grill, I'll get us started. Nikon should be back with Da shortly, and we can all eat."

Ciara holds the fridge open while Sloan pulls things out and sets them on the counter. "It was good of Nikon to take Lugh and Lara home and help Wallace get his supplies. The Greek is an amazing guy."

I agree. "Nikon's come through for us more times than I can count. Still, maybe we should store a set of medicinal crystals and remedies in the apothecary downstairs so we have things on hand."

"Great idea," Emmet says, returning from the back deck. "Between Sloan and I having disciplines in Health and Healing, having a stocked apothecary for us to work healing stuff with would be cool."

"Work healing stuff with?" Sloan repeats.

"You know what I mean."

Sloan nods, and for the first time in hours, we're smiling. You gotta love Emmet.

CHAPTER SIX

Things will look better in the morning. Thankfully, the adage is true. After a solid eight hours, most things seem less scary and more manageable, even a complication in pregnancy requiring bed rest.

Aiden posted an update on the family WhatsApp chat around eleven o'clock. He told us Kinu was released and they were coming home. She was ordered straight to bed, and he said no visitors until she got some sleep.

We all had one drink to toast her and the babies' safe return home. Then we went to bed.

"Good morning, *a ghra*," Sloan says as I make my way downstairs. "Did ye sleep well?"

I join him behind the counter for a hug. "I did. Today's a new day, amirite?" I look at the stack of dragon books on the table and smile. "Did *you* sleep well?"

He dips his chin. "I managed a few solid hours but didn't want to wake ye with my fidgeting. I thought being productive was a better solution."

"Is your dad still sleeping?"

"Och, no. He's an earlier riser than me, and with the time change, he was up and about at the crack."

"Where is he now?"

"He took his medical bag and hustled next door the moment Aiden texted that Kinu was awake and ready to be examined. They're on monkey time next door."

"They are. It's good that he's with her."

"Aye, it is. Da is a wonder at what he does. He can't fix things that are running a natural course, but he can certainly help and make sure Kinu and the babies are comfortable in the meantime."

I look at the bowl of batter mixed by the griddle and smile at the raspberries and strawberries washed beside the sink. "Berry pancakes?"

He lifts a shoulder and smiles. "I know yer father makes pancakes as comfort food for yer family. I thought it might help."

I kiss his cheek and pull the syrup and juice from inside the fridge door. "You're the best, Mackenzie. How did I get so lucky?"

"Perseverance on my part, more than luck, I'd say."

I take my glass of juice to the table. "You get full points for foresight. I'm glad you persevered."

"Me too. Do ye want yer pancakes now or in a bit?"

"Now would be great, thanks. I'm starving."

As Sloan works on the pancakes, I peruse the dragon books and find a notepad with four pages of notes.

TTGFS-Thank The Goddess for Sloan.

Collecting the notepad, I flip to the first page and study what Sloan gleaned as pertinent. Damn. This is good stuff. "Reason number two hundred and twelve of why I love Sloan Mackenzie —his note-taking skills."

Sloan chuckles while sprinkling cut berries into the beige discs of batter on the grill. "Two hundred and twelve, is it? Are they written out somewhere or locked in that complex mind of yours?"

I tap my temple and wink. "Locked in the vault."

"What about if I add a few chocolate chips to accompany the berries? Would ye like that?"

"Reason number two hundred and *thirteen* of why I love Sloan Mackenzie—his instinct to put chocolate chips in my pancakes."

The two of us are still laughing when Wallace joins us and we sober. "Don't stop on my account. It does my heart good to see the two of you having fun."

"How are Kinu and the twins?" I set the notepad back onto the table and stand. "Are they *really* all right?"

He sets his bag down on the floor beside the table and grips my arms. "Yes, Fi. They are really all right. Mother and young are doing fine. Kinu does need to stay off her feet for the next few weeks so they stay that way, but if luck be our mistress, things will be fine."

"If we need luck then there *is* a problem."

He gives me a reluctant nod and steps over to the breakfast bar to watch Sloan cook. "Placental abruption is three times more common in a pregnancy of multiples due to the increased stretching of the uterus as it expands to accommodate the extra babies."

"Okay, but what does that mean?"

Calum and Kevin come downstairs at the same time Emmet and Ciara jog up from the basement.

Wallace doesn't seem intimidated by the rush of a curious family. Thankfully, this is his wheelhouse. He deals with stuff like this on the daily. "Placental abruption means the placenta begins to detach prematurely from the wall of the uterus. The detachment may be mild and partial, happening slowly over time, or begin suddenly as in Kinu's case."

"But it's still attached?" Emmet asks. "The babies are still in there, and their bubble of nutrients and stuff is still keeping them safe, right?"

"Yes, all is well. And, if all goes as planned, Kinu will stay off her feet, and her doctor will monitor things very closely."

I swallow, easing onto one of the barstools at the breakfast bar. "And if all doesn't go as planned? What happens then? Worst-case scenario."

Wallace doesn't seem keen on getting into it, but he's reading the room and knows we're not about to let it slide. "In the worst case, pain and bleeding would accompany a complete abruption. This would require an immediate and emergency delivery of the babies by C-section."

"But we're not there," Sloan says, meeting my gaze. "In more mild cases, doctors can monitor the pregnancy and determine what's best fer the babies, including an early delivery to avoid potential dangers. It's too soon to panic."

I sigh. "Oh, it's too late not to panic, hotness. I don't think any of us will relax until those babies arrive and Kinu is healthy and recovering."

"If Kinu's on bed rest, we'll have to make sure the kids are kept busy and taken care of," Kevin says.

I nod. "I'll talk to Myra about setting up a few more sleepovers with Imari."

"There will be plenty to occupy them once Dart arrives." Sloan dishes me a plate of pancakes.

Crap on a cracker. "We still need to get ready for Dart. Oh, Emmet, Pip is pregnant and needs things for her nesting. She told Dora a few things, but can you talk to her and confirm what she wants? She asked if we could make her a proper home."

Emmet nods. "I didn't know they needed anything more than they have."

"Maybe it would be a good idea to poll all the fae and find out if their needs are met," Calum suggests.

"Didn't you have a book from Gran for that?" Emmet asks.

"I do. I'll bring it down, and we can see what it says too." My phone buzzes and I check out the attachment. "It's the lab reports from the U of T homicide. Garnet had them run an analysis on the blue lipstick. Does anyone speak bloodwork?"

"I do," Wallace says. "Would ye like me to have a look? It seems ye have a lot on yer plate already."

"Yes, thank you." I hand him my phone and reach for the syrup. "For the next three minutes, the only plate I want to think about is this one. Thank you, hotness. These are amazing."

I'm still chewing my first bites when Wallace *harumphs* and shakes his head. "Something's not right here. Not at all. If this is accurate…my God. Who would do such a thing?"

Aw hell. So much for enjoying my pancakes.

After plowing a plate of chocolate chip and berry ambrosia into my mouth, Sloan, Wallace, and I *poof* to the sterile corridor of the Guild's medical arts building to follow up on Wallace's concerns with the lab report.

I laugh and point at the graffiti addition to the sign to make it a medical *f*arts building. "Apparently, people in Garnet's world still dare to have a sense of humor and lighten the mood."

Sloan grunts. "I'm sure that won't end well."

"Oh, maybe it's new, and we'll get to see his reaction. That would be amazeballs."

Sloan chuckles. "You're so easily amused."

"True story."

The first time I was here, Imari's birth mother exploded like a pizza pocket too long in the microwave. The second time, a dark wizard had pretty much fried Calum, and my brother almost died.

Needless to say, it's not my favorite place.

Adding some humor is a welcome change.

Garnet comes through the double doors and strides toward us, his long, ebony hair flowing wild behind his shoulders. When he sees the sign on the wall, his eyes flash gold, and the air fills with a long rumble of his lion's displeasure.

It's awesome.

Shaking his head, he storms up to me, and I hold up my palms. "Wasn't us. It was a farts building when we got here."

He mutters something about biting off heads as he eyes me more closely.

"We didn't tag your sign," I repeat so he can smell the truth of my words. "Someone else has pranked you, not me. I knew nothing about it until I read it just now."

He stands down then, and I'm not sure if I should be flattered or insulted that he thinks I would fart his sign. "Hey, thanks for letting us have access to your lab people. You didn't need to come. We could've updated you later."

He gives me a classic Garnet scowl and lifts his chin toward Sloan's father. "Garnet Grant," he says. "You must be Wallace Mackenzie."

Wallace shrinks a little as Garnet thrusts his hand forward. Not that I blame him. Before I knew Garnet well, I thought he was intimidating as hell. Now I know he's just a growly pussy cat —that kills people who piss him off.

Meh. We all have our things, amirite?

When the introductions are over, Garnet leads us farther down the hall, past the emergency rooms and morgue to the lab. I recognize the faces of the two Guild scientists in lab coats and nod. "Thanks for coming in on a Sunday. A few things in your report about the trace chemicals of the lipstick raised questions."

"For us as well," one of the scientists says. "We ran the test three different times with the same result."

"Which is what, exactly," Xavier says, directly behind me.

I jump and turn, my heart thundering. "Seriously, dude. You did that on purpose just to be an ass."

Xavier pegs me with a cold glare. "You mean to hear your heart rate triple as you *yip* like a pathetic schoolgirl? I don't know what you mean."

I chuff and gesture at the newest arrival. "Xavier, Vampire

King of Toronto, this is Wallace Mackenzie, Master Healer of the Ancient Order of Druids."

The two exchange a cool glance and I get the feeling Wallace isn't a fan of vampires either. Smart man.

"I'm sorry, I don't know who that is." I gesture at the pretty Asian woman standing behind him. "Otherwise, I would introduce you."

Xavier throws me a dirty look and ignores my comment. He also doesn't introduce the woman. "Why was I called down here at this unholy hour of the morning? Have you found something?"

"I didn't call you so I couldn't say."

Garnet frowns. "I thought if your father-in-law had concerns about the results of the lab reports, Xavier might be interested in being part of the discussion."

Whatevs.

"Go ahead, Wallace. Ask your questions."

He does. At first, I try to listen and understand but when they get into the breakdown of lipids and leukocytes and percentages of basophils all I hear is Charlie Brown's teacher from Peanuts.

Wah wah woh wah wah.

Still, I try to look intelligent and nod when the others do. Sloan seems to be holding his own in the conversation and manages a few questions which they seem to consider relevant.

Gah… he's so freaking smart.

If I'm ever on *Who Wants to Be a Millionaire*, he's my phone a friend guy, fo shizzle.

"Are you getting any of this?" a woman whispers from behind me. It's the girl who came in with Xavier, and when I meet her gaze, she smiles and holds out her hand. "Hi, sorry, I'm Karuna. I probably shouldn't have bothered you, but you looked as lost as me."

I grin. "I was going for contemplative and informed. That wasn't coming across?"

She chuckles. "No. Sorry."

"Not your fault. You're right. I'm getting none of this." I look the woman over and wonder what I'm missing. "Sorry. Is it taboo if I ask if you're a vampire? You came with Xavier, but you seem so...."

"Normal? Human? Laidback?"

"All of the above."

She tilts her head toward the corridor, and since the men's conversation has now moved to endorphins and adrenaline and ghrelin hormones, there's no hope I'll catch on to what they're saying.

My shield is quiet, so I accept the prompt.

After closing the door behind us, I point at the plastic chairs along the wall.

When we're settled, I find she's studying me now. "You don't seem like such a pain in the ass."

I laugh and relax a little more. "Thanks. I'm Fiona, by the way."

She nods. "Oh, I know. Xavier told me I'd be meeting you this morning."

"He did, did he? So what's this about?"

She sweeps her hair off her neck and tucks it behind her ear. The movement draws my attention to the two puncture marks on the side of her neck. "He comes off as cold and unforgiving, but that's his way. It upsets him that you judge him on things you don't understand."

I sigh, the situation becoming clear. "You're one of his feeder sheep, and he brought you here to convince me you're not being taken advantage of."

Her smile dims. "I'm not one of his feeder sheep—I'm his chosen human companion. I fulfill his blood needs when he requires more than supplementation and in return, he fulfills my needs and will continue to do so for as long as I live."

I try to wrap my head around that. "So, you're saying you're genuinely happy being his juice box?"

"Wow. You're as rude as he said."

Being called out hits home. "Sorry. I don't filter well but me not being a fan of vampires is more their doing than mine."

"How so?"

"Vampires kidnapped me and my bestie a few months ago. They bruised us up, delivered us to two different hostile assholes, and when we ceased to be of use, they tried to kill us. I would be dead if my friend didn't jump in front of the bullet. As it was, he almost died."

She has the decency to look appalled. "I'm sorry. Were they vampires from Xavier's seethe?"

"Aren't they all? Isn't he the head honcho?"

"He is, but there are seven seethes of vampires in the GTA. One size does not fit all in the vampire world."

"Are you saying he's not the violent kind? Because if you are, I think he's snowing you."

She frowns. "I'm not being snowed. I know there is violence and bloodshed in Xavier's world, but that's not the side of him I ever see."

"Lucky you."

We sit quietly for a moment, and I realize she's rethinking telling me whatever it was that she coaxed me out here to say. I can either dig my heels in or try to salvage this olive branch. "So, tell me. Who is the Xavier you know?"

She offers me an apologetic smile and turns the ring on her thumb. "Xavier is a man born in a time and of a culture that believes in proper decorum and Confucian principles. Life may have changed him in dramatic ways, but his core beliefs remain the same."

"You realize your man of decorum is a straight-up crime lord, right? And the people of his seethe help him run his organization."

She presses her lips tight and sighs. "Sometimes life takes you down paths you weren't destined for. You adapt or die. You can't know Xavier's motivations, and you certainly don't know how he does business."

"You're right. Normally I try never to judge, but watching my best friend bleeding out made an impression on me—a powerful and negative one."

"I understand. But now you're part of the investigation into our family. I've known Jasper, Orion, and Gustov for more than a decade. Destroying them over something they would never do because of prejudice would be so wrong."

The tenderness and empathy in her voice surprise me. She's a beautiful woman who seems smart and articulate. How did she end up the feeder of a vampire?

"What about your family? Do they know where you are and why you're there?"

"Why would I care?"

"Because they're your family?"

Her rich, brown eyes cloud over when she looks at me. "My mother left us when I was a child and when I was eight, my father traded me to a man in my village for two bags of heroin. After four years, that man sold me into human trafficking. Xavier rescued me from a life of drugs, fear, and abuse. The companions in our family all have similar origin stories."

"I'm sorry. That's horrible."

"It's my first life. Like the vampires we're paired with, companions have past lives and our second lives. My second life with Xavier has given me everything. I take courses at the university and have friends, money in my wallet, and travel the world. Anything I need he provides. I am his companion *because* of who he is not despite it."

"And it's the same for the others in his seethe?"

Karuna nods. "Xavier ensures it. He has very strict rules about how his vampires treat companions. We are their lifeblood, and they treat us that way. Feeding is a private and reverent exchange of power. There is no way vampires from our family would ever lose control as they did. There's more to this."

I think about my father and all the years he's worked to support the legal system with unbiased dedication. Then I picture Themis holding the scales of justice with her eyes blindfolded.

"You're right. I have good reasons not to like vampires, but it's rude to judge. It isn't my place. I'll do my best to figure out what happened and once we have all the facts, we'll see what the Guild of Governors says."

She accepts that. "I don't know why it matters to him that you understand the way of things, but for some reason it does."

I'm not sure either, but something tells me Xavier is shrewd enough to realize Karuna would get through to me better than he ever could. "It's been a pleasure talking to you, Karuna. I hope we get a chance to visit again sometime."

"I hope so too."

When I stand, I pull one of my Guild Governor cards out of my phone case and hand it to her. "If you ever need anything, or want to grab lunch or come to our family pub for a beer or anything, give me a call."

"Thank you. I will.

CHAPTER SEVEN

The security protocols of the Batcave entrance flash green and the system clicks to allow Sloan, Wallace, and me through the reinforced glass doors. "Welcome to the Team Trouble headquarters, also known as the Batcave." I hold the door open and let our guest enter first. "This is where the magic happens."

Maxwell exits his office to greet us, and I gesture at him from across the room. "Here's the man who tries to organize our crazy cast of characters to keep us out of trouble."

John Maxwell is handsome, tall and with his silver hair, bears a striking resemblance to Anderson Cooper. He's also one helluva cop and all-around good guy. "*Try to* organize you is the key part in that sentence."

"True story." I tuck my pendant back under my shirt and unhook the strap of my purse from over my head. "So, what's up?"

"First off, I apologize for calling you in on a Sunday, especially when you have company. I considered letting it wait until tomorrow but thought you'd want to see this."

"That's fine. We were already out and about. Criminals don't take Sundays off, so why should we? Oh, introductions, sorry. John Maxwell, this is Wallace Mackenzie."

Maxwell offers his hand, and they shake. "It's good to meet you, Wallace. Your son has been an invaluable part of our team. You should be very proud."

Wallace casts a warm glance at Sloan and smiles. "Aye, I am."

I drop my purse on the conference table in the middle of the room and notice the photo array on the electronic wall. "Oh, you found our Goth girl."

Maxwell joins me at the table and picks up the remote. With a couple of clicks, the screen splits so her picture remains, but a data box opens with her deets. "Meet Galina Romanov. Daughter of one of the most powerful crime families in the Eastern Bloc."

I don't love the sound of that. "Is it wishful thinking to hope she's only in Toronto visiting friends?"

"It is, I'm afraid. From what I've gathered from my office, the DEA, and Guns and Gangs, she started making connections in the crime circles of the city two years ago and moved into a position of power not long after."

"What's her criminal focus?"

"Guns and sex. The RCMP believes her father's organization is grabbing up young girls from remote villages in Europe and shipping them here for Galina to utilize in her Canadian startup."

"A family business. Lovely."

Maxwell nods. "Unfortunately we have no proof and have never been able to put anything but circumstantial events together. As wild and reckless as she seems to be as a woman, she's shrewd when it comes to how she runs her organization."

"Maybe daddy keeps a tight rein on her."

"That's certainly a possibility."

"Do we know where her home base is?"

"No. From what the agencies can gather, she's nomadic. They've never been able to nail down a base of operations for her. They consider her a ghost."

"A ghost coming after a vampire. How cute."

"I have facial recognition working to scan public feeds and traffic cameras. If we're lucky, maybe we can piece together what she's been up to the past few months and how that led to a string of student murders."

"We came from meeting Garnet at the Guild lab and have some insights on that."

He sets the remote back on the table and gives me his full attention. "Did you find anything interesting?"

"We did." Sloan offers Maxwell the file folder containing the lab results. "The chemical breakdown on the blue substance found on the three victims indicates the lipstick is a catalyst used to alter the victims' DNA subtly. In essence, it alters the scent of the person kissed enough to make them a living beacon to trigger a vampire feeding frenzy."

"Inventive."

"What's more inventive," Wallace adds, opening the front cover of the folder to point at the DNA diagrams, "is that she designed the beacon so specifically that only one siring bloodline will feel its effect."

"Xavier's," he says.

I nod. "From what Garnet's scientists found, there is a rare stars aligning kind of mythical event in vampire life called *cântând sânge* or singing blood. It's said to be overpowering to the extreme and undeniable for a vampire in its thrall. Even those who are well-fed and well-conditioned to resist the violence of their instincts are mindless animals once the blood sings to them."

Maxwell flips the page and frowns. "It can't be a coincidence that she's targeting U of T students two city blocks away from Xavier's nest. The woman has done her homework."

"Agreed. She knows the kids she kisses either live or attend school close by and when one of Xavier's seethe catches the scent, instant murderous frenzy."

Maxwell closes the folder and sets it on the table. "Why target Xavier's seethe?"

"Rival vampire mafia?"

"Did someone say rival vampire mafia?" Dionysus appears beside me, grinning from ear to ear. "That's the kind of stuff we deal with, right? Vampire murder is part of our crime beat?"

I pat my chest, my heart thundering in my chest. "Holy crap, you scared me."

"Sorry, Red. I heard the conversation unfold and came down to see what we're working on. Vampire murder sounds fun. It just so happens that my day is clear."

Maxwell frowns. "Who are you?"

"This is Dionysus." I smile at his Sherlock deerstalker hat. "He's part of the team now."

Maxwell's frown intensifies. "I'm supposed to vet new members of the team."

I shrug. "He's Dionysus...*the* Dionysus. Greek god. Son of Zeus. God of wine and fertility. I'm not sure how you'd vet him? Wikipedia? Britannica.com?"

Maxwell's mouth opens as if he's about to say something but can't quite grasp the words.

I chuckle and pat the guy's arm. "He's a friend and a good guy. There's nothing to vet. He is who he is, and he's new to the time and the city. He finds our turmoil entertaining, but he's solidly Team Trouble material."

"I took out Minginippe in the last big battle," Dionysus says, grinning. "Dillan and Calum say it was epic."

"True story."

Sloan nods. "We were getting our asses handed to us at the time. Dionysus was the key player in our win."

Dionysus brightens, standing taller. "It was a temporary win. We still don't know where Minginippe is."

"No, we don't, but Samuel, Quon Shen, and Ahren are working on that. So much to do. So little time." I gesture from the Greek god to the others. "So, anyway, this is Deputy Commissioner John Maxwell, our RCMP liaison, and Wallace Mackenzie, Sloan's father."

Dionysus has already moved on from introductions and is scanning the photo array. "Yummy. Who's the hottie in leather?"

"A Romanian crime lord's daughter turned Toronto vampire tormentor and murder inducer."

"Murder inducer," Dionysus says, his brows arching. "That's not a descriptor you hear every day."

"Thankfully, no."

"So, are we taking her down? Bringing her in? Shining her on? Working her over? Roughing her up? What's the plan for this bad girl?"

I chuckle. "All good thoughts, but for now, figuring out why she's targeting Xavier and how she knows about vampire genetics would be our first step."

"I'm guessing it's knowledge from the old country. The Romanov crime family started in Romania, specifically Transylvania," he says.

"That might do it. So she gets here and wants to dominate Toronto, but there's a vampire kingpin in her way. She studies him, somehow figures out he's a vampire and uses old country knowledge to solve her vampire problem."

"She has guts," Sloan says. "To figure out Xavier is a vampire and target him through the siring line of his family is dangerous and bold."

I agree. "As unique of an approach as it is, it draws a lethal line in the sand. She has to know if he figures out who she is, he'll come for her."

"I think she's counting on that," Maxwell says.

"What makes you say that?"

"Attacking his family is personal, not professional. When profiling female assailants, the most common motivations are power or passion."

"So, ye think they've tangled in some way?"

"Definitely. If not romantically, then something he did in the course of his business dealings has struck a personal chord. She wants not only to take him down, but her chemical assault on his family says she wants to make him suffer as well."

Wallace steps around the table to take a closer look. "Maybe her hatred stems from him being a vampire at all. Growing up near the epicenter of vampire origins, she may have a family history with the race. If so, her assault could have less to do with Xavier and more to do with wiping out a nest of vampires she came across during her relocation to Toronto."

Maxwell nods. "I'll start a full background check on her family history and see if anything comes up that looks like it could've been vampire-related."

"I am *soooo* not a fan of vampires," I say, "but using innocent students to weaponize her revenge gives us no other option but to take her down hard and fast."

"Oh, there's no doubt about that, Fi," Maxwell says. "Protect and serve supersedes any vigilante motive no matter how compelling."

"Do ye think she knew about the singing blood and the chemistry behind triggering it because she's a vampire herself?" Wallace asks. "Maybe that's her grudge...that someone back home changed her."

Maxwell shakes his head and calls up another screen on the electronic wall. "She was admitted into the hospital five months ago with life-threatening injuries. I've got the surgery log, all the medical files, and the police report. There's nothing odd about any of it. She's human."

"Other than the fact that she claims she took three bullets after surprising an intruder in her home," I say while reading the police report. "That's personal. Any chance Xavier or his men had anything to do with that?"

"Possibly, but it would be nearly impossible to tie him to it if she wants revenge."

Sloan nods. "She won't point her finger at him if she's got her retribution sorted and is taking care of things herself."

I frown at the last notation in the police file. "It says she was unavailable for further questioning. What happened there?"

"After leaving the hospital, she went back to Europe for a month to recuperate. Once she returned, the surveillance teams lost track of her operation."

"Shoot me once; shame on you. Shoot me twice..."

Sloan smirks. "Perhaps her trip home wasn't about recovery. Maybe that's when she sought out the chemistry information on how to create singing blood."

Maxwell shrugs. "We can't prove it was anything more than wanting her mama's homemade meatball soup to make her feel better."

We might not be able to prove it yet, but my gut says we're on the right track. "Whether or not Xavier put her in the hospital, it's hard to believe he didn't recognize her when I showed him her picture. The two of them are heavily involved in the same crime circles. Know your enemy, amirite?"

"Ye said Xavier denied knowin' her in front of Garnet," Sloan says. "The lion would've smelled the lie."

"But *did* he deny knowing her?" I think back to what was said, second-guessing our acceptance of that. "His exact words were, 'I can't help you. I wish I knew how someone like her could manipulate members of my bloodline into the frenzied killing of innocents.' That's not a denial of knowing her."

Sloan sighs. "Yer right, but we can't call the Vampire King of Toronto a liar without proof that he knows who she is."

I point at the new set of photos filtering onto the screen and grin. "Score! Hey look, Xavier and Galina Romanov chatting outside the Gooderham Building. Oh look, there they are again at the Eaton's Centre having ice caps."

The five of us stare at the photos a few seconds longer before Sloan breaks the silence. "Ye better forward those photos to Garnet, *a ghra*. I'm sure he won't be happy to learn Xavier mislead him."

"Pants on fire, Xavier." I open a message to Garnet. "What are you up to, Vampire King?"

Sloan throws a globe of faery fire into the coffered lighting trough by the ceiling and the room bursts into a warm glow. He gestures at the interior of the Shrine of Toronto's Objects and Antiquities and draws a deep breath. "This is it, Da. This is what I've been working on the past months."

Wallace steps further into STOA and smiles at Sloan's budding dream.

"I realize there are still a lot of empty shelves," Sloan says, falling into step with his father. "And it's certainly not as impressive as the shrine Lugh keeps for the Order, but I'm hoping it might be someday."

"It will be." Wallace runs his finger over a petal blade and picks up a fire drake wand. "Even in its infancy, ye've got a couple of fine pieces here."

Sloan places his hand on the security panel beside the locked vault and opens the next room. "I have my eye on a couple of things coming up on auction next month. If I'm lucky, I'll pick up a band of bees and maybe even a lantern of hope. Those will be handy with the darkness in store next winter."

"Aye, yer right, there. They will." Wallace casts another appraising gaze around the shrine and nods. "Ye've done well, son. Yer coming into yer own and it's a lovely thing to see. This shrine is a dream of yer own making, and yer passion is obvious."

Sloan's expression softens, and I see how deeply his father's words touch him. "Thanks, Da. That means so much."

Wallace steps in and opens his arms. The gesture of physical comfort takes Sloan off-guard, but in the beat of a racing heart, he meets his father chest-to-chest. "I'm so very proud of ye, my wee man. I'm only sorry it took this long to see who ye truly are and what ye need."

I'm blinking against the sting of tears because both of them are tearing up and it's long overdue.

I turn to step back into the main room of the shrine and Wallace catches my arm. "Och, there's no runnin' away from this, young lady. Yer the one who stirred up all these emotions and showed us what we were missin'. Yer part of this too."

Wallace pulls me into the embrace, and it's the three of us hugging. Sloan's hold isn't as solid as it usually is and I squeeze him harder to lend him my strength.

After a moment, I pull back and kiss Wallace's cheek. "Thank you for being who he needs now. It doesn't matter how long it took to get here. This is where we are, and it's all good."

With that said, I leave the two of them and make my way out to browse the shelves of Sloan's happy place.

Yes, he wanted to come to Toronto for me, but he also wanted a chance to find his purpose, and it's a beautiful thing to watch. I run my gaze over a few items and make a note to find him something exceptional to add to his collection.

I look at the chakram Sloan used against Melanippe. It's a little worse for wear since its exposure to the detonation of Dionysus's RPG, but hey, lots of antiquities are banged up.

The thought that the Amazon and Mingin got away to regroup is unsettling. Aside from crisscrossing the world following every spike in dark energy, there's nothing to be done unless or until they resurface.

My phone buzzes in my pocket and I smile at Dora's message.

How to Train Your Dragon 101 is beginning. Don't keep the teacher waiting.

We wrap up our tour of STOA and Sloan *poofs* us to the circle of standing stones not far from our home. Built by the Barghest in a flat clearing within a small forest, the necromancers of Toronto originally warded it to prevent human discovery while performing human sacrifice. Putting an end to that was one of my first accomplishments as an urban druid.

Now it is what it was always supposed to be—a place to celebrate a reverence for nature.

Seventeen rugged stones, each reaching about eight feet from the ground, encircle a raised stone slab used as the altar.

"The resemblance to Drombeg is incredible." Wallace scans the landscape. "The Barghest built it, ye say?"

I release Bruin to stretch his legs and walk toward the altar stone. "Yep. Although we confiscated it from the first wave of Barghest after they tried to kill us."

Sloan shrugs off his jacket and joins me. "They almost succeeded in sacrificing Fi on that altar stone, but true to form, she fought her way free."

"I didn't do that alone. I had help."

He winks. "Then she and Nikon came back and spelled the altar stone so the Barghest could never use it for sacrifice again."

I giggle. "It was the first mission of mischief. Nikon made it so the harm of spells cast on the altar reflects at the one wielding the ill intent while the innocent victim remains unscathed. He called it the old Leviticus theory."

Wallace runs a hand over the stone slab. "Fracture for fracture, eye for eye, tooth for tooth; anyone who maims another shall suffer the same injury in return."

"That's the one."

Sloan winks at me. "Once Droghun lost a couple of men during sacrifices, they realized this was no longer a place for their evil dealings and lost interest."

Wallace *harumphs* and shakes his head. "I remember Droghun from decades back. He was a skilled druid but never held the reverence needed to be a great druid."

"So, he and who knows how many others turned to necromancy to give them the power boost they were after to be more than they earned."

Wallace sighs. "Do ye honestly believe there's a connection with Barghest and Riordan McNiff? I know ye said it on a whim a few months ago, but Sloan mentioned it's still a working theory."

I run a hand over the stone slab and tilt my head from side to side. "Part of me does, yeah. Beyond the obvious connection of Barghest being a large black dog and the McNiff surname translating into 'black dog,' there are all the other little things that add to that."

"Like what?"

"Like his arrogance and quest for power."

Wallace chuffs. "There's no shortage of arrogance in the empowered world, Fi."

"I get that. He also had a book on Hunter-gods when no one else had ever heard of them. He knew about the seam to the Neitherlands being in Newgrange tomb and the dark souls trapped there."

"Riordan is a well-read man."

"Tad said Riordan was furious when he found out he lent the text to me."

"He might not approve of his son taking his possessions and loaning them out."

"He is also an elder, so he knew the super-secret equinox ritual and what it would mean if the druids didn't perform the fertility ritual."

"I don't want to think it, but one of the fae races who attend might've let the word of that slip. I have a hard time believin' that one of our own would sabotage a sacred ritual."

"Well, he also knew where the nine families live for the kidnappings. To get all of you in a coordinated attack, Barghest had to arrange a lot of moving parts."

Wallace frowns. "Riordan is a powerful man who comes from a powerful lineage, Fi. Be careful who ye offer this theory to."

He's not wrong. I know that.

"As I said, it's just a theory. I don't *want* it to be true. Tad's our friend. The last thing I want is to accuse his father of being a traitor to the Order."

Wallace nods. "Don't forget, they kidnapped Riordan along with the rest of us."

"True, but it would've raised too many red flags for him not to be. And why weren't any of you more hurt?"

He chuckles. "I'm rather pleased we weren't."

"Oh, yeah, I'm super thankful you're all well and back to normal, but think about it. If Barghest is truly our enemy, why keep the nine of you alive and tucked away in a mansion? If they wanted to undo the druids in Ireland and they had the nine elders of the Ancient Order of the Druids, why not get rid of you while you were unable to defend yourselves?"

"I can't say," Wallace says. "I suppose I thought you kids rescued us before they had the chance. You foiled their plans."

"I hope that's it, but my instincts tell me no."

"Yer instincts are usually spot-on, *a ghra*."

"I know. That's what worries me."

CHAPTER EIGHT

W hile Bruin and I give Wallace the grand tour of the stone circle and the forested area beyond, Sloan *poofs* across town to gather Dora and bring her back to join us.

When they arrive, I hold my arms out along the horizon. "What do you think of this as a training area? It's open and already spelled for privacy. I think it might be a perfect place to allow Dart to spread his wings while he develops."

Dora considers it for a moment and smiles. "It has potential. We'll have to expand the privacy spell to include the air above here so he can land and take off without being seen—and he'll only be able to fly in the dead of night anyway—but yes, I think this will work."

"Awesomesauce."

Wallace scans the area and nods his agreement. "I'm certain yer Western will thrive here. Stone circles have long held deep ties with dragons. It's fitting you chose to train him here."

"A fine point, Mr. Mackenzie," Dora says. "You're referring to the days when ancient megalithic circles were also dragon portals?"

"Hubba-wha?" I blink. "Is that a thing?"

"Och, aye," Wallace says. "There were myths that's how dragons escaped persecution as long as they did. When hunters set upon them, the caregivers devised a way to link circles and transport them away to somewhere safe."

This starts sounding familiar, and I smile. "Fionn mentioned something about this when we were back in the days of Camelot."

"Is that somethin' we could do, Dora?" Sloan asks. "Maybe link the real Drombeg in County Cork with this replica Drombeg?"

"To what end, hotness?" I ask.

"Och, many reasons. To connect Dart with the Dragon Queen and his brood. To allow him an avenue of escape if I'm not around to transport him out of a tough situation. To give him the chance to travel home once he's full-grown and too big for me to transport him."

I hadn't thought about that.

Yeah, I guess when Dart is fully grown and super-sized for good, he'll be too big for Sloan and Nikon to transport back and forth to Ireland. "The next question is do we know *how* to do it?"

Wallace frowns. "If it ever was more than a myth, I'd say the knowledge died centuries ago. Maybe next time you speak to Fionn, you could ask him about it."

"That's one option." I turn to Dora. "The other might be to ask a friend who might know how to do it already."

Dora flutters her glittery eyelashes and flashes a coy smile. "I might be able to dust off a few of my old spell books and do that for you."

I reach up and hug her. "You're the best. Thanks."

"Don't thank me yet, cookie. If I'm taking on some of the care responsibilities of Dartamont's life here, I'm going to be tough on both of you. It doesn't do a dragon any good to be an enabler. They respond best when they have clear boundaries and expectations."

I stiffen my fingers and touch my forehead in a military salute. "Yes, ma'am. Whip us into shape, ma'am."

Dora rolls her eyes. "Goddess help me. What am I agreeing to? My life was a great deal simpler before you tromped into it."

"Meh, simple is boring. With me, you're back in the swing of things like you were always meant to be."

She sobers and lays her arm across my shoulders. "I admit, it's good to be back."

With our plans progressing and the weekend coming to an end, we *poof* Dora back to the apartment over her drag club, then Sloan takes us home. I can honestly say I've enjoyed having Wallace stay over, which is both a relief and a happy surprise.

Sloan deserves to have his parents see how amazing he is. I haven't given up hope that Janet will come around. If Wallace talks us up, maybe his mom will give Sloan's new life a chance.

"If ye don't mind waitin' on dinner a few minutes," Wallace says, grabbing his medical bag. "I'd like to check on yer sister-in-law before it gets too late."

I release Bruin and hug Manx. "That sounds perfect. I'll come too and check in."

"We'll make it a family affair then," Sloan says. "Lead the way, *a ghra.*"

The three of us make the quick trip next door and find my brothers lounging in the family room at the front of the house. "Hey, how are Kinu and the babes?"

Aiden sets his beer down on his coaster and stands to greet us. "Day one of bedrest has gone well. Dillan moved his TV into our room, and the kids snuggled in with Mommy and watched Moana. Then Calum and Kev took them to the park so she could have a nap. They're picking up a bucket of chicken if you're interested."

"Thanks, but I'm taking the Mackenzie men to the top of the tower for dinner. Wallace wanted to check in before we go."

"If she's sleepin' and ye'd rather not disturb her—"

Aiden cuts that off with the wave of a hand. "No. We're thankful to have you here. If you have time to look at her, we'll accept the offer with thanks."

Wallace checks his watch and meets my gaze "Is twenty minutes all right? I'd like to strengthen the connections of things internally and check in with each of the wee ones."

"Take your time. Honestly, if it takes all night, I'd rather you do that than worry about dinner. Kinu and the twins are the priority."

Aiden escorts Wallace upstairs, and I catch the weird vibe passing between my brothers. "What did we miss?"

Emmet takes a long sip of his beer and shrugs. "I was saying to them we should be better druids. After performing the Alban Eiler at Drombeg, I think we should recognize and celebrate all the druid holidays."

I snort. "Alban Eiler was a disaster all around. Why would we want a repeat of that shit show?"

Emmet frowns. "Your part might've been a disaster, but our Ostara ritual was life-changing."

Dillan barks a laugh. "Says the guy who got uber laid while high on god powers. Not all of us were so lucky. We were battling evil smog and fighting Barghest assholes while you and Ciara were exploring your Adam and Eve reboot."

"D is for dick." He gives him the finger. "I'm not saying we have to make it huge, but something."

"With the vampire killings and Kinu having trouble with the twins, don't you think we have enough going on without taking on a ritual celebration we've never done before? I'm supposed to bring Dart here this week too."

Emmet can be like the sweetest, happiest puppy dog ever, his tail and tongue wagging, his ears perked at the mere thought of having fun.

Seeing him deflate breaks my heart every damn time. "Never mind. Forget I brought it up. Yeah. We're too busy to worry about it."

Except his words and his energy are sending out opposite messages.

"Em? What's this really about?"

He drops his gaze and picks at the label of his beer bottle. "Ciara's family takes the druid traditions seriously. When she asked me what we have planned for this weekend, and if she could be involved, I wasn't sure what to say. I told her she was more than welcome to join us."

"You lied to her?"

"No. She is more than welcome. We just don't have anything planned yet."

"Aw, Em, why weren't you straight with her? Now you're all twisted up?"

His sad gaze sears me right to my soul. "I don't want them to think we're half-assing it."

"Half-assing it?" Dillan snorts. "We've done more druiding in the past eight months than the druids in Ireland, hands down. End. Of."

He nods. "I know, but not the holidays. It's cool, though. I'll explain to her that with Kinu having troubles it's a bad time."

Part of me wants to take the excuse and let the idea of a Beltane celebration die its last death. Ciara certainly doesn't need another excuse to come hang out with Emmet. And it's not an excuse. We *are* overwhelmed with stuff coming at us from all sides.

Another part of me remembers the Tarot reading.

Nine of Wands.

I'm the point of obstacle. I honestly don't want to be. I want

Emmet to be happy. I want all my brothers to be happy...gloriously, deliriously happy.

"Hello? Fi? Where'd you go there?" Dillan asks.

I shake off my mental wandering and smile at Emmet. "Yeah, a Beltane celebration sounds great, Em. We should for sure do something. Maybe it's small, but we'll do something."

"Maybe something at the stones," Sloan suggests.

Emmet's happy puppy excitement returns in full force. "The stone circle is a fantastic idea. I'll do research and see what we can do. Irish? Maybe you could help me a little? You know what Ciara will be expecting. Maybe you could keep me from looking foolish?"

"Of course. I'd be honored to help. Beltane has several simple traditions we could incorporate like having a maypole and going a-Maying and burying wish boxes."

Emmet's enthusiasm is catching on.

I get on the bandwagon and squash my inner nay-sayer. "It sounds like tons of fun, Emmet. Maybe we can even get Gran and Granda to come."

"And Da," Sloan says. "Maybe he'll come back too. Ye never know, maybe he can convince Mam."

I nod. "You should definitely invite them."

Sloan grins. "All right, Em, you look up what you can, and we'll start making a list tonight after we get back from dinner. We haven't much time. May the first is less than a week away."

Emmet lays a heavy arm over my shoulder. "If there's one thing Clan Cumhaill excels at, it's pulling together a bash in a flash."

"Bash in a flash." Dillan nods. "We should get t-shirts."

I laugh and roll my eyes. "If we got t-shirts every time one of us said 'we should get t-shirts,' we'd have no room in our dressers."

"True story." Emmet steps back to pull out his phone. "Cool.

I'm telling Ciara we're on for Beltane. She'll be jazzed. Thanks, guys. I appreciate this."

Emmet rushes off to spread the good news, and I have to admit, the idea of a druid celebration without darkness overwhelming and ancient prisoners escaping the Neitherlands sounds good.

"Welcome to the top of the tower, 360 Restaurant." Our server sets down a basket of breadsticks and hands us our menus. "Have you been here before?"

"I have. They haven't." I drape my napkin over my lap, happy to be treating my guy and his father to a meal at the top of the CN Tower.

After all the crazy of the past twenty-four hours, I hope to send Wallace home with a smile on his face and a great meal in his stomach so he can put in a good word with Sloan's mother.

Not that it's sure to work, but hey, I'm an optimist.

"360 Restaurant is known to provide one of the country's finest dining experiences while providing a panoramic view of the city. As you dine, the tiered table areas rotate around the column of the tower while you enjoy locally sourced, fresh-market, Canadian cuisine."

I sit up straighter and smile. "Which is a fancy way of saying it's good food while we spin in a slow circle."

Wallace chuckles and accepts his menu. Sloan orders a bottle of wine for the table, and we settle in for some much-needed downtime.

"I'm sorry we haven't had more time to relax during your visit." I set my menu aside and unfold the napkin covering the basket of breadsticks. "I'd like to say it's not usually like this, but that would be a lie."

Sloan chuckles. "True. This weekend isn't much different than any other, I'm afraid."

Wallace accepts the basket, takes one, and passes it along to Sloan. "Then, I suppose it's good yer young and have the energy needed to deal with the mayhem. No offense, but I prefer the tranquil pace of my clinic in the Irish countryside."

"Och, there are moments of chaos there too." Sloan chuckles. "I remember more than one emergency knockin' on our door that kept us scramblin'."

Wallace lowers his chin. "True, but I think maybe with more quiet time between emergencies."

"Aye, I'll give ye that."

The wine arrives, and we place our orders.

"Wonderful," he says, marking down our selections. "I'll be back with more breadsticks in a moment."

"Excellent. Thanks."

When it's the three of us once more, Wallace checks that our conversation is our own and leans in. "Do ye truly think yer friend can link the stone circles for dragon transport? The magic of standing portals is arcane knowledge. I'd hate to see things go wrong and yer wee dragon get hurt."

I peer out the glass windows as our table inches across the Toronto skyline, looking for places I recognize. Sloan's father doesn't know about Dora's first life, and it's not our story to share.

Still, I can see his point of concern when all he has seen is her razzle-dazzle. "Dora has arcane knowledge and power held in reserve. There's a lot more to her than cheetah print fabrics and wild wigs."

"Och, I didn't mean to imply otherwise."

I wave that away and hand my empty wine glass to Sloan to fill. "It's fine. Sloan and I know a great deal about Dora's past, and I can honestly say, whatever she says she can do, she can."

"There we are, *a ghra*." Sloan hands me my glass. "Yer locked and loaded to take on the world once again. A lovely red, for my lovely red."

I accept my glass and hold it in the air. "To wine, family, and a break in the chaos long enough to enjoy it."

"Och, that's a good one." Sloan raises his glass to share the toast.

Wallace lifts his glass too. "It is. I'll drink to that."

The *chink* of crystal is still ringing in the air when Dionysus appears sitting at our table. "Hey Red, Irish, father of Irish. Um... I think you need to come with me—like right now—and before you say anything, it totally wasn't my fault."

CHAPTER NINE

"Oh my God. What did you do to him?" I'm staring at a very naked John Maxwell dancing in Dionysus's apartment. I can't for the life of me figure out how he went from being the straight-laced, silver-fox leader of our band of merry men to a handsy exhibitionist in the span of only a few hours.

Well, obviously it's Dionysus, but beyond that.

"Who are all these people?"

Dionysus scans the room. "Just a few fae and ancients I invited over to enjoy my new apartment. Eros. Pan. Herne. Lugh."

"Fiona! Sloan!" John waves vigorously from the other side of the apartment, and I studiously keep my focus on his face. "I missed you."

"Hey, John. Come here for a moment, will you?"

Two pale green women with webbed fingers and pointed ears don't want him to leave. They paw at him when he starts to heed my call, and when I head over to intercept, they hiss and bare their pointy serrated teeth. "You can't have him. He is ours. We claim him."

Well, well, possessive much.

I rake my fingers through my hair and laugh at the absurdity of my life. Fiona Cumhaill, battling evil wizards, unseelie princes, and horny green women.

There's no way around it, so I go through it.

Stomping past the naked elves and gnomes on the dance floor, I make my way over to Maxwell.

"A good time was had by all, but the party is over."

I take his hand, and he lurches forward, hugging me and petting my hair. "I love you, Fi. You're so pretty."

"Uh-huh. Thanks, Maxwell."

He kisses my forehead and grins. "Forget Maxwell. Maxwell is boring. I'm Mad Max now."

"Mad Max!" the others shout, a round of shots appearing in their hands. They tip them back on one and the glasses disappear with another round of shouts. "Mad Max rules."

"Yes, I do! Thank you." He grins, giving a queen's wave to his fans. "I love you all so much."

Grappling a nakey man is awkward enough without him being your supervisor and friend...and slicked in some kind of massage oil.

Fighting the crush of the crowd and the loving affection of a handsy Maxwell, I lose my grip and close my eyes. I don't know what I brushed over, and I don't want to know. I refuse to think about Maxwell's male bits.

Didn't happen.

When a hand cups my boob, I throw a glare over at Sloan, taking it all in from the sidelines. "Are you part problem or part of the solution, Mackenzie?"

He laughs and strides into the fray. "I was admiring my girl in her element."

"How is *this* my element? Wrestling Mad Max away—"

"Mad Max!" they all shout again.

This time a shot glass appears in my hand too. "Seriously? Now I'm part of this?"

Whatevs. I down the shot and let the liquid burn the back of my throat. The glass disappears and signals another round of shouts. "Mad Max rules."

Maxwell chuckles and kisses Sloan's cheek. "Irish, I'm a drinking game."

"Ye sure are, sham." Sloan helps me tug him free of the crush, and we make our way over toward Dionysus and Wallace standing by the arcade.

"Get your hands off him." One of the green girls pushes me back onto a giant inflatable swan. The shove catches me by surprise, and I trip on the swan's chunky webbed feet and assplant.

Before I can get back to my feet, the other one bends and spits a massive amount of water in my face. "We claim him."

I wipe the briny water from my eyes, launch to my feet, and punch Miss Spit in the face. She flies backward over an inflatable panda and bounces ass over end until she crashes into a bumper car.

The sister-wife hisses and launches at me.

I call Birga, stab the swan, and flip the staff to club her with the blunt end. After I untangle my feet from deflated wings, I swing my spear. "Step the hell off you...whatever the fuck you are. Damn. You smell like swamp water."

"They're nixies." Dionysus grins, obviously thinking he's helpful. "Swamp nixies to be exact, but you already guessed that. You have a good sniffer, Red. I'm impressed."

I growl at him and send Birga back to her resting place. "It's not so much a sniffer thing as a 'swamp spit is covering my face' thing."

Sloan and I usher John to another part of the apartment, and if his behavior didn't already tell me, his gaze says he's majorly tripping.

"What did you give him? He's all love and laughter so it's a party drug, right? Molly? What was it?"

Dionysus makes a face and scuffs his foot on the concrete floor. "Promise you won't get mad?"

I shake my head. "No, dude. I don't promise that. Tell me what happened. I need to know what he's on."

"Well, after you left, John asked me about being an immortal Greek, and he mentioned he didn't know much about the fae world and was eager to learn more. I invited a few friends and thought we could have some bevvies and...you know...educate him."

"And you roofied him?"

Dionysus scrubs a hand over his face. "Arynol and Faust asked if I am a fan of ecstasy and I said I love ecstasy—because, duh, who doesn't and it's part of my dominion. When they gave me little pills, I was fascinated. I didn't know people in your realm could contain ecstasy in a pill. I was eager to see how it turned out."

"Oh for shit's sake. You gave him ecstasy?"

"I didn't *mean* to. They are slippery little suckers, and I had just finished my round of Jell-O wrestling against Pan. I may have dropped a couple of pills while I was making drinks."

I groan as I look around the room, searching for John's clothes—which is an impossible task because there are two dozen half and fully naked people in the apartment, and there are clothes strewn everywhere.

Releasing Bruin, I set him on it. "I realize you are not a bloodhound. However, I will be forever grateful if you can find Maxwell's clothes, buddy."

Bruin lifts his head and grunts.

Sloan barks a laugh. "Ye know it's a room of fae when the sudden arrival of a massive grizzly bear doesn't even rank a double-take."

"Let me have a look at yer friend," Wallace says.

"Get your hands off our betrothed." One of the swamp nixies rushes Wallace, and I lose my shit.

When she opens her mouth to spew, I raise my hands. *"Tidal Wave."*

A wall of water hits her in the face and knocks them both flying across the concrete floor. The inflatables catch the rush of water, and suddenly Dionysus's living room is a skinny-dipping wave pool.

"Back at you, bitches."

Sloan's biting his bottom lip, chuckling, but I miss what he finds funny about any of this.

"You, laughing boy, *poof* Maxwell and your dad home. The boys can help him on that end. I'll grab Bruin and Maxwell's clothes and be ready for you on the return trip."

"As ye wish, luv." Sloan grins. "Mad Max has left the building!"

My mouth falls open. "Seriously?"

"Mad Max!" the room shouts as Sloan *poofs* away, busting a gut. I down my shot and like before, the glass disappears. Rolling my eyes, I raise my fist into the air and join the mantra. "Mad Max rules."

The moment the nixie twins recover from my tidal wave and realize Maxwell is gone, they become unpleasant—well, more unpleasant. They start rhyming off edicts and proclamations of possession, and I'm lost in the sea of screeched legalese.

"Does anyone here know what the hell these women are going on about?" I shout.

"I can help you." I follow the sultry voice and meet the gaze of a tall, Mediterranean man with shoulder-length ebony hair and swirling silver eyes.

Okay, wow. "And you are who?"

"Eros."

The way he says it, I take it I'm supposed to know who that is, but I don't, and I don't have time to Google him right now. "And you understand what these nixie bitches are going on about with their claiming?"

He nods. "I do. I hold dominion over all things love, desire, and sex."

"Aha, and that's why you're friends with Dionysus." I look at Dionysus sulking to the side and can't stand him looking so distraught. He's like the biggest, most powerful kid I've ever known.

I draw a long, steadying breath and open my arms. "Come here. You big goof."

He rushes in for the hug. "I'm sorry I broke your friend, Red. Honest."

"You're forgiven."

"Forgiven? You're sure?"

I chuckle and hug him tighter. "Forgiven by me anyway. I can't say how Maxwell will feel about you come tomorrow morning, but we'll deal with that together."

He holds the hug longer than is necessary, so I let him have a moment. "But you and I are okay? I'm still an honorary Cumhaill?"

I bark a laugh. "Oh, dude. The first thing you need to understand about being a Cumhaill is that we stand by our own. You'd have to screw up *waaay* worse than this for us to reconsider."

"Oh, that's good to know because I screw up a lot and often bigger than this."

"You get a lot right too." I ease back and kiss his cheek. "S'all good, Tarzan. I am forever your Jane."

I memorize the joy on his face and remind myself to revisit it when the collateral damage for this fiasco hits and I want to throat punch him.

"There's bound to be a learning curve to modern-day living, but let's go over it just so we're clear. Your kind of ecstasy—good. The chemical kind—bad... especially bad for men very high up in law enforcement like John Maxwell."

"Understood."

I draw a deep breath and then turn back to Dionysus's friend.

"Now, Eros, tell me what to do to negate their claim and get these nixies off my friend's back."

"Well, the first thing you'll need is a talented preternatural lawyer."

I pull out my phone and call up my directory. "Luckily, I have one of those."

Andromeda Tsambikos, Team Trouble's legal counsel, arranges for her brother to pick her up at the courthouse and snap her to the scene of chaos a few minutes later. Nikon's sister is as amiable as she is intelligent as she is beautiful. She's the whole package. And she's everything I want to be when I grow up.

I fill the two of them in on what happened, and Andromeda frowns at the water-soaked fae. "Is he all right? I don't know a lot about how drugs affect mortals."

"Yeah, he should be. Ecstasy is a happy-happy club drug. It's only a nightmare if you mix in other chemicals. The base drug MDMA alters sensations to increase energy, empathy, as well as heightened pleasure. He's going to love everyone for a while."

"Thank the gods. As long as that's all it is."

"Yeah, it could've been worse." I look at the mess in the apartment, and I can't believe the day got so out of hand. "Shit. I *am* sorry about the tidal wave. I wrecked Dionysus's fun pad and murdered his swan."

Dionysus waves his hand. Magic tingles over my skin and tweaks my nipples. Of course, his magical signature has a sexual element to it. I cross my arms and watch as the damage vanishes, and the swan reinflates. Once it's fully upright again, its orange beak turns up in a smile. "You fix my mess, and I'll fix yours."

"Done deal." I gather his hand and squeeze. "I'm going to take Maxwell's things home and see how things are going there. Come over with Andromeda when she's finished if you've finished up here with your friends and want to say hi. If not, we'll have a drink soon and laugh about all this."

I'm not sure Dionysus will laugh about this one.

Poor guy.

"Thanks, Fi. I didn't mean for any of this to happen. I wanted Max to meet some of my more interesting friends so he'd know more about us. Faust brought the nixies. He has questionable taste in friends."

"Your heart was in the right place."

"We'll have to figure out how to remove traces of the drug from his system," Andy says absently. "The RCMP does random testing, and we can't let him face scrutiny over something that wasn't his fault."

"I'm sure Wallace can help with that."

Dionysus sighs. "Humans are so much more fragile than I'm used to."

"Live and learn." Nikon pats his shoulder.

Andromeda nods. "Now on to the next problem. Tell me about the nixie claim."

I wave over Mr. Love, Desire, and Sex and introduce him. "Eros, this is Nikon and Andromeda Tsambikos of the Isle of Rhodes."

"Eros?" Andy says, eyes wide. "Well, imagine meeting you at a Toronto house party."

He leans close to Andy's neck and draws a long breath. "You smell divine, *agape mou*. You're what, second-generation immortal?"

"Third, actually."

He arches a brow. "Third? I'm impressed. The scent of your prana signature is strong for third."

The look that passes between them is awkward, and I'm not sure if he's flirting or if his designated dominion in the pantheon simply makes it seem that way.

Not my circus. Not my monkeys.

I pick up the pile of clothes Bruin found for me and pat my bear's shoulder as Sloan *poofs* in. "You ready to roll, buddy?"

"Ready and steady."

He takes his place within me, the shift of him settling a familiar flutter in my chest. When we're all set, I take Sloan's hand. "Home, James."

Even with the world gone crazy and my living room filled with family and chaos, it's great to be home. The power of Sloan's wayfarer magic tingles over my skin a moment before we appear in the middle of our main floor. "How are things—"

"Fiona, I missed you," Maxwell shouts, jogging over to nakey man hug me again.

I manage to side-hug him and avert my gaze. "Couldn't someone get some boxers on him in the past half-hour?"

"You have his gitch in your hand," Dillan says.

"You could've found some here to cover him up."

Emmet makes a face. "Guys don't share underwear. Do girls share underwear? That's weird."

I roll my eyes and pick through the clothes in my arm. "Fine. These are his boxers. Any takers?"

Cue the sound of crickets.

"You big chickens."

"Guys don't touch other guy's junk," Dillan says.

"Speak for yourself," Calum says.

That gets a round of laughter, but no one moves to getter done.

"How are things on the nixie front?" Wallace asks.

"Andromeda will take care of everything," Sloan says. "Fi explained that Maxwell was under the influence of a psychoactive drug given to him without his consent. Add that to the fact that he's human and newly exposed to the empowered world and she is confident she can mop the floor with the nixie claims."

"Andromeda is so beautiful," Maxwell sighs. "I love her. How do I get her to love me back?"

"I bet getting dressed would help," I say, holding out his Calvins. "Let's start there."

"You're sweet, Fi." That's all the warning I get before he grapples me into another full-body hug and is back to petting my hair.

I pat his bare shoulder and try unsuccessfully to extricate myself. "You're pretty great yourself."

"I love you guys."

Sloan takes the clothes from my hands. "Thanks, babe. I knew you wouldn't—" He steps back and Calum and Dillan start taking pictures. "Seriously, you guys?"

Kevin smacks Calum as he passes and grabs the boxers from the pile of clothes. "I'll help you, Fi."

Calum laughs. "You just want to get up close and personal with the naked man on a love drug."

Kevin grins. "I don't know what you're talking about, but the man does have an exceptional ass."

"I like your ass too," Maxwell says.

Kevin laughs. "Thanks. I work at it. Now, let's get you decent, shall we?"

"I'm so thirsty."

I wriggle in his embrace. "If you let me go, I'll get you a drink. How about that?"

His hold loosens enough while he considers that for me to escape. As I spin out of his love lock, I push Sloan into my spot and giggle when he gets sucked into the wake of naked affection firsthand.

Maxwell is hugging Sloan close and grips his jaw to look deep into his gaze. "Your eyes are so pretty, Irish."

Sloan arches his brow and throws me a look. "Do ye feel better now?"

Maxwell brushes a hand across Sloan's abs and lays his head against his chest. "I love you."

I giggle and take a picture of my own. "Yeah. I do. A lot better. Thanks."

CHAPTER TEN

The next day, Garnet frowns through my retelling of what happened to Maxwell, and I know I'm going to get the blowback. I invited Dionysus into our lives, and now Maxwell is not only known to the fae community but is kind of famous—at least in a very small circle.

The growl of the angry lion is something I'm getting used to. It's still unnerving, but I don't worry he's going to rip me to shreds any longer.

"Tell me, Lady Druid. Did you forget the part where we decided John would only be safe from the violent empowered communities if his knowledge of our existence remained a secret?"

"I didn't forget. Dionysus appeared here, and I introduced the two of them. I didn't plan any of this."

"I don't suppose you did, but the result remains the same. Did you express to your friend that Maxwell's identity was privileged information?"

"No. I didn't think of it at the time."

"Well, thinking of it now doesn't help anyone, especially John Maxwell."

I run my fingers through my hair and drop my forehead onto the conference table. "I'm sorry. You know I'd never intentionally put one of our own in danger."

"We know that," Andromeda says, her tone much more reasonable. "I've broken the claim on John by the swamp nixies, but their magistrate isn't happy. He says you intentionally humiliated two members of his community and he wants an apology."

I blink. "You mean the two crazy bitches who spat in my face and snapped their teeth at me?"

"Yes, them."

"And *I'm* supposed to apologize?"

Garnet growls. "No, not supposed to. You *will* apologize. We have enough bad blood between empowered species already. With what you learned in Ireland about the coming of the Culling during the Winter Solstice, we need to build our allies not create enemies."

"There is strength in unity," I say, bumping my head a couple of times against the table. "Yeah, I remember."

Ní neart go cur le chéile.

Ever since the rocking chair lady told me that a few months ago, it seems to be hitting me in the face every time I turn around.

"You'll need to take one for the team on this, Fi," Andromeda says. "It's the only way we can leave the Mad Max episode behind us."

I chuckle. "I don't think I'll ever leave it behind me. How do I look at Maxwell again without revisiting him naked and rubbing up against me?"

"I don't know. He's an attractive man. I can't imagine it was too scarring." I hear the amusement in her voice, but there's also something else…interest maybe?

Intrigue?

I make a mental note to revisit that later when it's only the two of us. "So, when do I meet the magistrate for those nixie psycho bitches and fall on my spear?"

Garnet arches a brow. "You've already met him. In fact, you've rebuffed him on more than one occasion. Which is likely why he's exacting his pound of flesh."

"Rebuffed him?" I try to think of anyone I've met and crossed words with green skin and smells like a swamp. It hits me like salty spit in the face. "Oh, you've got to be kidding—Malachi?"

Garnet flashes his teeth in a broad smile. "See, more than a pretty face and a forked tongue. She's smart too."

"Malachi is a putztastic schmuck."

"And the fact that you're so free with that opinion is why you're in the situation you're in. Play nice. Eat crow. Make Malachi happy."

My eyes roll closed, and I sigh. "Fine. I'll say the words, but I won't mean it. Those bitches deserved what they got and more."

"Nixies have no lie detection so have at it. As long as you lay it on thick and Malachi thinks he's won, you're off the hook."

"Awesomesauce. Where and when?"

Garnet stands and holds out his hand. "There's no time like the present. Let's put this to bed and focus on more pressing matters."

"Hmph, I suppose next to blood-lust crazy vampires killing innocent students, my pride taking a hit is inconsequential."

"Glad you see it my way." Garnet clasps my hand and extends his other to Andromeda to include my legal counsel. "Quick and painless."

"Where are we?" I ask once we're standing on solid ground. Well, it's not one hundy percent solid. We're on the sand of a beach. I do a half-turn and look at the massive body of water to my right. "Lake Ontario?"

"Right you are, Lady Druid. Stephenson's Swamp to be exact. It's the wetland at the mouth of the Highland Creek Watershed."

"Huh, swamp, creek, and lake. I guess Malachi's got all the water nixie bases covered."

Garnet nods and sends a quick text. A moment later, Anyx arrives with John Maxwell. It's the first time I've seen him since Nikon and Andromeda collected him at our place last night.

"Oh, shit. John, I didn't know you were coming, or I would've prepared an apology."

He holds up a finger to Garnet and pulls me aside so we can have a private conversation. "I'm angry, I'm embarrassed, and I'm ready for this all to be over, but I don't need an apology from you, Fi. I don't blame you."

I run my fingers through my hair and capture the blowing strands in the elastic I'm wearing around my wrist. "That makes one of us."

"Fi, you introduced me to a Greek god, and I took my eye off the ball. I was so eager to learn everything there is to learn I forgot about simple common sense."

"Dionysus is really sorry. He's only been in this time a few days and didn't know about synthetic drugs."

He shakes his head. "I don't blame him either. It's ironic really, he's new to the human world and made a blunder out of eagerness and excitement, and I did the same being new to the empowered world. Quite a pair we are."

I chuckle. "You were the life of the party if that helps. Hey, I've never had my own drinking game."

He groans and stares out over the open water of Lake Ontario. "I remember being jazzed about that."

I squeeze his wrist and send him what I hope is an encouraging smile. "My brother Brendan used to say life is about gathering experiences. They won't all be good, but if you're able to take away even one gem from each moment, then it was worth it."

He smiles. "That's the brother you lost last year?"

"Mhm. Brenny would've thought this whole Mad Max stuff was hilarious. He lived hard, loved with abandon, and died much too young."

"That's often the way of things."

Sadly, it is.

"He was the second oldest of your family?"

I nod. "Yeah. We're alphabetical, Aiden, Brendan, Calum, Dillan, Emmet, and me. Mam thought it was orderly. Da said it helped them narrow down names."

He grins. "Are you and Sloan starting at A or G?"

I roll my eyes. "That's crazy talk, Mr. Maxwell. It's way too early in the game to be thinking about babies."

He sobers. "Speaking of babies, Andromeda mentioned Aiden's wife had a scare. Is everything okay with the three of them now?"

"So far. We hope it'll stay that way."

He gestures to where Garnet and Andromeda are waiting. "That's what's important. The health and safety of those we love are what deserves our attention, not some drunken ecstasy debacle. Let's end this and refocus on what matters, shall we?"

I let out a long sigh. "I'm so relieved. I didn't want you to hate us and give up on the team."

He toes the sand with his shoe. "Not a chance. Like your brother said, even that one gem makes it worth it. We have more than a few gems on our team. It's definitely worth it."

"Yes, it is."

Garnet leads us on a little jaunt inland, and while we're walking the sandy path, I figure we might as well be productive. "What did Xavier say when you confronted him about knowing Galina Romanov?"

Garnet casts a glance over his shoulder. "What makes you think I confronted him?"

"You didn't?"

"No."

"Why not? It's obvious he lied about knowing who the lipstick psycho is. He flat-out omitted the truth when I asked him. Shouldn't we call him on that?"

"Think it through." Garnet raises a hand and sweeps away a low branch so we can pass. "What happens if I confront him? He admits to knowing her and says he didn't say anything because it's *his* bloodline she's targeting and his reputation she's messing with."

"But he'll go after her on his own, assuming he hasn't already."

"Of course he will. If I were in his shoes and I found out a rival targeted me and mine, there's no way I'd allow someone else to move in for the kill while I sit on the sidelines."

"We're allowing that? Violence begets violence. In a lifetime of listening to my father, I know the spillover of things like a rival mafia turf war affects innocent bystanders."

"Possibly," Garnet says, not sounding too worried, "but on the off chance Xavier can catch Ms. Romanov unaware, he might end this before it truly begins. She likely wasn't suspecting us to put together the lipstick with the boy's photo and figure out what she's doing."

I read Andromeda's expression, and while she's not offering her opinion, I think she's as skeptical as I am that this won't bite us in the ass.

"What happens if she sees Xavier coming and uses her mutating lipstick to get him to start killing people? Neither he nor anyone of his bloodline should be allowed to engage with society until we have a way to counteract the blood singing."

Garnet frowns. "I don't disagree with you about sequestering him and his bloodline, but sometimes we take a calculated risk if there's a chance for a quick resolution. If we hold Xavier back,

Galina has time to plan her next move. She might kill other innocents anyway."

"So, let's go after her as Guild enforcers. She's an empowered member of the community within our city. Let's take her on within that capacity."

"We don't have enough intel yet. How big is her organization? If she knows about vampires, what else does she know? Does she have fae on her staff? Traditional law enforcement can't find her. Where is she? How is she operating within the boundaries of the city without being found?"

"Those are all good questions," Maxwell says.

"Trust me, Lady Druid, Galina Romanov is in our cross-hairs. We'll stop her one way or another, and it'll be very soon. Swift justice is coming, I promise."

I don't like it, but I get it. "Have we at least got her under surveillance to make sure she doesn't go clubbing and kissing people?"

"There's been no sign of her," Maxwell says. "We can't watch what we can't find."

Garnet stops outside a thick hedge with an iron gate. "The team in the lab have two serums we're working on to counteract the effect of her lipstick chemistry. By the end of the day, maybe tomorrow, we'll distribute the antidote to Xavier's bloodline."

Good. That's good.

When the conversation falls quiet, I draw a deep breath and suck it up. "All right, let's getter done. One heaping helping of eating crow, coming up."

Maxwell chuckles. "If it helps, I'm forever grateful that you fought for my right to choose."

"It helps. If me taking a hit to my pride releases you from a lifetime with the spitty twins, I'm happy to be the nixie punching bag."

"So dramatic." Garnet chuckles.

"Easy for you to say. You won't be the one choking on your words."

"You had to what?" Dillan raises his dual daggers over his head and catches the downswing of Birga in the crux of the two blades. The *thunk* of wood against steel echoes throughout the stone circle and the vibration of the hit rattles my bones.

The contact would worry me if I didn't know that like me, Birga is a lot tougher than she looks. No ordinary blades will damage her.

She's enchanted.

I push with all my might, getting nowhere against Dillan's strength. "I had to make amends to the nixie magistrate, who also happens to be a fellow Guild Governor I may have spouted off to a few times."

He grunts as he pushes his block.

The thrust knocks me back. I shift my footing to steady my balance, and he tries to sweep my leg out from under me.

It doesn't work.

I backflip and land in a crouch, shifting to offense.

Launching forward, I spin Birga over my head and come in hard with the staff, going for his ribs. "In the grand scheme, it was fine. My pride will recover, and I can honestly say I went over and above to appease the phantom rocking-chair lady."

"*Ní neart go cur le chéile,*" Dillan mutters, catching my attack. He throws it back at me and ducks to avoid a follow-up strike to the side of his head. "Do you think the nixies will be the allies we need to hold the balance of good during the purge?"

"No idea. What are nixies even good for?"

The buzzer goes off, and I hold up my hand. "I'm done, Em. I want to check on Dora and see how she's doing with the expanded warding."

I release Birga from my hold and return her to the tattoo on my forearm. Grabbing my towel from our pile of supplies, I dab my face dry and catch my breath. "If we're adopting this property as a spot to train, do you think we should build a little shed or something to keep some supplies on site?"

"Are you suggesting we erect a Rubbermaid shed at the sight of our sacred stone circle?"

I giggle. "Maybe something less urban and more druid. Maybe we erect a stone dome or something by the car parking area."

"It couldn't hurt. As long as we don't leave anything too important." Emmet gathers up the weapons from the pile and starts stashing them into the hockey bag we use for transporting them.

When Dora crests the rise of the plateau and enters the clearing of the stones, Emmet and I head over to chat. She's looking sensible and sassy in gray bell-bottoms, leather boots, and a glimmering zebra sequined top. Completely sensible for hiking around outdoors.

"So, how goes the warding?"

"I have to admit that the Barghest practitioners did a decent job at warding this property. Other than adding the element of height to the spellwork, I didn't have much to do at all."

"Excellent, and thank you for doing this. I appreciate you joining in and helping us make this work."

"It's my pleasure, girlfriend. It's been fun to get back to my roots. I think my past left such a bitter taste in my mouth that I forgot how fun it could be simply to be a druid."

Emmet grins. "That was an amazing segue into something I wanted to talk to you about."

Dora arches a brow and chuckles. "Oh? And what is that, cookie?"

Emmet tells her about his plan to start hosting druid celebrations here at the stone circle and how he's been researching and picking Sloan's brain. "I wondered if you might like to be our Mistress of Ceremony?"

"That's a fantastic idea." Dora grins. "I haven't been to a good Beltane celebration in years. I would love to be involved. Are you finished planning? Can I help with that too?"

Emmet presses his arm against his waist and bows. "I would be honored to have your help, of course."

She grins. "Oh, baby. Beltane won't know what's coming. I'm busy tonight, but if you want to get together tomorrow, I'm free through the day."

"I'm starting nights tomorrow, so that works."

She nods. "Excellent. Text me any time after ten in the morning, and I'll be alive and receiving visitors."

Emmet lifts his knuckles for a bump. "Thanks, Dora. I'll bring my notes, and you can help me iron out the details."

"Lady Druid," Garnet says, appearing in the circle by the altar. He strides toward us, positive energy charging the air around him. "Good news."

"Yay, I like good news. Lay it on me."

"Maxwell's facial recognition search caught Galina Romanov heading into Copacabana for dinner. Is anyone hungry? Dinner's on me."

Noice.

Dora waves her hand and opts out. "I have plans and am looking forward to a quiet dinner with a dear friend."

Awesome. "You do you, girlfriend. Enjoy."

Garnet looks us over and takes in our post-workout state of sweat. "I'll flash you all home. You two have five minutes to invite Sloan and get cleaned up."

"Yes." Emmet pumps his fit in the air. "An all-you-can-eat steak house stakeout. I love it."

CHAPTER ELEVEN

The Copacabana Brazilian Steakhouse is one of those restaurants we never got to go to as kids because it's wildly too expensive for one person to pick up the bill. Feeding six kids on a cop's salary was tough enough without paying fifty bucks a head to eat endless amounts of meat.

Once we were old enough to throw in our share toward the tally, it became a place we enjoy at least once a year on special occasions.

I suppose catching a Romanian crime queen counts.

It's casual chic, so it doesn't take long for us to toss our workout clothes, do a fast face-cloth refresh, and throw on some deodorant and clean clothes.

"Can someone iron my emerald blouse?" I yell down the stairs.

"On it!" Calum says. "I got you, sista."

"Thanks. Love you, forever." I jog back into my room and pull on a pair of black slacks and frown at my closet.

"What's the problem, *a ghra?*" Sloan asks, buttoning a baby blue dress shirt that looks so good against the warm brown of his skin it should be illegal.

"Heels would be more fashion-conscious, but if it comes down to a confrontation, I won't be nearly as stable as I would in everyday shoes."

"Form follows function. Wear what ye need to hold yer own against a criminal murder mastermind."

"Heeled boots," Kevin hollers from across the hall. "It'll give you the height on Irish's arm and the fashion sense you're looking for, but still give you the ability to kick ass."

"Can't argue with that," Sloan says.

"Thanks, Kev." I wave as I jog past their open bedroom door. "Love you."

"Represent, Fi."

I grab the newel post of the staircase and run downstairs. Garnet frowns as I zip past him in my bra on my way to the next flight of stairs.

"Clothes would be a good thing, Lady Druid."

I giggle and keep going.

Calum meets me at the top of the basement stairs with my blouse. "Here. All done."

"Awesome." I accept the hanger and sling the blouse on in front of the mirror at the back door. When I'm buttoned up, I grab my black boots out of the hall closet. Jogging back to the living room, I sit on the ottoman and pull on my boots. "How are we doing for time?"

Garnet checks his watch. "Still good. They've been there less than fifteen minutes."

"Copa is an hour or two experience," Calum says. "Lots of time to catch up on what's going on."

Once I've zipped my boots, I stand and tuck in my blouse and am good to go. "You ready to roll, Bruin?"

"Is there any doubt?"

"Nope. Not ever." Once Bruin is in place and Sloan, Dillan, and Emmet rush down the stairs, we're all set.

"Safe home," Calum says.

The four of us nod, and Garnet flashes us out to spy on a mafia queen.

"Welcome to Copacabana Steakhouse," one of the hostesses says as the five of us step inside the glass doors. "Do you have a reservation?"

"We do." Garnet is damp-panty dapper in his Tom Ford suit jacket and black slacks, and I'm not the only lady in the small entrance to notice. "The table was arranged under the name Grant. I believe some of our party has already arrived."

The woman, wearing the customary Copa tight black sheath dress, checks her reservations screen. "Yes. This way, please."

Copacabana has three service floors, and I'm not sure where Galina is seated for her dinner. If tonight is about food, she'll likely be on the main floor. If there are private things to discuss, being up or downstairs would make more sense.

From the ground floor entrance, there is a bar and lounge area down the stairs to our left and the main dining room up six or seven stairs straight ahead. From there, an open staircase leads upstairs to another dining room that is used as an overflow seating area or for private parties.

When Clan Cumhaill makes reservations, we ask to be seated on the main floor because that's where the buffet bars are. Closer to the buffet means a shorter distance to the slices of bread, soups, salads, and sides.

Which, if I'm honest, anyone who knows how to eat here pretty much avoids. Not that they aren't good—they're awesome—but this restaurant is all about meat. You don't carb up or fill your tummy with veggies.

As the hostess leads us up the first steps, it strikes me that it's only Dillan eyeing the back of her legs.

Garnet, Sloan, and Emmet seem oblivious to how attractive

she is. Garnet and Sloan not paying much attention doesn't surprise me, but Emmet's lack of interest is new.

Even when he was dating Sarah, his gaze wandered.

"Everything all right, *a ghra?*" Sloan rests his hand over mine as we take the top step.

"Perfectly. Just thinking about love and how it changes the way we see the world."

His mouth quirks up at the sides in a sexy smile. "Well, as long as it's nothing too deep."

We pass the stairs and stay on the main floor. Part of me cheers for being closer to the buffet. I get that's not why we're here tonight, but hey, I'm a Copa professional.

Our table is past the stairs and away from the open layout of the main floor dining room. The hostess leads us to a run of three tables set along the sidewall and tucked away from the mainstream bustle of the rest of the diners. The wall itself is one long, brown leather bench, and the three tables with chairs run along it.

Anyx and Zuzanna are already seated, and I make a conscious effort not to look at Galina and her party as we pass to get to our table. Instead, I focus on my footing so I don't trip and draw undue attention— which, who's kidding who—is totally something I would do.

When we arrive at the table, Garnet takes the chair at the end of the table facing Galina. I slide along the bench seat next to Zuzanna and Anyx, Sloan takes the chair opposite me, and Dillan and Emmet take their seats to the left of him.

Sloan adjusts in his chair and greets Anyx and his wife. "Zuzanna, you look lovely this evening."

"Thank you for saying so," she says before looking at me. "How is your sister-in-law? Andromeda mentioned there was trouble with the pregnancy?"

"Still pregnant." Dillan knocks his knuckles on the table.

The rest of us do the same.

"The doctor confined her to bed for the foreseeable future," Emmet says.

I nod. "We're counting that as a blessing and are hopeful everything will work out."

"Well, we'll send the three of them positive energy."

"Thanks. We appreciate that."

Our server arrives and drops off two tall glass pitchers of water. "Have you been here before?"

Anyx, Zuzanna, and Garnet all nod, so I answer for the table. "All of us except one. This is new for Sloan."

She turns her attention to my guy and smiles. "Welcome, you're in for a treat. Do any of you wish to order off the menu?"

"That's crazy talk," Emmet says.

We all laugh, although Sloan likely doesn't understand why it's funny. The beauty of Copa is the dining experience of being served sizzling meat for two hours.

Our server meets Sloan's gaze and smiles. "The way things work is you visit the buffet bars for any appetizers and side dishes you want. Everything is all-you-can-eat. The waiters will bring hot rotisserie skewers of meat to the table and will slice you pieces to order. You'll pinch the meat with your tongs as they slice and place the meat on your plate. Don't pull. Allow them to cut it free."

Emmet picks up his tongs and gives Sloan a demo.

"In front of your plate, you have a double-sided coaster. Everyone has blue facing up to start, which signals the guys to serve you. If you flip it to red, they know you're taking a break or are finished."

"Pacing yourself is important," I say.

She nods. "Other than that, let me know if you want drinks other than water, and if you're waiting on a particular cut or type of meat that hasn't come around, I'll track someone down to bring it to you."

"Can you bring us warm cornbread?" Dillan asks.

She nods. "Each seating time is two hours, so pace yourself. Washrooms are upstairs or downstairs. Don't touch the dancers. That's about it. Enjoy."

Sloan watches her go and blinks. "This is an interesting restaurant. And what does she mean, don't touch the dancers?"

I grin. "There will be samba dancers in feathers and heels shaking their money makers for you in a bit."

He laughs. "A *very* interesting restaurant."

"It's Latin chic," Anyx says, "and very popular with the Moon Called."

Zuzanna chuckles. "Scantily dressed dancers in feathers plus all-you-can-eat meat. What more could a male ask for?"

"As much fun as all this is," Garnet says, pegging us with a look, "let's not forget why we're here."

I casually glance to my left and check out Galina sitting at her table. She's alone on the bench seat, sipping wine and eating a plate of salad. She has three burly escorts seated at the table between us who are chowing down on meat and one standing against the wall beside her table taking in everyone coming and going.

Dillan checks with the table. "Even with a task ahead of us, it would look suspicious if we didn't fill our plates, wouldn't it?"

Garnet chuckles. "I suppose it would. Cumhaills go first. We'll take the buffet in shifts so someone's always at the table."

"Done deal." Emmet stands. "Although, I can't guarantee there will be much left for you when we finish."

Dinner progresses as any visit to Copa does. I eat too much and have to flip to red to ward off the attention of servers bearing gifts of parmesan encrusted filet mignon, glazed salmon, prime rib, and cheese infused top sirloin. I hate to turn them away, but unless they have roasted pineapple, I can't accept.

"I don't think I've ever eaten so much meat," Sloan says an hour later. "Honestly, I don't think I've ever seen so much meat."

"Cheese-stuffed prime rib?" The waiter places the metal saucer onto the table and then rests the point of the rotisserie skewer into it to cut.

Sloan and Dillan raise their tongs and take a couple of pieces. Zuzanna and I pass. Then he shifts to the other end of the table to cut for Garnet, Emmet, and Anyx.

Dillan discreetly undoes the button of his pants and sighs with relief. "Have you ever suffered from meat sweats before, Irish?"

"No. I can't say I have."

"Well, they're coming." He turns his coaster over to take a break. "You gotta push through."

Garnet chuckles. "Please remember you all might have to jump up and tackle someone at any moment."

"Oh, barf," I say, thinking about that. "Yeah, I did *not* consider that early enough in the process."

"Garlic sirloin?"

I pass, and the others all turn their coasters to red.

"I think we're taking a break," Dillan says.

"How are things smelling?" Emmet asks.

Garnet, Anyx, and Zuzanna are each lion shifters. They have the heightened senses to sort through the smells of lies, emotions, and other nifty tricks that help in a stakeout sitch.

"Unfortunately, the richness of the air negates any advantage we have here," Zuzanna says quietly.

Well, that's unfortunate.

Lucky for her, Ms. Romanov picked a restaurant that fritzed out the Moon Called sniffers.

Someone drops a plate at the buffet. The shatter and smash of ceramic has Galina's bodyguards abandoning their plates and jumping to their feet.

While they're up, Galina stands, and two of them follow her upstairs toward the ladies' room.

Sloan reaches across the table and spins the bone ring on his finger. "Are ye enjoyin' yerself tonight, *a ghra?*"

We've been down this road before. When he thumbs his ring like this, it's a message for me to join him in a fae reveal. I slide my hand into his, and the moment his fingers close around mine, the room bursts out in a roar of fantastic colors and auras.

Sloan's ring of fae sight chose him and has come in handy more than a few times.

The first thing I notice is that we're not the only empowered folks having dinner here tonight. There is a djinn couple at the salad bar, and the woman with the scarf tied over her head is an elf.

What I think is of the utmost importance though, is what I see when I glance over at Galina Romanov as she turns to climb the stairs.

"Oh, dear. That's unfortunate, isn't it?"

"I thought so."

Garnet is watching us, and I reach my free hand down the table. "Thank you so much for treating us to dinner. We should do this more often."

Garnet takes my hand without prompting. I'm not sure if I've ever explained Sloan's ring to him, but he's a shrewdly intelligent man, and he understands without missing a beat. "It's my absolute pleasure. It's always illuminating to spend time with you and your family."

"Chimichurri steak?"

"No, thank you. I think we've finished here." Garnet signals to the waitress to come over. "Can we get our bill settled up, please?"

He releases my hand and casts a casual glance toward Anyx and Zuzanna. Their gazes gloss over with a faraway daze. I've wondered about it before, but I'm now certain that is a sign that

Garnet's alpha status allows him to speak telepathically with the Moon Called members of his pride.

Other than a slight tension around Zuzanna's mouth, neither show any outward signs of the danger Sloan just uncovered.

Galina's knowledge of targeting a vampire's siring line likely had nothing to do with myths of the old country and everything to do with her and her bodyguards all being vampires themselves.

Five vampires against three Moon Called, four druids, and one battle bear. The odds could be much worse. Still, we have to pass. We might win in a fight, but it wouldn't be easy, and there are too many innocent civilians in here who might get hurt in the process.

I understand Garnet's instinct to leave, but I also think it's a wasted opportunity if we cut our losses and retreat.

"Roasted pineapple?"

Damn it. Now I don't want to leave. "Maybe just one slice while we wait for the bill."

The server steps between the tables to slice me roasted decadence and all is right in the world. "Did you know that pineapple helps in digestion and makes you feel less—"

My shield explodes into a five-alarm warning.

A woman screams by the stairs at the same time the high-pitched discharge of a magic weapon explodes in the air.

I try to see what's coming, but the others screen my view.

A rapid-fire spray of bolts hits our section. The pineapple server convulses as he's hit. He collapses half on me and half on the table, blood splattering me like a gory Jackson Pollock.

I expect it to be Xavier gunning us down.

It isn't. Six men with wide, flat noses and black bandanas covering their heads are targeting Galina.

Hobgoblins.

The vampire bodyguards launch to defend, and I lose visual. I struggle to free myself and engage. It's awkward with the server's blood slicking my hands. He's heavy, and I'm in a bad position, trapped behind a table.

Sloan, Dillan, and Emmet are barely on their feet and turning before another round of high-pitched discharge sounds.

Another sweep of rapid-fire bolts hits.

I lift my arms to block dinnerware shrapnel.

My guys are exposed. Sloan grabs for my brothers but doesn't make contact before they're hit and thrown back. Magical bolts riddle the three of them.

The sound that peals from my throat is deranged.

Anyx flips the table, and it lands on my brothers. I lunge to get to them, my sobs ripping from my throat.

The restaurant is a war zone.

I lose track of Garnet and the lions.

I need one of them to flash my guys to the guild medical building.

"Garnet. Help me!"

"It's too late," Garnet growls. "Fight!"

The vampires are moving at a blur of speed. Snapping necks and punching their hands into chests and ripping out vital organs.

Innocent people are getting trampled.

I can't breathe.

Panic presses my lungs and grips my guts and consumes my conscious thought. I'm numb. I'm lost.

They're dead...

CHAPTER TWELVE

"Garlic sirloin?"

I blink at the server standing at our table, and my mind crashes inside my head. My brothers and Sloan reach forward and turn their coasters to red.

"I think we're taking a break," Dillan says.

"How are things smelling?" Emmet asks.

I gasp, tears rushing hot down my cheeks as I gasp for breath. "What's happening?"

"Fi? What's wrong?" Dillan's alarm brings everyone's attention to me.

I can't breathe. They're alive...but they weren't...or won't be.

"Her scent is horror and grief," Zuzanna says.

Sloan reaches forward and grabs my hand. "*A ghra?* You're scaring us. What's wrong?"

Someone drops a plate at the buffet. The shatter and smash of ceramic have Galina's bodyguards abandoning their plates and jumping to their feet.

I swallow. "I...uh, I think I had a premonition." I scan the restaurant and when Galina stands and signals for two of them to escort her upstairs toward the ladies' room I know I'm right.

I turn to Garnet and try to make sense of it. "Six hobgoblins with black bandanas—they come in and mow down our section with magical assault weapons. It starts a bloody massacre. Stop them."

Garnet, Anyx, Dillan, and Emmet are on their feet and striding for the door without question.

I'm trembling and snotty. "I need a minute."

Sloan gets up when I do and has one hand behind my back, supporting me as we climb the stairs. The memory of those horrifying moments might no longer be a reality, but the grief still heaves in my chest.

At the top of the stairs, we turn toward the washrooms. By the time we get into the short hallway, I can't take it any longer. I curl into Sloan's chest and hold on tight. "I lost you," I sob. "You, and Dillan, and Emmet. All of you... killed right in front of me."

His arms are tight around me, and he presses his cheek against the top of my head. "It's all right now, *a ghra.* I'm sure you changed the course of that path."

"But what if it had been real-time and not a glimpse?" The trembling isn't getting any better, and a full emotional fall-apart is barreling down on me.

"Let me take you home. I'll finish up here and bring yer brothers with me as soon as we see what happens."

"No. I won't leave you—none of you."

"All right. Then splash some water on yer face, and we'll gather yer brothers and head home together."

I'm reluctant to be separated from him even for a few minutes but can't cling to him like a traumatized koala for the rest of the night.

"I need to go home and hide with you in the safety of King Henry."

"Whatever ye need. I'll wait right here."

I swipe my tears, step around the man outside the washroom door, and head inside to get a grip.

The ladies' washroom at Copacabana is a five-foot-by-ten-foot area with two sinks and two invisible doors hidden in a floor-to-ceiling art wall opposite the mirrors. The first time I came in here, I thought someone was punking me, and there weren't any toilets. Luckily a girl came out of one of the private stalls, and I figured it out.

With the emotions of the premonition roiling within me, I stand at the vanity, cup my hands, and splash water over my face. I let it run through my fingers and repeat the process a couple of times before one of the stall doors opens behind me.

Galina steps out.

Right. With the massacre shaking my foundation, I forgot she was up here.

Galina Romanov is a European beauty. She was a stunning brunette before her transition and is even more entrancing with the empowered genetics of the undead.

Sadly, when I look at her, all I see is Elliot VanClay lying dead and hollowed out on the ground.

She eyes me up and down and frowns. "Tears is a new approach."

I step over to the hand towel dispenser and pull a couple of sheets free. "I don't know what you mean."

She chuckles. "Please. I may not know who you are, but everyone in the city knows Garnet Grant. You're here for me. The only thing I wasn't sure of is if you were here to observe or engage."

I pat my face dry, and thankfully, this confrontation is pulling me out of my funk. "Observe."

"Well, you'll be disappointed. I texted my dinner guest the moment Grant's right-hand killer sat down at the table next to ours."

"You calling Anyx a killer is rich."

She flashes me a red-lipped smile and moves to wash her hands. "I'm sure I don't know what you mean."

"Don't know what I mean because you're pretending you're not a killer or because you don't know which killings I'm referring to? I suppose a woman in your business loses count."

The water cuts off, and she turns for a towel. I shift out of her way and check myself in the mirror.

My shield is tingling hot but nothing like the fiery inferno I experienced five minutes ago downstairs. Gah, even the thought of it makes me want to curl into a ball and wail.

"Listen. I'm not sure what the protocol is in this situation, and I don't possess the patience to play coy right now, so I'm going to go with honest."

"Save your breath. There's nothing you can say that I want to hear."

"Fine, be bored and listen anyway. I'm the one investigating the murder of innocent U of T students and know all about you, your chemistry experiment, and how you targeted Xavier's bloodline. You're busted."

The widening of her pupils tells me she didn't see that one coming.

"I also know targeting him is personal, but using your Goth lipstick is over now. We have a serum to counteract your lipstick, so that ride is over. FYI, Xavier knows it was you, and he's pissed."

She swallows, and I'm not sure if I'm hitting the nail on the head or blowing it big time.

"Also, it wasn't him who attacked you on New Year's Eve if that's what you think. It was the hobgoblins. They planned to attack you again tonight, but we moved in and stopped them. You're welcome."

She huffs. "Oh, little girl. You need to fact-check. Kartak of the Narrows and his thugs were wiped out last September by some kind of wild beast loose in the underground tunnels."

I release Bruin, and he materializes beside me, taking up the majority of space in the washroom. "Galina, meet Killer Claw-bearer... the wild beast of the tunnels."

She hisses and bares her teeth, her fangs extending like they're spring-loaded. "Get that thing away from me, or I'll rip you to shreds."

"Watch what you say. He's very protective, and I can't always control him."

To punctuate my point, Bruin sniffs the air near her and lets out a long, rumbling growl.

"Sorry, buddy. No killing the vampire lady tonight. I told her we're only observing. I'm a woman of my word." I pat my chest and Bruin returns to his resting place within me.

"Don't threaten me, little girl."

"Don't underestimate me, vampire lady."

We stand there for a moment, and I let her assess me without flinching. When I figure she's had enough time, I continue. "So, this is my take on what happened. Kartak came after me in September and was surprised when he and his men ended up dead."

"I heard it was brutal—an inhuman massacre of dismemberment."

"I can't say. I was out of the country at the time, and he took it upon himself to defend my honor. But yes, my boy is very efficient."

"And you scoff at me and call me a killer."

"Those hobgoblins took me prisoner and tried to kill me. The human students you targeted were innocent. There's a big difference."

"You're hardly in a position to judge."

"That's not what this is about. We assumed the hobgoblins were all dead, but they weren't. You expanded your organization to fill the vacuum left by their sudden absence. A few survived, or maybe they immigrated here to assume control. Either way, they used the belief that they were extinct to take a run at you on New Year's to reclaim their territory."

She shakes her head. "You're wrong."

"I'm not. I overheard the hobgoblins say you should've died on New Year's Eve and they wouldn't fail again."

There's a knock on the door, and I realize we've been in here a while.

"Everything is fine, Andrei."

"Yes, Mistress."

"You good too, *a ghra?*"

"All good, hotness." I chuckle at the thought that our guys are out there staring each other down. "I suppose we should wrap this up and get back to them. I honestly didn't come in here to have face time with you, but I'm glad we got a chance to talk."

"I don't believe a thing you said," she says.

I shrug. "Then it's your funeral. I'm telling you who truly tried to kill you. Ignore me, and maybe they'll catch you unaware and get the job done. In the meantime, stop targeting innocents to attack Xavier. If you want to take him down, grow a pair and go at him head-on."

She arches a manicured brow. "You're a mouthy bitch. You know that?"

"You're not the first person to say so, and I'm sure you won't be the last."

Her smile surprises me. "In a different world at a different time, I could see us as friends."

I doubt that very much but decide not to burn that bridge. "I understand you're new to the empowered community, but if you don't want Garnet and the Guild of Governors coming at you hard, stop targeting humans."

She chuckles. "Why should we care about humans? They are food. Weak. Stupid. Inconsequential. Do you mourn the lives of the animals who died to feed you and your group tonight? No. You don't."

I chuckle. "How soon they forget. You were a measly human only three or four months ago."

"Physically maybe, but I knew what I'd become before that. If I had my way, I would've transitioned more than a year ago. Then, I wouldn't have been cut down and almost killed. Then I would've been feared and respected, and your precious students would still be alive. So, in actuality, it's Xavier's fault they're dead."

I rush from the restaurant and cross Adelaide. My brothers are loitering in the public parking lot leaking plasma onto the asphalt. "What happened? Are you all right? Shit, you're bleeding."

"Where's Irish," Emmet says, licking at the swelling on his lip. "We'd like to go home now and didn't think we meet the Copa dress code like this."

"He went to the table to collect Zuzanna and settle the bill. We almost dined and dashed."

I check on Dillan next, who looks more pissed about me mothering him than the fact that he ripped his shirt and he's banged up. I don't care. My patched-up emotions spring a leak when I have the two of them in front of me.

"Just so you know, in my premonition, I watched all three of you get gunned down and die in front of me. I'm going to be extra emotional. I need you to deal with it."

"It wasn't real, baby girl," Dillan says when I suckerfish to his side.

"It was real to me. My heart is broken, and I can barely stand."

"Shit." Emmet hugs me from behind. "This sounds like a Fi Oreo moment."

I grunt a laugh but don't escape before they have me squished between them. They lock their arms around one another and squish the air out of me, making me the filling in the Fi Oreo.

"How's our creamy filling feeling," Dillan says.

"Mercy. Do you know how much food I ate?"

"There's no mercy in Fi Oreo," Emmet says.

I'm still begging to be released when Sloan and Zuzanna join us and my brothers relent. I sag and lean over to catch my breath both laughing and crying. "Thanks, guys. I needed that."

"Anytime, baby girl."

I straighten and make sure my hours of meat are firmly settled. S'all good.

"Tell us what happened?"

Dillan shrugs. "Exactly what you said was going to happen. We got out here, and six hobgoblins were crossing the street and heading to the restaurant. Garnet and Anyx tackled one each and flashed them out. The rest scattered. We each took one and ran them down. Anyx caught up with us and took them too."

"But one got away?" Zuzanna asks.

"Yep. Five in custody and Copa massacre foiled. We're taking it as a win."

"It's a huge win." I hug each of them again. "Please don't ever die on me again. My heart can't take it."

Emmet touches his forehead to mine and his eyes cyclops into one. "Now you know how we feel every time you get into one of your life and death mayhem jams. We'll stop if you do."

Well, poop. "I'll try but don't hold me to that. The magic mojo of the fae world seems to have other ideas."

Galina and her bodyguards step out of the restaurant, and she glances our way. I raise my hand in a friendly wave. She doesn't wave back.

"She's playing it cool, but we're tight now. Almost in braid each other's hair territory."

A big, charcoal-gray Humvee with ramming bars on the grill rumbles down the street, and they all pile in.

"Check that beast," Emmet says.

"That truck is sick," Dillan says.

"Bruin? Follow that Humvee in spirit mode and find our vampire queen's home base. If Garnet won't act until we know more, we gotta step up the process before she kills again."

I release Bruin, and he propels himself down Adelaide in a rush of air to pursue.

Dillan chuffs. "Did I miss the part where the two of you are chummy?"

"Yeah, you know what it's like. Chatting it up in the washroom. Having a heart-to-heart. Becoming besties."

The three of them share looks of horror. "Yeah no," Dillan says. "Dudes don't do that. You get in, getter done, shake it, and get out. Eyes front, no chatting."

"Huh. Boys are so weird."

CHAPTER THIRTEEN

"Do we have to get up?" I drape myself across Sloan's chest to keep him pinned to the mattress and prevent his escape. "You said, whatever I need. I think I need a few more hours of you naked in my bed."

Sloan flashes me a sexy grin. "Yer insatiable, Cumhaill. I need food. Ye can't keep me chained to the headboard and demand I perform without refueling."

I laugh. "You make me sound like a dominatrix. If I recall correctly, you're equally invested in our horizontal hijinks."

His mouth quirks up in a crooked smile, and he lifts his head to kiss me. "Och, there's no doubt about that. I love every private moment. I do, however, require sustenance to do the job right."

His stomach chooses that moment to let out a long, hollow growl.

I smack his abs and laugh. "Hilarious. How did you time that so well?"

He brushes our lips together, and my heart trips in my chest. "I look forward to naked hijinks with you for decades to come, *a ghra*, but like it or not, we have lives to live and responsibilities and other physical needs we're required to meet."

"Poop. You are such an adult."

He closes the distance between our mouths and kisses the hell out of me. "I like being adult with you."

"That's what I'm talkin' about. Let's take a few more minutes in here while—"

"—Auntie Fi?" Jackson's voice is across the room but definitely inside our bedroom. With the five of us who live here, we don't lock our doors—there's no need to, and there's no telling when we might need to gain emergency access. A closed door is respected.

Unless you're five.

"Auntie Fi? Are yous here?"

A scramble in the sheets covers us up and gets me to the opening in King Henry's drapery. I slide my hand into the seam of the curtains and peek out. "Yep. I'm here, buddy. What's up?"

"Daddy falled asleep, and we's hungry. Can you make us special toast?"

"Yep, I sure can. Were any uncles downstairs to help get us started?"

"No, just Daisy girl."

"No one? How did you get inside?"

"We crawled through the Manxy door."

Right. We spelled the animal access to allow entry to Cumhaill friendlies. The kids are small enough to get in through the doggie door. "That was clever. Okay, sweetie. Give me one second to go pee and come downstairs. I'll get you guys set up."

"Auntie Fi?" he says, his expression screwed up in thought.

"Yeah, buddy?"

"Your jammies dirty? You don't have yous top on."

The mattress jiggles with Sloan's silent laughter. He has his lips pressed together, and I whip my hand back to smack him.

I check that the girls are properly hidden behind the drape of King Henry. They are. Everything that needs to be covered is covered, but Jackson is an observant kid.

"Yep, I need to do laundry. Don't worry. I'll find something to wear and come downstairs super quick. Give me two secs, 'kay?"

"Okay." He toddles over to the chair by the window and climbs up.

Hilarious. "Buddy, can you ask Daisy if she wants special toast too? I bet she's super hungry and Uncle Calum and Uncle Kevin will be happy if we take good care of her."

"Okay." He plops down out of the chair. "I'll ask her if she's hungry too."

"Thanks, hon. You're the best."

He forgets to close the door on the way out, but that's fine. I wait until I hear him on the stairs, then I flip the curtains open and bolt for the door. Once that's closed and locked, I hurry to my dresser.

Sloan whistles a catcall behind me. "Lookin' good, Cumhaill. Naked and hustling is a good look."

I giggle, grab my clothes, and jog toward the ensuite. "Get dressed, Uncle Sloan. We have minors to feed and impressionable minds to protect."

I get the kids set up with a round of cinnamon toast and find Manx lounging on his branch in the basement above an empty bear den. "Did Bruin not get back yet?"

Manx rubs the fur on his cheek against the bark of his branch. "I haven't seen him, no."

I sigh. "I hope he's all right."

"Och, I'm sure he is. He likely got sidetracked by a pan of whiskey or a fine, wide rump of a sow bear in the woods."

Those are two of his favorite things, but he was on an intel sweep, and I don't think he'd head out on the pull without checking in first.

"Okay, thanks Manx. Breakfast in five."

"I'll be there."

I jog back upstairs, look around for any note that one of the boys might've left with news of my bear, and leave the kids with Sloan while I jog next door to check on Aiden and Kinu.

It's not like them to lose track of the kids so Aiden is either thoroughly exhausted or something is wrong.

I find him slouched over on the couch snoring, and I relax. Thoroughly exhausted for the win.

I pick up a notepad and pen off the sugar bin and write him a quick note.

Fi and Sloan have the monkeys.

Get some rest.

I set that on the couch beside him and take my leave.

Water rushes down the pipes from upstairs as I exit the family room, and I detour upstairs.

Da is coming out of the washroom, dressed and ready for his shift. "Hey, baby girl," he whispers. "What brings you by?"

"We had a monkey infiltration next door, and I wanted to make sure no one here was frantic."

He frowns. "I just got up and into the shower. I thought yer brother had them downstairs."

"He's sacked out. Not a problem. Sloan and I can keep them for a few hours and take our turn."

"You guys don't have to whisper," Kinu says from the master bedroom. "I'm awake. Come tell me what's going on in the world beyond this bed."

Da kisses my cheek and hugs me before heading for the stairs. "I'm off to the station and have dinner plans with Shannon after. Call me if ye need me."

"Will do. Safe home and give Shannon my love."

I smile as he descends the stairs, the creaks and cracks of this house an old familiar friend. Our house next door is the same age, but it's been remodeled and reinforced and doesn't have the same worn-in feeling this house has.

Maybe in a couple of decades when our kids have raced up and down the stairs a few million times and hit the walls fighting and wrestling to loosen things up.

"Are you still out there?" Kinu asks.

I laugh and head in to see her. "Sorry. I was listening to the house talk and daydreaming."

Kinu is propped up in bed, looking much better than she has over the past couple of days. She's a petite, Canadiasian woman normally but being this pregnant with twins has taken up much more landscape on her belly than looks natural.

"That bad, is it?"

I settle on the side of the mattress and pat her foot. "What's that bad?"

"You looked at me like I'm a puzzle you can't quite figure out."

I grimace. "Sorry. I thought there isn't enough space inside you for all of this." I wave a hand over her belly and laugh. "It's bizarre seeing you like this."

"It's bizarre to feel like this." She adjusts a bit but doesn't look like she's any more comfortable. "What brings you by?"

I consider whether or not I should mention her babies being loose in the wild, but figure Jackson or Meggie will probably tell her anyway.

"Aiden crashed on daddy duty, and the monkeys ended up on my couch watching Paw Patrol and eating cinnamon toast. I came by to check that things are okay."

She frowns. "Well, that shouldn't have happened."

"Maybe not, but they didn't leave the property. They even knew enough to climb through the companions' doggie door to get in."

Kinu laughs. "That's Jackson, one hundred percent. He's probably been planning that since he first saw Manx and Daisy use it to come and go."

"Technically, that's what it's there for."

"Still, we'll go over the safety rules again. Sorry, and thanks."

I wave that away. "It's not a bad thing for them to consider the two houses their safe zone. We've spelled the property, and between the two houses, there is almost always someone to help gather them up. S'all good."

She rubs a hand over her massively round belly and smiles. "It's pretty perfect, actually. Aiden and I are forever grateful for Sloan buying that house for you and making this work. Being here and having the kids grow up with full-time access to your family is amazing."

"It was an inspired idea, that's for sure. Sloan has a lot of inspired ideas. He's way too smart."

"He has a lot going on in that pretty head of his."

"True story."

She adjusts the blanket folded over her lap and flattens things out. "Speaking of Sloan, I had an idea and wondered if either he or Nikon might help me."

"Yeah? What's that?"

"Aiden started nights last night and tried to get up and take care of the kids. Obviously, it's too much for him, and I don't want him sleep-deprived on the job."

"I'm with you on that. What do you need?"

"Are you still planning a trip to Ireland to pick up Dart?"

"That's the plan. I told Patty near the beginning of the week, but with the vampire murders and Maxwell getting roofied, there hasn't been a good time. Why?"

"Gran invited me to hitch a ride and stay there for a few days. She's offering to watch the kids and make sure I'm good to give Aiden a break. If there's a problem, I have her and Wallace there, or Nikon can have me back in an instant if I need the hospital here."

It's not a bad idea.

I'm not sure Aiden will be less distracted with her in Ireland than having her here, but that's not up to me. "Have you mentioned this to Aiden?"

"Not yet. It was something I was thinking about while lying here and Gran invited me with almost the same idea. Since you're heading there anyway, I thought maybe it would work."

"It sounds like a good idea... at least while Aiden's on nights. You talk to him, and I'll mention it to Nikon. I don't suppose he'll have a problem with it. If you and Aiden are on the same page, I'll make it happen."

By the time I get back, the kids have finished their toast and are using Sloan as a personal climbing apparatus. Not that I blame them. He's my favorite jungle gym workout, except for entirely different reasons. "Look, kids," he says. "Yer Auntie Fi's back. Yay! Let's play with Auntie Fi."

I snort. "You can't possibly be frazzled. I was gone less than ten minutes."

"That can't be true. I'm quite sure you were gone at least an hour."

I laugh, grabbing Meg off his leg and setting her back onto the couch. "Is your show over?"

"Again," Meggie says. "Sky got wings."

"Did she? That's amazing." I reclaim the remote from the crack between couch cushions and get her set up. By the way Jackson is talking Sloan's ear off, he won't be so easy to appease. "Hey buddy, I need to talk to Uncle Sloan for a minute. If you watch one more show, I'll get a bowl of fae treats together and take you to the grove after."

"Deal. Can I have more toast?"

"Absolutely. Sit quietly with your sister for a sec, and I'll get you set up."

As Jackson runs over and climbs onto the couch next to his

sister, I grab the bread and pop down another round of special toast.

"How'd ye do that?"

"Do what?"

"I asked if they wanted to watch another show and they climbed me like ants on honey."

I chuckle and flatten his upturned collar. "Years of practice. The key isn't to ask them. It's to suggest it enticingly. Then, if you don't think they're going for it, sweeten the pot with something they want more."

He rolls his eyes. "Who knew I'd need schooling on how to outthink two toddlers."

I chuckle, grabbing the toasted bread to top it off with butter and cinnamon. "Technically, Meg is a toddler, but Jackson is not. He's almost five and doesn't want to be confused with being a baby because he's a big boy, aren't you, Jackson."

"Ya-huh." I hand him his toast, and he grins. "Thank you."

"You're welcome." With the two of them set, I grab the leftover ham and cheese quiche from the fridge. "Did you eat?"

"No. I waited to see what your plans were."

I take the foil off the quiche and hold it up. "Quick and easy reheat. You may join me or fend as you wish."

"I'll join you." He opens the cupboard, takes out two plates, and sets them onto the counter.

I cut a wedge of quiche and put it on my plate. "How big for you?"

"Twice that."

I double the size of the next piece and set it on the second plate. "Has Bruin gotten back yet?"

"I'm here, Red." He lumbers up the hall. "I'm tired as hell, but I'm here."

I set the first plate into the microwave and cover it before turning on the timer. "Are you okay? I was getting worried."

"Yeah. I followed the vampire and have cracked the mystery of why no one can pin down where her base of operations is."

"Oh, yeah? Tell me. I'm all ears."

"After they left the restaurant, the driver went west along the lake for a bit and pulled into a shipping depot lot. Then they parked, and the woman got into the back of a long, highway truck with pictures of vegetables on the side."

"What was she looking at in the back of a semi? She seemed to like her salad last night, but I can't imagine her going out of her way to bother with the shipping of fresh produce."

The microwave sings its completion tune, and I climb up on one of the breakfast bar stools. Sloan slides my plate over to me and puts his in next.

"No. There wasn't any produce in the truck. It was all done up inside like an office closest to the back, then a den with a couch and a table and chairs, and a little bedroom nearest the truck's cab."

"A home base on wheels."

"Aye. When they slammed the door shut, I was sealed in fer the night. It was air-tight."

"What? They trapped you in the semi-truck?"

He drops his chin. "Aye, until they parked this morning to head off to get something to eat."

"I have so many questions. Was there a coffin? Did she get all vampirey?"

"Och, no. She sat at her desk and did paperwork and made calls most of the night. Vampires need very little sleep it seems."

"Did ye hear anything valuable while ye were in there?" Sloan asks.

"Not a great deal. She rarely spoke English. Not to her muscled men or on the phone. It sounded Russian."

That doesn't surprise me. "Maybe Russian or maybe Romanian. She could do business in her native tongue. It would eliminate a lot of eavesdroppers from understanding what she was saying."

"Even eavesdropping bears," Sloan says.

"Sadly, yes."

"Are we done?" Bruin asks, his maw opening wide in a long yawn. "Can I curl up in my den now?"

"You can," I say, "but did you forget we're headed to Ireland to pick up Dart? It should just be there and back with a pit stop at Gran's. You can pass—"

"Och, no. My den can wait. I'll rest well enough while we're bonded and not be worried ye'll get yerself mockered or kidnapped or changed into a bog monster by an angry swamp beast."

I laugh. "I'd argue if I didn't think any and all of those are possible."

"It's sad really. Ye can't be left alone for a moment."

I set my fork down and turn on my stool to face him. "So, is this your cantankerous way of saying you're coming aboard?"

"I suppose. Just try not to get worked up about anything. Ye know how yer heart racin' bothers me."

I grip his jaw on both sides and bend to kiss his nose. "I love you too, Bear. Sleep now. If you're lucky, maybe we'll get to battle and maim vampires when we get back."

"Och, ye sure know how to sweet talk, Red. From yer lips to the goddess's ears."

I chuckle as my bear takes his place within me and text the update on Galina's home base on wheels to Garnet to deal with while we're gone.

Maybe when we get back, he'll have a lead, and we can end the vampire mafia war before it begins.

CHAPTER FOURTEEN

"Hello, the house," I call as we arrive in my father's childhood home in the countryside of Kerry, Ireland. "We come bearing monkey monsters and overly-pregnant women."

Jackson laughs, and I let go of his hand. Nikon sets Meggie down, and I point toward the front hall. "Shoes off at the door and put your coats on the bench. You gotta be good for Gran if you want to have more fun visits."

The two of them take off like streakers on the pitch at a football game. They nearly bowl Gran over as she comes out of the kitchen and bursts into giggles. "Welcome. Welcome. I'm so glad to have ye here."

"You need to put me down before I break your back," Kinu says to Sloan. He has her in his arms, cradled against his chest. "Bedrest doesn't mean I can't stand. A girl gets to pee, you know?"

Sloan grins. "I'm under strict instructions from yer husband. All ye get is a trip to the jacks and yer back in bed."

Kinu looks at me and laughs. "Your brother is *so* bossy. He's even deciding when I can use the bathroom."

Gran laughs and waves that away. "Sloan, luv, take Kinu into the facilities and give her a moment. Ye can carry her to the spare bed after she's finished her business."

Sloan turns and marches off, careful to walk sideways as he gets to the back hallway.

"That'll be you someday soon, Red," Nikon says. "All knocked up and Sloan toting you around because you're too huge to waddle along and piss on your own."

I sucker-punch Nikon in the gut, and he doubles forward. "Someday soon, my ass. I'll take the someday. You keep the soon. And I'll never be so huge I can't pee on my own. Kinu's a unique case. Twins are cray-cray."

Jackson and Meg are back, and Gran kneels to love them up. "Granda and I are so excited to have ye stay with us a few days. In fact, he has a surprise fer ye in our bedroom. Why don't ye run back and see what he's workin' on."

Jackson looks at me, and I nod. "Be good and help Meg make good choices. While Mommy isn't feeling well, you gotta be extra good."

"Oke doodle, Auntie Fi." He takes Meg's hand and scurries off toward the bedroom.

When they're off, I hug Gran and slide their duffle off my shoulder. "What's Granda doing in your room?"

"Och, we didn't want the children to bother Kinu in her state, so Lugh put two cots in our room and is makin' them nice so the kids will settle in with us."

"They'll love that. They're Cumhaill kids through and through. They love any kind of adventure."

Sloan returns from the back a moment later and winks at me. "Kinu has settled and is quite enjoyin' the hot pad ye left."

"Wonderful," Gran says. "When I was pregnant with Niall, I had terrible backaches. A hot pad was such a blessing."

It still strikes a bit of a nerve that Da kept us from Gran and Granda all these years. I get that he and Granda had a heated falling out and that Da didn't want to be involved in the shrine commitments, but we missed out on having grandparents. Mam was an only child, adopted, and her parents both died young.

That's why she always wanted a big family.

The only consoling factor is that I get to watch them with Clan Cumhaill next-gen and imagine how they were with Sloan.

"Well, if you've got things well in hand, I'll pop in and kiss Granda. Patty's bringing Dart to the backyard soon and I'm anxious to get him home and settled."

"Och, must ye go so soon, luv? Ye just got here."

I hug her again and nod. "I can't stay this time. We have vampire mafia issues and all kinds of craziness going on, but I plan to spend a couple of hours when we pick up Kinu in a couple of days."

"Och, I don't think yer pickin' Kinu up, luv. I spoke to Emmet this mornin', and he said Tad's bringin' us to you for the Beltane ritual on Friday. He's quite excited fer us to be there."

"Oh, awesome. Yes, he's jazzed about starting a tradition for the rituals. He's been researching and planning for days."

Gran smiles a wide Cheshire grin. "Och, he's been researchin' all right. He's got some big plans, that one. Big heart and big dreams."

"Yeah, that's Emmet."

She points toward the study. "I have a couple of books fer ye to take back with ye on Lugh's desk. Sloan, be a dear and grab them, won't ye?"

"Of course, Lara. I'll—

I get distracted as my phone rings. "Hey, McNiff. How's life, dude?"

"Fi, help," he croaks, his voice rattling with liquid. "Da killed step-monster and tried to kill me. He blocked my power… I'm hurt and I can't portal."

"Where are you? We're coming right now."

"In the woods north of the cabin. Be careful. He's not alone and Fi...the evil detection stone is glowin'."

"Shit. Okay. We're coming right now." I hang up and meet the worried gazes. "Riordan's gone crazy and tried to kill Tad. He's hiding in the woods north of the cabin. Samuel's detection stone is glowing."

"Mingin's back?" Sloan closes the distance and takes my hand.

"Let me grab my boots." Granda stomps past us. "I'll not let ye take on Riordan alone if some evil entity possesses the man."

"Tad says he's not alone."

Granda utters curses beneath his breath. "Nikon, would ye like a weapon?"

"A short sword, dagger, scimitar...anything sharp and pointy would be great."

Granda takes a quick side trip.

I'm trying not to shout at my grandfather to hurry up, but that doesn't stop me from thinking it. I didn't like the sound of Tad's voice, and I worry about what he meant when he said he's hurt.

The moment Granda is back, Nikon, Sloan, Granda, and I join hands. A moment later, we're in the forest behind the McNiff family cabin, and my shield flares.

"Do you feel that?" My skin crawls with dark energy. It's like a colony of termites burrowing at my flesh. "There's some seriously dark power here. Riordan might not be Riordan at all. Be careful."

The four of us spread out and head deeper into the trees.

Bruin, Riordan is possessed and hunting down Tad. He's hurt.

This is why I need to stay close by.

You're not wrong. Try to find him.

Red, a grizzly can smell blood from a mile away. I've got this.

I heart you huge, big guy.

Yeah, ye do.

The subtle pressure of having Bruin within me releases, and I wish him luck on his hunt. Pulling out my phone, I text Tad. *We're here. Bruin's coming to you. Stay hidden.*

My creep-o-meter goes off as I scan the dense crush of trees. The power behind the darkness hangs thick in the air. I sense the "others" Tad mentioned and release my fae sight.

As my eyes adjust to the magic of seeing things in night vision, I pick up the blurs of evil in the distance. I call on the *Tough as Bark* armor Fionn gifted me, and my skin hardens. Then I call Birga forward.

Scout in Stealth. Moving to scan the trees before we set out, my feet make no sound and my connection to the forest grows stronger. I draw a deep breath and absorb the energy the trees and creatures offer.

The forest feels the presence of evil and doesn't like it. It wants us to remove it.

That's what we're here for.

The magical signatures of Granda and Sloan tingle in the air. I wait for them to signal that we're good to go.

Sloan jerks his chin, and Granda nods as well.

When Nikon signals he's ready we get the search party started. The four of us stick together, weaving through the shadowed maze.

Sloan, Granda, and I have the benefit of druid abilities to see in the dark. Nikon doesn't.

I would ensure he stays tight to me if I needed to. I don't. He's sticking close and doing his best not to make noise and give our position away.

Not that he needs to worry.

"Incoming!"

Three men rush in from my right and two come at us from the left. I duck the blade of a sword and swing Birga to stop them from taking another swipe at me. A creeping vine wraps around my left foot, but I'm too busy defending to untangle from it. When the first man rushes, I sink Birga's spearhead into his stomach and swipe left.

An orb of orange magic screams past my ear and explodes against the tree by my head. It detonates like a short-circuiting snowball. I smell the tainted magic it releases and stop inhaling immediately.

"Whirlwind Force." I swipe my hand through the air and blow that funky stank back the way it came.

My peripheral vision catches Nikon getting his feet pulled out from under him. He lands hard on his back and falls still. I hope he's only winded and stunned. He's immortal so dead only means his body will disappear, and we won't see him for a few days.

Dammit.

I evade the hit from one of our attackers and roll to the ground to assist. Dropping to one knee, I yank on the vine twining around his legs. He blinks and groans, stirring back to awareness.

I counter the *Creeping Vine* spell, but it doesn't help.

My shield flares hotter, and I spin, bracing Birga with both hands to block the downward strike of the incoming staff. The other two attackers take advantage and come at us. Shit. They've got—

"Guns!"

I throw myself over Nikon and grunt at the weight of someone landing on top of me. We topple to the side, and I don't have time to react before we *poof.*

We reform somewhere else in the forest with Sloan on top of us, breathing heavy. "Gotcha."

"Thanks, hotness. Good move. Let's practice that more later."

He laughs and rolls off me, releasing Nikon from being pinned as well. "Find Tad. I gotta get back to Lugh."

He *poofs* off, and I scramble to check on Nikon. "You with me now, Greek?"

"If 'with you' means pissed, then yes, I'm very much with you." He hacks at and pulls away the rest of the vine around his legs. Then he's on his feet, and we're off again.

I found him, Red. He's at your three o'clock about six hundred feet out. You'll see a rock that looks like it's had a bite taken out. He tucked himself in the gaping space.

Got it. Thanks, buddy. Have your fun.

If you insist.

I race through the trees with Nikon at my back, and we cut the distance quickly. I'm searching the forest in front of us for a rock that looks like someone took a bite out of it when my shield flares.

I spin, searching the darkness in a quick circle.

Nothing.

The hit comes from above as someone drops from the forest's canopy and tackles me to the ground. I pinch my lips shut to keep from eating dirt, and other than cracking my face against the scrub, I absorb the hit pretty well.

Even with the violent force behind the attack, I barely feel the impact—Fionn's armor is the bomb.

Nikon grunts as he kicks the guy on top of me and frees me to get to my feet. I reclaim Birga from the dirt and settle back into a fighting stance.

Standing in the shadows, I see nothing of the man and only what my fae sight shows me. It's like a heat signature. Only, instead of seeing his outline in the indistinct orange-red silhouette of thermal energy, he's a toxic olive green with clawing swipes of purple.

I recognize it for what it is—evil.

I've got the creepy tree tackler, Greek. Find Tad at the base of that rock and snap him to Wallace's clinic.

You're sure?

145

Abso-smurfly.

Kick his ass, Red. You da man. When Nikon moves off, creepy shadow stalker guy *harumphs* and shifts to intercept.

I get in his path. Then it's on.

The pounding rush of footsteps has me bracing for impact. The power of his darkness grows with each step he draws nearer. It's like a physical grip tightening around my throat...choking me.

By the time he's close enough to engage, I'm gagging on the acrid tang of sour-milk evil on my tongue.

It's *soooo* gross.

I worry I might retch, but then he's upon me and the focus of surviving trumps evil queasy.

"What do I have to do to get rid of you?"

The voice is distorted yet recognizable. Same goes for his face...sort of. He still has the strong features of Tad's father, but his eyes are glowing, and there's this freaky black spiderweb veining on his face. He's also giving off a smoky black smog that I recognize from inside Newgrange tomb.

"Damn, McNiff. You look like shit." I brace my feet, send Birga back, and prepare to engage in a close-quarters melee.

The sitch is complicated. I can't kill Tad's father—not even if he's Mingin infected.

Especially if he's Mingin infected.

I can, however, distract him. The longer I keep him busy, the better Nikon's chances of finding Tad and getting him to Wallace's clinic. Riordan is a dirty fighter—no surprise there—but not practiced.

Too long on the sidelines thinking himself the biggest and baddest has made him slow.

If this were a straight fight, one opponent against another, I'd wipe my ass with him.

It's not, and I can't, so it's taking a lot out of me.

This is why Sloan has us overtrain until our arms almost fall off. I take another hit and manage a ball-busting front kick to the groin. He barely registers the hit, and that's when I know for sure he's more dark possession than man.

Even the toughest of men registers a jimmie kick.

All Riordan does is exhale another puff of smog. "If the saying is true that when you lie with dogs, you get fleas, who exactly have you been laying with?"

Warning tingles across the back of my neck, and I scan my surroundings between blocks and thrusts. I can't see who's coming. It feels like something more than a few thugs hanging out with Riordan.

It feels more sinister than that.

I strain to see into the darkness.

Bruin. Feels like someone's targeting me. What do you see?

The roar of my bear explodes in the distance. At the same time, five gunshots ring out.

CHAPTER FIFTEEN

"**B**ruin, you all right?" Despite the panicked volume of my shout, he doesn't respond or roar in fury. I dig in against Riordan, needing this to end. I won't be stuck here smacking an evil smokestack if my bear's hurt. "Bruin, talk to me, buddy."

I push down the gag pushing at my gorge and focus on ending this bullshit game of push and pull. If it comes down to Tad's father or Bruin, I pick Bruin.

Letting the fates decide what happens next, I call Birga and lunge forward. The wicked-sharp marble spear point clinks against his abdomen and skitters off.

"What the hell?"

"Try this, asshole." Nikon slaps the glowing rock Samuel left with us against Riordan's face. "Checkmate, asshole."

I exhale and am about to break into a happy dance when I realize nothing changed.

He's not unconscious.

He didn't fall to the forest floor.

Riordan tips back his head and laughs. "Stupid children. You think a track and trap stone will work on me?"

I shrug. "We did until you ruined the moment. You're not a team player, are you?"

His grin is too creepy for words. "You can't subdue me because I'm not possessed. I welcomed the dark power of the banished Hunter-god within me. We are one."

I blink, my cognitive hamster stopping in his little wheel and canting his head to the side.

Hubba-wha?

Nikon chuckles beside me. "Hearing yourself say that out loud, do you still think it was a wise choice?"

I sense more than see Granda in the darkness behind Riordan. I can't make out what he's doing, but I'll give him whatever opening he's hoping for.

Backing up, I double my efforts to keep him distracted. Birga sings through the air as I spin her, showing off a little fancy spear work. "Tad said you killed your wife. Was that a planned end of nuptials or did Mingin clear the path for his beloved Melanippe?"

I can't tell if Riordan regrets that or not.

I'm not sure how much of him even remains now that the two of them have merged.

"There can be only one," Nikon says. "Bigamy is illegal after all."

I chuff. "So is murder, Greek."

"Yeah, there's that too." Nikon swings Granda's short sword, and Riordan turns to block. I come in at the side, and he has to shift to evade.

Riordan has his head on a swivel, watching Greek and me at the same time. I'm not sure how we're going to end this, but it needs to happen soon. I still don't know what happened to Bruin, and until I see my furry bear smiling at me, I can't think of much else.

Samuel was the one who knew what to do against this much darkness. It's him we need in this battle. Sadly it's also him who is galivanting across Europe searching for Melanippe.

My focus is split, and I miss the shift in Mingin's stance. Out of nowhere, he has me by the shoulders and is throwing me up against the tree.

My head cracks hard against the bark of the trunk, but it doesn't rattle my noggin much because my armor protects me from any damage.

The forest around us explodes in another wave of fighting, and it's pretty clear that Mingin's backup forces have arrived.

The two of us scrap it out, me clawing him and him trying to get a proper grip on me. "Give it up, puny female. You're mine now."

Ha! I've fought off more determined foes than him. Nobody wants to strangle you and make you cry mercy more than brothers.

They likely even used that line on me.

The two of us tangle and topple, landing awkwardly over a bunch of roots.

The bleeding edge of a blade glints in the moon's dim light. I don't panic when he pulls his arm back and jabs. He thinks he'll stab me but—

I gasp as the blade punctures my skin and tears through the muscle of my side.

How? But my armor…

My heart rate triples. Fear and fury overtake the usual strategic chaos. He's emboldened and evil. I'm pinned and punctured. He takes another jab at my stomach, and all I can do is try to grab the blade. It slices into my hands, and I scream as it penetrates.

The forest stirs…enraged and empowered.

I connect to the energy of the roots and trees around me and call for help. A rumble against my back signals the forest's answer.

Tree roots spear through the forest floor, snaking around my attacker.

They peel Riordan off me while he curses and hacks at them. The roots are unaffected.

Undaunted.

Whatever these men did or brought to the forest, it's unwelcome. I gasp and cough blood.

Trying to stop the bleeding in my side is futile. My hands are just as bad. They're slick and hot, but the rest of me is cold.

All I can do is empower the forest to fight for me. And it does. The earth heaves open, and the roots tug Riordan into the depths. He's cursing and kicking but contained, at least for the moment.

I lose focus as the earth reforms, and I press my palms to the forest floor. "Thank you."

Nikon's there a second later, and he curses. "Okay, Red. I've got you.

"Is yer basement dry, bright, and comfy?"

"It is. What's wrong with that?"

"Where's the character in that? Where's the meaning behind things?"

"Where's your head? Wait, there it is—stuck up your Irish ass. Do you honestly think you're better than me because you have mold in your basement?"

"I do."

"You're an idiot."

I rouse from unconsciousness, chuckling at the remembered convo Sloan and I had, way back at the beginning of things.

At first, I wonder why my brain is burping that oldie up. Then I draw a deep breath and know exactly why—Stonecrest Castle.

"It boggles my mind that ye wake from bein' poked full of holes and nearly dyin'—*again*—with a smile on yer face and chucklin' to yerself."

I open my eyes to find Sloan lying next to me in bed, and all is right in the world. Stripped to my undies and bra and comfy cozy beneath a mass of blankets, if I didn't know better, I'd say I was at home in bed protected by the thick draperies of my beloved King Henry.

The 'ode to old and slightly musty' places us solidly at Stonecrest Castle, Sloan's childhood home.

"Hey, you."

"Hey, back."

"I got stabbed."

"I noticed that."

"Is Tad all right?"

"Physically, yes."

"Is Bruin okay?"

"Everyone is fine."

I stretch under the covers and look up at the carved panel above our heads. King Henry has a lovely depiction of forest animals and grapevines and a large stag with a massive rack of antlers. I've used every "nice rack" joke I could think of over the past months.

Just. Can't. Stop.

This bed has an upholstered ceiling but is almost as nice—almost. It's less hard-core masculine.

I shall call her Anne Boleyn.

I could go with one of the Catherines or Anne of Cleves, but after watching *The Tudors*, that bodice-ripping scene between Anne and Henry…

OMG. That's what I'm talking about.

Yeah, baby.

I'm grinning, reliving the passionate pleasures of that one in my mind when he taps my forehead and I realize he's watching me mind-spin.

I pull my dirty mind from the gutter and get back to the moment at hand. "I take it your parents didn't convert your room when you moved out."

"No. I think there are enough rooms in the castle if they need space to expand.

"What would the mighty Janet Mackenzie warrior woman do if she set her inner crafter loose? Do you think she's more of a scrapbooker or a knitter? Maybe a painter? She could probably benefit from journaling."

His silent laughter jiggles the mattress. "No. My castle. My room. Though now, I've tried to make it more *our* room. Da and I agreed a while back that we should furnish it to make us comfortable when we visit."

"Or get stabbed and need saving. Which, all kidding aside, is likely to happen more than regular visits."

"I'd like to change that, but yes, yer probably right."

I shift my legs and wriggle a bit. Everything feels like it should below the covers. Holding up my hands, I check for damage, and there's nothing but a few pink lines where flesh is still knitting together.

"Your dad does excellent work."

"He's had a lot of practice."

"Do you mean with me specifically or in general?"

"Both options are accurate."

I tuck back under the covers and turn to face him. "I didn't mean to get hurt. My armor failed. Dark Riordan stabbed right through my *Tough as Bark*."

"All armor can fail, *a ghra*. It's there as a layer of defense, not a safety net. Yer Unseelie Prince Keldane got through yer armor too."

"*You* are my prince. Keldane is a bully dickwad."

"My point remains the same. Extremely powerful foes will be able to breach your armor. Commit that to memory and make adjustments to keep yerself safe."

"Yes, Da."

He smiles, not a bit riled with my teasing. Good. I don't want him freaking out every time I get hurt.

Calm and loving Sloan is much better.

He taps my forehead again and smiles. "Go have yer shower and get dressed. Ye've got family and friends worried about ye, colleagues waitin' to talk to ye, and a bear and a dragon waitin' to see that yer all right."

"Dart's here?"

"He was. He felt yer struggles and arrived at the forest pretty much when Nikon snapped ye here. He's more than a bit upset. He waited outside with Bruin while Da worked on ye and once we knew everything was all right, Nikon took them both to spend the mornin' with Lara and the kids before we leave."

"Oh, my poor blue boy. Okay, I'm up."

"Almost up." He rolls over me, presses me deeper into the mattress, and kisses me softly. "I'm glad yer not dead, *a ghra*."

"Such a romantic."

The connection is too short. The moment he rolls off the bed, I want to go back ten minutes and fill our time doing more of that.

He winks and points toward the stone wall opposite the footboard. "That's yer dresser. I took the liberty of fillin' it on the off chance we end up here, and ye find yerself without something to wear."

"Good call, sweet prince. I love how you anticipate my needs." I meet him chest-to-chest and clasp my hands behind his neck. "Though I do have a few aching needs unmet."

He chuckles. "Those must keep until we have the time and privacy to explore them properly. Now, get dressed. I'll go tell the others yer up an about and come back to get ye."

I reach up on my tiptoes and steal one more kiss before he gets away. "I heart you hard, Mackenzie."

"How could ye not. I'm feckin' fabulous."

I burst out laughing and push him on his way. "That's it. You have officially been hanging out with my brothers too much."

Fifteen minutes later, Sloan escorts me through the ancient corridors of Stonecrest Castle. We find the gathering of family and friends he mentioned in the receiving room of Sloan's wing.

Patty is chatting with Granda.

Tad is sitting on one of the sofas looking rather beaten up by life.

And Nikon is having a lively discussion with Samuel, Ahren, and Quon Shen about what we are facing trying to put Dark Riordan down.

Maybe not doing that in front of his son would be a good idea. Especially after the past twenty-four hours.

I head over to him first, sink onto the couch, and twist so I'm facing him. "Hey, McNiff. It's a tough day in the life of you. Are you hanging in?"

He looks up at me, and I understand Sloan's comment earlier. Yes, physically Wallace patched up whatever the damage his father's attack left him with. Emotionally, he looks pretty much wrecked.

I sigh and try again. "I'm so sorry about your dad. Your step-mom, too. I know you didn't get along with them, but family is family, and losing them is hard."

"I didn't lose my father, Fi," he snaps. "The asshole embraced dark power over the life he built with us. He was so eager to move on that he wanted us dead."

I want to lean in and hug it out, but as a professional hugger, I sense it's not time yet. He's angry and hurt. He's not ready to be comforted. "I believe the violence against you and his wife was more Mingin's doing than his. He may have been a hard ass, but he loved you."

Tad lifts his shoulder, and I can tell he's had as much pep talk as he can handle. Reaching forward, I squeeze his knee. "Come stay with us for a while. You could use a change of scenery, and there's always lots going on around our place to keep you distracted."

He manages a half-smile and fingers his hair back and out of his face. "I appreciate the offer, Fi. First, I need to figure out what to do about Lena's murder. Yer granda said he'll help me figure out how to put it to rest so it doesn't come back and bite me in the ass."

I pat his leg and get up. "Then get yourself sorted and come. It might get worse before it gets better, but there are people who care about you who have your back."

After a quick hug, I leave it at that.

Next, I move over to Patty and Granda. "How's the craic, lads?"

Patty pushes his rimless glasses up his nose with a stubby finger and winks. "Och, not much craic when yer gettin' torn down by the evils of life, I'm afraid. Maybe it's a good thing Dartamont is coming with you. It's believed having a dragon bond is good luck. Seems to me ye could use some, Red."

I chuckle. "Well, I'll never turn away the opportunity for some luck. I hear having a Man o' Green on your side is good too."

Patty nods. "Ye have that, fer sure. Don't ye ever doubt it. If ye need me, I'll be there."

I bend down to hug him and kiss his cheek. "How'd I get so fortunate?"

"I believe Baba Yaga kidnaped you. Ye didn't think it was so lucky at the time."

"Live and learn, amirite?"

"Aye, yer right."

I hug Granda and assure him that I am whole and healthy. "Don't worry about me. I come from tough stock. Your job is to worry about Kinu and to keep those monkeys out of trouble."

Granda smiles. "Och, I think I'm man enough to do both. Worryin' about yer kids and grandkids comes second nature."

"Especially with grandkids like her," Patty adds.

"Yer preachin' to the choir, my friend."

I wave away the teasing, leaving them to talk about me behind my back while I head over to my fellow Hunter-gods.

"Hey, guys." I hold up my fist and we knuckle-bump a round of greetings. "So, how did things end up with Mingin? The last thing I remember is helping the forest suck him into the depths. I'm sure that didn't last long."

"Sadly no," Nikon says. "But it gave us enough time to get you clear of the danger. Once Dart arrived on the scene, Riordan lost a bit of his bravado. I'm not sure if he is afraid of dragons or what, but he evaced PDQ when your blue boy got there."

"That's because my blue boy is fierce and intimidating. Was he supersized?"

"Yeah. Feeling you all worked up had him tightly wound and ready for a fight."

"A dragon with a true Irish heart," I say. "My brothers are excited to see how he adapts to living in the city. They have a few wagers on things they expect to go wrong."

Samuel laughs. "I have a feeling you'll handle whatever comes your way."

I take the encouragement to heart and get back to the current problem. "Knowing Mingin merged with Riordan, can we assume he'll head toward Melanippe as soon as he can? He has a body now. I'd guess he is eager to claim his lover and get his dark and dirty on after centuries apart."

Samuel nods. "That's our take on things too. We managed to find Melanippe's place of origin but still aren't sure if that's where she resurrects."

Ahren sighs. "For all we know, she regained her physical form weeks ago in another part of the world and is waiting for Mingin to join her."

It's all such a muddled mess.

Leaning closer, I lower my voice. "Is Riordan still in there?

When we send Mingin back to the Neitherlands, will Tad get his father back?"

Samuel shakes his head. "Possession like what happened with the ones we cleansed and returned to their lives is different. They were overtaken. They never agreed to be suppressed by the dark entity and therefore remained two separate consciousnesses."

"But Riordan welcomed Mingin and his power to merge with him."

"Right. There is no Riordan and Mingin anymore. They have truly become one."

I sigh, my heart hurting for Tad. "So, how do we take him down and get him into Newgrange to seal him behind the veil?"

Samuel makes a face. "We can't. At least not until the next spring equinox when we can access the seam."

"The next spring equinox? That doesn't work. If the Culling is happening in December and bad guys are amassing strength, we can't have something as dark and powerful as Dark Riordan hanging around and gaining followers. He needs to be gone."

"Then we need to figure out somewhere else to stash him before that," Quon Shen says.

"Exactly. We'll find another preternatural prison to stick him in and lock him down."

Samuel opens his palms, looking skeptical. "All right. Where are you thinking?"

I frown. "Yeah no, I've got nothing."

CHAPTER SIXTEEN

Once Wallace checks me over and gives me the seal of approval, we all go our separate ways. Samuel, Quon Shen, and Ahren resume the hunt for Melanippe and Mingin, who is now Dark Riordan. Granda goes with Tad to start sorting out the mess that is his life. Patty, Nikon, Sloan, and I head back to the Irish Shire to gather my boys.

We materialize on the wide green backyard behind my grandparent's house, and I spot Dart at the same time he sees me. If you've never seen a dragon barreling at you, it's much like standing in the path of a St. Bernard the size of an elephant in a stampede, but instead of floppy ears, it has pumping wings.

I brace myself for impact and am thankful for my druid training or else I would likely have a few sprained or broken parts.

When the momentum is absorbed, and my feet are once again on the ground, I hug him. "Hey, buddy. I missed you too."

His tongue is like a cat's tongue. He gives me a dozen lashes, exfoliating my cheeks to the point that they're a little raw. Doesn't matter. S'all good.

"Yer dragon's comin' to live at ours house."

I giggle at Jackson's accent. He's been here one day and is talkin' the Irish like an oul man. "Yes, he is. Dart's our family, and he's going to sleep in the new part of the grove we made."

Jackson reaches up Dart's side and pats his blue scales. "That's cuz we's druids."

"Partly, but there are lots of druids who aren't lucky enough to have a dragon."

"That's cuz we's amazeballs druids."

I laugh. "Yep. That's what it is."

Bruin comes in for a hug, and I wrap my arms around the wide column of his neck. It never ceases to amaze me how thick and soft his coat is. I press my cheek into his fur and breathe in the scents of evergreen and the great outdoors. "Hey, Bear. Love you."

"That goes both ways, Red, but yer a tough one to love. Yer hard on the heart."

"Sorry about that. How about we go home, and I fill up a roasting pan with whiskey for you?"

"Whiskey? Not beer?"

"Nah, I'm springing for the good stuff today. You know, to ease your aching heart."

"Och, well, I'll not turn ye down. Whiskey it is. Let's be off then, shall we?"

I chuckle and hug Gran goodbye. "Are you okay with everything? Kinu's good? The kids are behaving for you?"

Gran waves that away. "I'm in my glory, luv. I'm sure I'll sleep well for the next few nights, but I'm enjoyin' every second of havin' them here."

"Awesome. I'll assure Aiden all is well."

"Do that." Gran hugs me again and moves to Sloan and Nikon, then Bruin and Dart. "All right now, off ye go. I'm sure ye've got things to do and places to explore. The wee boy finished off a wild boar a short time ago, so he'll be full fer a few days at least."

"Excellent. A full tummy is a good thing." I pat Dart's side and hug Patty one last time. "Then I guess it's bye for now. We'll see you Friday for Emmet's big Beltane gathering, right?'

"Wouldn't miss it."

I hug my dragon boy the moment we arrive in the druid circle and scrub my knuckles between the three horns on his snout. "Welcome to your new home, buddy. Are you excited to finally be here?"

He thumps his spiked tail on the ground hard enough for us to bend our knees and brace our footing.

I take that as a yes.

"You're going to live at our house and sleep in my grove, but this is where we'll be training."

He doesn't seem to have any objection.

He nudges me again, and I give him another big hug and rub his scales until he makes the sweet coo that means he's truly content. "I missed you too. From now on, we won't have to miss each other at all. You're officially a Cumhaill now."

Sloan chuckles. "Yer like a rolling snowball gathering the lonely and forgotten of life as ye go."

I nod. "Everyone does better if they know they belong somewhere. It's important."

"Yer not wrong."

"No, she's not," Nikon says. "Considering we both fall into that category, I'd say we're pretty lucky she snowballed over us."

Sloan chuckles. "Agreed."

I hug Nikon. "Thanks for the quick round trip to Ireland and the side adventure in the forest."

"Anytime, Fi. I mean that. My life got a lot more interesting since you've been in it."

"Interesting is one word for it," Sloan says.

I wave away their teasing and grab Dart's wing. Holding my

other hand out, I wait for Sloan to make the connection. "Home please."

"Yes, dear."

I'm showing Dart his nest area in the grove and introducing him to Pip and Nilm and Flopsy and Mopsy when my phone *pings* in my pocket with an incoming text. "It's Garnet. He wants to catch up on a few things."

"That's a good idea," Sloan says. "Da sent a stabilizing solution to be added to the vampire serum fer the Guild lab techs. Apparently, they're havin' trouble with one of the proteins reactin' to the altered plasma in Xavier's bloodline, and he said he'd do what he could."

"He's a wonder, that dad of yours."

Sloan pulls the vial of clear fluid from his pocket. "Maybe this will help end Galina's and Xavier's vampire mafia war."

I snort. "I can't believe we're even saying that phrase. Vampire mafia war sounds crazy."

"Agreed. Yet this is the life in which we live."

True story. "I'll text that we're in the backyard if he wants to pop over or that we'll meet him in a bit if he's busy."

Busy or not, Garnet steps into the shade of the grove a moment later. He takes a beat to scan the new section of the grove and nods. "I'm impressed. You've done a lot of work back here since the last time I stopped by. Myra said it was expansive with the new section."

"It is. It may not be as big as some of the Nine Families' sacred groves, but it'll do us and our fae just fine."

"There are still a few additions to make," Sloan says, "but it's progressin' nicely."

Garnet nods.

"I'm quite sure you didn't come here to talk about our grove. What's up?"

Garnet grins. "That's our girl. Straight to the point. You're right, there are several things I want to cover, and none of them is your grove. First, I think an in-person meeting with your dragon is a good idea. I'd like an introduction because odds are, someone will learn you brought a dragon to Toronto and lose their mind."

"Why?"

"Because you brought a dragon to Toronto."

"Oh, is that all? I thought you were anticipating dragon prejudice or something."

"Is there such a thing?" Sloan asks.

"Sure. People hunted dragons to near extinction. That's not the action of dragon fan clubs."

Sloan chuckles. "Right ye are."

"So, the introduction," Garnet says, tilting his head to where Dart is snuggled in his nest, trying it out.

"Oh, yeah, sorry. Come here, baby boy. Dartamont, this is my friend Garnet Grant. He's in charge of Toronto and needs you to be a good boy, okay? He's important—like your dragon mother. And also like your dragon mother, he's scary when he gets mad."

Garnet arches a brow, but I don't course correct. It's good for Dart to see Garnet in a respectful light... maybe even trepidation. Dora says dragons need strict boundaries when it comes to the hierarchy of power to keep them in line and well-behaved.

"I assume you've warded your property and spelled it to prevent any exposure of the empowered world."

I nod. "Yes, and Dora has double-checked and reinforced things to be sure. She's also going to help with his training. She said he's almost old enough to glamour himself, at which point, it eliminates a lot of the danger of exposure."

"What about feeding?"

"We have a few plans in motion."

"Such as?"

"Andromeda created a shell company that disposes of roadkill and made inquiries with several rural road works departments. They are pleased to have someone assume the responsibility for large carcasses."

"Good. And what else?"

"Anyx and Zuzanna are friends with a Prime Puma up near Algonquin Park. He works for Fishing and Wildlife and specifically game enforcement. He says they confiscate kills a couple of times a month from illegal poaching. When they do, he'll give us a call, and Sloan can *poof* up and pick up the animal."

That seems to meet his criteria.

"And if we run into trouble or our network of food falls through, Gran and Granda said they'll supplement. Don't worry. I don't want a hungry dragon in Toronto any more than you do."

"You might think you understand my concerns, Lady Druid, but until you see a hungry dragon raze a small village and eat its citizens, you can't truly understand."

"Yikers. Then I hope I never truly do."

"Me too."

Dart tilts his head to the side as if asking me something, and I guess it. "You can go back to your nest or explore more if you want, buddy. Thanks."

He nudges me with his head, and I scrub his horns before he trots out onto the lawn to meet up with Bruin, Manx, Daisy, and Doc.

It does my heart good to see them welcome Dart and to see my dragon so happy.

"What about Galina? Were you able to track her down with the description of her semi-truck and where she parked it?"

"No. There are thousands of produce trucks in the city, and without a physical address, we weren't able to narrow it down. Now that you're home, do you think Bruin could retrace his steps and show us where?"

"When he travels in spirit mode, it's as the crow flies. I don't know if he could find it again."

"We'll certainly ask," Sloan says. "I have this fer the scientists working on the final stages of the vampire serum. My father has been working in conjunction with yer lab techs to iron out a few last-minute issues."

Garnet accepts the vial and holds it up to the light. "That's thoughtful of him."

"I hope my bluff about the serum already being in play will keep her from using her lipstick on anyone else, but who knows?"

He holds up the vial. "Do you want to come to the lab and the immunizations, or would you rather enjoy your time with your family and your dragon and consider the vampire problem delegated?"

As good as it sounds, I'm not sure I'm the delegating type. I catch bad guys and either put them down or away—especially Goth vampire mafia chicks.

But... Dart did just arrive.

"You go, *a ghra*," Sloan says. "I'll go over the boundaries and the rules with Dart. Then ye can test him later when ye get back."

I blow Sloan a kiss and heart my fingers against my chest. "You get me, Mackenzie."

He nods. "Aye, I do. Now, don't ye dare leave without Bruin. I'll not hear the end of it from him or yer brothers if they find out ye've gone off without yer bear again."

I chuckle. "Look at you getting all autocratic and forceful. I like it, hotness. Boss me around later when we're alone."

Garnet groans.

Sloan rolls his eyes.

Once I gather Bruin, Garnet flashes us to the medical lab of the Lakeshore Guild of Empowered Ones headquarters. "I come bearing gifts," he says, handing over Wallace's vial. "Mr.

Mackenzie said you were having difficulties with part of your serum?"

One of the techs accepts the vial and holds it up to the light. "We are. There's something about the breakdown of proteins and how they respond to the vampire DNA that is thwarting us."

I giggle. "Well, hopefully, it will thwart you no more. Good word, by the way. Two points to you."

Garnet frowns at me. "Now, while they work on this, we'll meet with Xavier and explain to him how he should trust us and allow us to inoculate his bloodline."

"Is there a chance he won't allow it?"

"A good chance. He's concerned that as well as curing Galina's trigger of the singing blood, we're lacing the injection with some dark and devious side effect."

"What kind of side effect?"

"Who knows...microchipping, changing their DNA, turning them into vegans."

I laugh. "Seriously?"

"You'll find most of the empowered community are paranoid and untrusting of other races and species."

"Why can't we all just get along?"

Garnet chuckles. "Maybe that's what we should be dosing people with—a get-along drug."

I point at the lab techs. "Get on that. Let's have everyone playing nice by the end of the year, shall we?"

The techs look at me confused. Do they think I'm expecting them to invent an injectable world peace? "Kidding. Wow, you guys work too hard."

Garnet takes my wrist. "Can we leave before you break them?"

"Sure. Sounds good."

Garnet's assistant stands the moment we stride through the lobby of his office. He's a wiry male with snazzy style and a haircut that frames his chiseled jaw and shows off his piercing yellow eyes. If physical features indicate species, I'd bet he is Moon Called and possibly...a coyote or a jackal?

It hits me as I scan the metropolitan chic space.

I don't think I've ever come in through the door.

"Martin, this is Fiona. I'm not sure the two of you have ever met."

I lift my fingers to wave as we pass, but it seems the introduction wasn't meant for an actual meet and greet.

"Has Xavier not arrived yet?"

"No, sir."

Garnet frowns. "It's unlike him to be late. I'm sure he'll be along any moment. Please show him right in."

"Yes, sir."

We arrive at the door, and Garnet leans around me to open our way into his private office. He grips the handle and—

My shield ignites into a blaze on my back.

Switching into full reverse, I lift my foot and push against the doorframe, taking Garnet with me.

The explosion is massive.

The power of the blast throws us backward in a tornado of heat and debris.

Even catapulted through the air, Garnet's alpha protector instincts kick in. He cages me in his arms and rolls to take the hit of the landing.

We tumble in an uncontrolled tangle until Garnet's back hits Martin's desk. The halting stop is jarring. My bells are still ringing when his lion lets out a furious growl. He shifts to roll off me, then curses, tightens his hold around me, and rolls.

Bang. Gunshots start ringing out and don't stop.

Garnet's body jolts against me from the impact. He's taking heavy fire with me pinned under him, and my brain is fritzing.

Get them, Bruin. I release my bear to do what I can't. The homicidal roar of my battle beast has never sounded so sweet.

Screams ensue. Crunches echo. Snaps explode.

There's some meaty *thunks*, some smashing glass, and the world falls silent—except for the breathy grunts of my bear.

I force myself to move. *Ah, fuck, that hurts.*

The wave of pain nearly knocks me out cold. There's no time. Garnet's on top of me, and he's not moving. My clothes are too warm and too wet.

Surely someone heard that and is coming to help us.

I listen for a few more breaths but don't hear anyone. With my arm out of commission, I can't pull out my phone. I can't—

"Yer pendant, Red. Press yer pendant."

Good one, Bear. I use my left hand to fish it out of my shirt and click the emblem.

Okay, cavalry. Where are you?

CHAPTER SEVENTEEN

"Garnet! Fiona! I need you both to open your eyes." I shake myself awake and blink, thankful to have Anyx and Thaos cursing and growling over me. "I'm okay...dizzy. I think I hit my head. Help Garnet."

"Och, *mo chroi*, what have ye done to yerself now?"

I gasp as they lift Garnet's weight off me and flash out with him. Hallelujah, I can breathe for the first time since he shielded me. "It wasn't me. Bruin got them...didn't he?"

I roll to the side to get up and holler as my right shoulder moves. "Fuckety-fuck."

"It's dislocated." Nikon frowns at me. "Any chance Irish's healing powers include a knack for getting a popped shoulder back in place?"

"Let's hope," I grunt.

"I'll get him." Nikon snaps out.

I try to shake myself inwardly, but the dizziness remains. "How'd you get here so fast, Da?"

"I was at the Batcave with Andromeda and Nikon when yer emergency call triggered."

Thank the foresight of Garnet Grant to have locator jewelry made for us.

"Yer covered in blood, Fi," Da says. "Are ye certain yer not hit? Shock and adrenaline can mask injuries. Ye need to be sure."

I start to take stock of things, then Sloan arrives. He looks at me and scowls. "Fer mercy's sake, woman. I need to wrap ye in cotton and lock ye in the house. Seriously. I just got ye out of the clinic a few hours ago from bein' stabbed."

"What?" Da snaps. "What happened?"

I give up on trying to sit up and rest my head on the floor. "Riordan merged with Mingin and went dark. Blah, blah, he tried to kill everyone. I'm fine."

Dionysus snorts, joining the fun. "Did I hear you say, blah, blah, he tried to kill everyone? I love how you think mass murder falls under the category of blah, blah. You're the best, Fi."

"Glad you're amused, dude."

Sloan is trying to see my stomach and arms, but Garnet's blood plastered my shirt to my skin. "Yer a feckin' mess. I need to strip ye down and hose ye off to see what I'm dealin' with."

"You take her," Da says. "I'll work the scene and try to figure out what happened."

"I'll help," Dionysus says. "I'm part of the team now, right?"

"What *did* happen?" Nikon asks.

I swallow and try to think through the woolly blanket around my brain. "Garnet and I were headed into his office to wait for Xavier. He grabbed the handle of the door, and my shield flared. I pushed us back, and we escaped most of the blast, then Garnet cursed and rolled over me. Lots of shooting. All I could do was release Bruin."

"That was the perfect thing to do," Da says. "He mopped the floor with some very dead assailants and saved yer life. Ye win the day yet again, Bear."

"Yay, Bruin," I say, eyes closed and head spinning. "You're my hero, Bear."

"I see now why the universe put us together, Red. Ye need a full-time battle bear."

I chuckle and groan when my shoulder moves. "True story."

Sloan lets out a throaty Irish grunt and pats my sternum. "If yer comin' home with us, Bruin, now's yer chance. This train is leavin' the station. I have to get this shoulder in place before the swelling sets in worse than it has."

"Someone find out about Garnet," I say. "Oh, I gotta tell Myra."

"I'll take care of Myra," Nikon says. "You focus on letting Sloan patch you up."

I let out a long sigh. "Sounds good."

Sloan *poofs* me home, and we materialize on the floor of our ensuite bathroom. I release Bruin and ask him to check on Dart. Being his first day here, I don't want him freaked out and panicked if he felt my turmoil during the attack in Garnet's office.

Consider it done, he says across our private communication channel. *Don't worry about a thing.*

Except I *am* worried—about a lot of things.

"It was smart if you think about it," I say absently. "Garnet and I were both too dazed and distracted by the bomb to defend ourselves against an immediate raining down of gunfire."

Sloan has medical scissors and is cutting off my shirt. "Calum? Kevin? Is anyone up here? Can I get a hand here, please?"

My ears are still ringing, sounds rushing at me one moment and hollowing out the next.

"Yeah, we're here," Kevin says in the bedroom. "What do you need, Irish—oh, fuck, Fi. Are you all right? *Calum,* get in here. It's Fi."

Kevin is on the bathroom floor next to me a nanosecond later. "Shit. What do you need?"

Calum's socks slip on the bathroom floor as he rushes through the door. "What happened? Fuck, that's a lot of blood."

"Not mine," I say.

"We'll get into that in a moment," Sloan says. "One of ye help me cut away her shirt so I can examine her and put her shoulder back into its socket before the swelling gets too bad. The other one, get the flexible ice pack from the freezer and some water and a couple of the Tylenol 3 we have from her last disaster."

Kev is already helping with the shirt, so Calum runs downstairs.

"I don't think I'm shot." My voice sounds funny coming out of my mouth, and I tell them that.

"Ye were in close proximity to a bomb explosion, ye hit yer head, and people were shooting at ye at close range. I'd be surprised if yer hearing *wasn't* wonky."

"Holy shit." Kev peels the front section of my new shirt away. "Where was this war zone?"

"Garnet's office," I say.

Sloan and Kev ease my shirt off in pieces, and Sloan wipes me down with a warm cloth. He has to rinse often to get anywhere, but my guy is focused.

"There's a lot of blood on me," I say, watching him do his thing. "Like, a *lot* of blood."

"Yes, luv, I noticed that. I need to be sure how much of it is Garnet's and how much of it is yers."

I swallow as my stomach revolts. "I'm gonna puke."

Kevin is quick to grab the little garbage can, pull out the bag, and get the plastic bin to me before I hurl. I retch to the side and cry out as the tensing of my body moves my shoulder, and my field of vision darkens.

"I'm gonna pass out."

A cold cloth is on my forehead by the next pounding beat of my heart, and the world settles.

"Bless you."

"Okay, she's right. She's not shot anywhere, so I'll need one of you to tend to Fi and the other to help me get her shoulder set. I'm going to do a bit of magic prep work first."

Calum opts to help Sloan, so Kevin takes over the cold cloth. "This will be over quickly, Fi. Then you'll be good as new."

I swallow, but the sour acid taste in my mouth makes me regret that soon enough. "Sorry to always be the source of drama."

Kevin chuckles and shakes his head. "We'd all take you on the worst days rather than spend a single day without you. Life would be boring without you."

"True story."

Sloan and Calum are talking about their game plan, and I try not to listen. I've seen the movies. I know this will hurt. Once it's back in place, life will be good again.

"Tell me something to distract me."

Kevin smiles. "Your brother and I started planning our wedding."

"Yeah? That's amazing. Tell me everything."

"We're working on having a small ceremony down at the beach at the end of June before it gets too hot. We're thinking sunset vows and the reception at Shenanigans. Calum talked to Shannon, and she's checking their bookings to give us free dates. Then we're making it happen."

Calum wraps a towel under my armpits and tightens his hold on my left. The tingling of Sloan's magical massage ends, and he grabs my upper arm on my right. "I'm sorry, *a ghra*. This will hurt. Feel free to swear at me."

I look back at Kevin, my heart rate rising. "Keep talking. Cake? Colors?"

"The cake will be vanilla with Chantilly icing and raspberries

—Calum's favorite. And we think—"

The boys pull, and Sloan shifts my arm.

I shout a very unladylike, albeit deserved, string of curses a pissed-off trucker would be proud of.

I'm not sure if I pass out or if it's just a close call, but the next thing I know, Calum's wrapping the icepack over my shoulder, and Sloan is holding a glass of water and two tablets in front of my face. "All right, *a ghra*. Things will get better now. Take these and I'll get ye dressed, and we'll go check on Garnet."

I lean my head against Kevin, and being the angel he is, he presses the cold cloth to my head once again.

"Best support team, evah."

"Fi! Are you all right, duck?" Myra jumps up from her seat outside the Guild operating room and rushes toward me, her lovely cat's eyes red from tears.

I step back to avoid her hug. "I'm battered, but I'll be fine. Garnet shielded me from the worst of it."

"How is he?" Sloan continues along the sterile corridor toward Anyx, Zuzanna, and Nikon.

Anyx stands. "He took four bullets to the back and a couple to the arms and legs. They're working on the ones that hit his core first."

"Would it be of any help fer me to go in?"

Anyx lifts his shoulders. "Feel free to offer. I'm not sure what you can do."

"Well, I'm not my father, but I am a decent healer."

"He's more than decent," Nikon says.

"Go see if they need help," I say. "Maybe you can work on the damage to his limbs while they focus on what they're doing."

Sloan nods. "At least I'll offer."

When the door bumps shut, I focus on Myra. "How are you?"

She shakes her head. "I'm a bloody mess. How did this

happen, Fi? He's so careful. A bomb in his office? Gunmen waiting for him? How did they even know he'd be there? He flashes around the city so much putting out fires that he often doesn't go to his office for days at a time."

"That's a good point." I look at Anyx, my mind turning over a few things. "He was expecting Xavier for an update, but he hadn't shown up yet."

Anyx frowns. "He didn't show up during the aftermath either. Why do you suppose that is?"

I shake my head. "I don't know, but I think we should find out."

Anyx frowns. "I'll take Thaos and visit Xavier. You look like you just lived through a bombing and need to sit down."

"I did live through the bombing, and I think I deserve a chance to face Xavier if he was involved. Besides, we were supposed to immunize his seethe to eliminate Galina's hold on their singing blood weakness."

Anyx doesn't like the idea of me joining him, but he doesn't have much choice. "If you leave me here, I'll have Nikon or Sloan take me. You might as well take me."

His brow arches. "I see why you annoy him."

"Now you're getting it." I side hug Myra and rest my head on her shoulder for a second. The painkillers are kicking in, and my body is warring between drowsy and dizzy.

It's been quite a day.

"Fi!"

The world goes topsy-turvy, and when things settle, I'm blinking up at the fluorescent lights. "Why am I on the floor?"

"Because you found standing upright too much work?" Nikon says.

I look around, and Anyx is gone. "Shit. Did I miss my ride?"

"You did, duck. I'm fairly certain that despite your best intentions, neither Nikon nor Sloan will be flashing you to take on vampires at the moment."

I groan. "It's the stupid T3s."

Nikon laughs and helps me sit up. "It's more likely the bomb and the fact that your brains got scrambled during the fallout. But, hey, if you want to blame it on the Tylenol, that's up to you."

"*Mo chroí?* Feckin hell, what now?"

I wave that away and struggle to get to my feet, which only happens because Nikon helps me. "Nothing. It was a reenactment of what happened upstairs. S'all good. Nothing to see here."

Da frowns at me. "Home to bed, now. And save yer snark. I've had enough of yer stubborn will fer one day. Where's Sloan?"

"Helping with Garnet's surgery."

Da turns his attention to Nikon. "Take her to her beloved bed. Tie her down if ye have to, but she doesn't step out of that bedroom until she's steady on her feet and clear in her head."

"Da! You can't—"

Da holds up his finger and gives me the "one more word out of you" glare that makes us all pee a little. "Bed. Now. Yer not helpin' here, Fi. If anything, yer distractin' us from dealin' with things."

I sigh. Dammit. "Fine. I'll go lay down until my head stops spinning but then I'm back in the game without argument. I won't let you sideline me from my case."

"I wouldn't dream of it." He meets Nikon's gaze. "If ye need to leave, ask one of the boys to watch her. She's a sneak, and she's stubborn. Don't fall fer her promises."

Nikon wraps an arm around my hip. "I've got her. Someone tell Sloan she's at home in bed when he comes out."

"Will do," Myra says. "You go home and get some rest, duck. And don't forget to wake her up every hour in case she has a concussion."

Nikon nods. "Will do. Say goodnight, Gracie."

I give my father, Myra, and Zuzanna a little wave. "Goodnight, Gracie."

CHAPTER EIGHTEEN

The morning sun is streaming through the windows the next time I open my eyes. Sloan's side of the bed is rumpled but empty, standard operating procedure around here, and Manx lays stretched out along the bottom of the bed.

"Sleeping Beauty awakes at last." Manx yawns wide. "I bet yer hungry."

I pat my belly and yeah, the pit is empty. "Ravenous. Wow I guess I slept through dinner."

"Ye did. Ye've been out almost twenty hours."

"What? Why didn't somebody wake me?"

"Och, they did. The boys took turns wakin' ye every hour fer the first long while, then Sloan gave ye the all-clear to sleep undisturbed. It seems yer recent ordeals took more cut of ye than ye realized."

"Apparently."

Rolling out of bed goes better than it has in a few days, and I stretch my shoulder out and twist my ribs where Dark Riordan stabbed me. Huh, time does heal all wounds.

Grabbing a fresh outfit, I get sorted in the ensuite and head downstairs fifteen minutes later, feeling strong and ready to tackle the world.

Sadly, it seems the universe has other plans.

There's a Cumhaill sibling meeting, and I'm late to the party. I find Sloan standing against the window, and he shrugs, giving me nothing. "What's going on? Why does everyone look like they're losing their minds?"

Emmet throws up his hands. "I told them about a decision I was excited about, and I'm getting shot down from all sides. There's no sense telling you because you'll hate it too and then I'll just feel ganged up on."

That doesn't sound good at all.

I sit on the footstool in front of Emmet's chair. "All right, I'm listening. I promise I'll try my best not to jump to conclusions and to see it from your side."

Dillan makes eyes at me and bites his bottom lip. "Brace yourself."

Emmet scowls and faces me. "You know how I've been researching Beltane for tomorrow's celebration, right?"

"I do."

"Well, I had an idea. *No.* It was more than an idea. It was an epiphany."

The way Emmet's mind works, him having an epiphany is a scary thought. I keep that to myself. "All right, lay it on me."

"Did you know Beltane is the celebration to honor the Great Wedding of the goddess and the god?"

"No. I didn't."

"Well, it *is.* Over the centuries, it has become a popular and revered time for pagan weddings."

Aiden grips his fingers and starts snapping his knuckles one by one. It's his tell. Emmet talking about weddings isn't making me happy, but I said I'd listen with an open mind, and I try.

"It's a time for pagan weddings, *and?*"

"And pagan weddings are called handfastings. The hand-fasting celebration binds a couple in a traditional betrothal for 'a year and a day.' After that, they can choose to stay together or part without recrimination."

"And you think we should suggest this to Da and Shannon?" I put as much hopeful energy into the suggestion as I can.

Dillan barks a laugh. "If only. Them I could understand but—"

Emmet turns on him. "Butt out, D. I get to do this."

Dillan lifts his palms, and I can tell it's killing him to keep his opinions to himself.

Biting our tongue is not a Cumhaill strength.

"So, not Da and Shannon."

Emmet shakes his head. "No, but I agree the two of them tying the handfasting knot makes a lot of sense. I'll suggest it to them. No, I'm talking about Ciara and me."

I swallow the bit of barf that crawls up the back of my throat. "Okay, I'm trying not to tailspin here."

Dillan snorts. "Yet we still see the steam coming out of your ears."

I throw him a dirty look. "There is no steam, but yes, I am concerned. The two of you have been dating less than six weeks."

Emmet nods. "I get that. It's been the best six weeks of my life, and honestly, I hate that we're so far apart. We both do. We miss each other like crazy and want a full-time relationship."

"I get that. It was hard having Sloan so far too. Still, if you both feel the same way, you could invite her to stay with us for a bit. You don't have to get married to take things to the next level to see if she's the one."

He sighs. "I *know* she's the one. The problem is her parents won't let her move across the world to 'shack up' with me. They say if we're going to play at being adults, then we need to treat our relationship as responsible adults would."

"But marriage?"

"Handfasting," he repeats. "A year and a day. It's perfect. The two of us know we're more than a fling, and over the next year, we can prove it to the rest of you. I know you don't love the idea, and I'm not sure you even like Ciara, but she's different than she was, Fi. I really want you to give her a chance."

I look at Sloan for support, and he shrugs. "The length of commitment is reasonable. Handfasting can be dissolved in a year or can often be for life. If it works the way they plan, everyone's happy."

"And if it doesn't?"

Emmet frowns. "If it doesn't then there's no recrimination. I don't need my feelings to be blessed by a church or sanctioned by a government. This commitment is between the two of us. Next year at this time, we'll decide if it worked, and we'll be the ones who decide whether to stay together."

"Have ye asked Ciara? Is this a thought you're considering or a plan in motion?"

He straightens. "The second. Ciara told her parents today and invited them to our celebration tomorrow."

Tomorrow. Hokey-doodle that's soon.

"Fi. I want you on my side for this. If it's a mistake, it's mine to make. Ciara and I make each other happy. To make her parents happy, we're signing papers saying if it washes out, we each leave with what we came with. No fault. No foul."

My mind is fritzing. "Unless she gets pregnant. You can't prenup a baby, Em. What happens then? Parents on opposite sides of the ocean are no good."

He shakes his head. "Absolutely not. We're firm on that. We're too young, and it's much too soon for that."

Well, that's good.

"It sounds like ye've given it serious consideration." Sloan's tone is soothing and reasonable. It's the voice I equate to him talking down a cornered animal about to pounce. In no way do I miss the implication that *I* am the wild animal in this scenario.

"I can't say I'm thrilled," I say, trying for reasonable yet honest. "But Myra reminded me the other day that it's not my place to form an opinion. I don't belong in your love affair any more than you belong in mine."

A light of excitement flashes in his green eyes. "So, you're with me?"

This is one of those pivotal moments in a relationship that either builds up or tears down the foundation of trust. I'm not willing to lose that with Emmet over this.

Sloan's right. Emmet has thought this through.

I swallow. "I'm always with you, Em. If you're set on giving your relationship with Ciara a real go, I'm behind you."

His smile lights up my heart. "Thanks, Fi. I knew you'd understand. What do you think, guys? Can you get on board?"

I cast a hopeful gaze toward Aiden, Calum, and Dillan and try to help Em's case. "Yesterday, a friend of mine turned a doorknob, and it blew us up. It was a close call that could've ended both our lives."

"Thank the goddess, it didn't," Sloan says.

There's a round of knocking on wood, and I continue. "My point is, we live dangerous lives and we have to celebrate each moment. If Emmet's happiness is in Ciara's hands, I say they get to navigate how to celebrate that however they choose."

Aiden sighs and licks his lips. "I guess we'll know if it's the right decision in a year and a day. It's not the path I took with Kinu, but I wish you both all the happiness the two of us have found over the years."

Calum shrugs. "I think you're mental, but I'll get on board. Not everyone waits a decade to make it official."

Kevin grins. "Everyone's journey is different."

Emmet's smile grows, and he shifts toward Dillan. "Come on, D. Say you're not against me. You'll see I'm right over time."

"And if you're not?"

He shrugs. "If a year from now one or both of us wants to end it, we'll know we grabbed the ring and went for it. You gotta respect that, right?"

Dillan rolls his eyes and sighs.

"How's this. I officially give you the right to the 'I told you so' moment if it doesn't work out."

He lifts his chin and considers that.

"Yeah? And I can be brutal?"

"Sure."

"And you have to take it?"

Emmet sighs. "It's not going to happen, but sure."

Dillan leans forward and offers his knuckles for a bump. "Okay, fine. Not my circus, not my monkeys. I'll stash my negativity and wish you the best for now. I'm still not convinced, but I'll back off. I hope you know what you're doing, bro."

"I do." Emmet grins. "Thanks, guys. I knew you'd come through for me. It's going to be great, you'll see."

"Assuming you live through telling Da," Aiden says. "When's that?"

"I'm meeting him for lunch at Big Smoke Burger."

"Public place. That's smart," Calum says. "Although, I'm not sure it'll save you this time."

"Och, and don't discount Evan Doyle," Sloan adds. "The man might be portly, but he's wicked deadly with poisons and very protective of his daughter. I'd avoid sharin' a meal with the man until the shock of this dies down."

Emmet pales. "Thanks, Irish. Good to know."

After the dust settles on Emmet's handfasting bomb, everyone clears out, and Sloan and I are left to enjoy a rare moment of having the house to ourselves.

"You miss a lot when you sleep almost twenty hours. It's disorienting. Not to mention how hungry you get. Damn, I might be better off to eat the refrigerator and spit out the metal."

Sloan opens the stove door and pulls out the best possible solution. "I ordered ye an extra Hawaiian last night fer when ye woke up. Ye didn't wake, but it's still here waiting for ye."

"Oh, you beautiful man. Just when I think I can't love you more, you prove me wrong."

He chuckles and hands me the pizza box. "Well, I couldn't let the Greek get all the Hawaiian pizza praise. I have to protect my turf."

I snort, biting off the tip of my first slice. Second-day pizza is the bomb. The cheese and tomato sauce has merged and trapped the ham and pineapple in their clutches. *Sooo* good.

The key is *not* to put it in the fridge.

"Your turf, am I?"

"Most definitely."

I chew for a bit and swallow. "Well, your turf is secure. You have me locked down."

His smile turns contemplative. "What do you think about the handfasting idea?"

"I meant what I said. If Emmet wants to take their relationship to the next level and that's the way they decide to do it—"

"No. I wasn't askin' about Emmet. I was askin' about yer thoughts on it...fer us."

I stop chewing and carefully swallow so I don't choke. "Are you asking if we should get handfasted?"

"I am. No pressure... I'm not lookin' to move ye toward it. We're simply havin' a conversation."

I set my slice down and brush the crumbs from my fingers. "Then, if it's all the same to you, I respectfully decline. I love where we are right now and consider us a lock. I agree with Emmet's thinking that I don't need a church or a government paper to tell me I'm bound to you, but I also don't feel the need to jump on the handfasting bandwagon either. Is that all right?"

His expression is open and relaxed. "Perfectly. I simply wanted to gauge where ye stand."

I reach across the island countertop and take his hand. "You're mine, and I'm yours. One day, when it's time to consider kids and our future and stuff, I want a dress and a ceremony with friends in the grove and Niall Horan, and a drunken celebration at Shenanigans—but for right now, I don't want anything different than this."

I tap his Claddagh band and smile. "You and me and our house and our animals and my family. I'm one hundy percent content."

He nods. "As am I."

"Are you sure? If you want more or were hoping for a different answer, tell me. We're partners, and this is a simple conversation, remember?"

He picks up my half-eaten slice of Hawaiian bliss and holds it up for me to bite. "I am one thousand percent content to continue exactly as we are."

I laugh and reclaim my slice. "One thousand percent. Trying to outdo me, eh?"

"It's tough to raise the bar around here. I gotta take a win when and where I can."

I take a bite and go back to chowing down. "Good. It's nice to be on the same page."

"We usually are, but yes, it's nice."

He joins me in the ode to cold pizza for breakfast, and we eat in silence for a while. Then I figure I'll broach the one issue I've been skirting the past six weeks.

With Emmet's handfasting tomorrow, there's no getting away from it now. I focus my intentions and cast a silence spell.

When the air pops around us, his gaze narrows.

"Since we're talking things through, I want a little privacy to get something off my chest."

Sloan hands me a napkin and grabs one for himself. "All right. What's on yer mind?"

"Ciara and you? Can we go over what happened there? Emmet's determined to bring her into our lives, and he noticed I'm not comfortable with her, and I think that's because—okay, no—it *is* because the two of you used to have sex."

"Och, Fi—"

I hold up my hand and get it all out.

"If she's going to live with Emmet and he lives with us, that means she's living with us, and that's stirring up questions and insecurities I don't usually have... And honestly, I want to be happy for my brother."

"Insecurities?" He rounds the island and pulls out the stool next to me. "Fiona Cumhaill, there is no one, male or female, fae or human, who should ever make you feel less than the magnificent female ye are."

I run my thumb over my Claddagh and nod. "Logically I know you love me and that she'll be here for Emmet, but it was only last summer that she was still into you and being a bitch to me because of it."

He takes a moment and, as always, gives my concerns consideration before he speaks. "In a perfect world, ye shouldn't be forced to deal with my mistakes in our home. I apologize fer that. Tell me what ye need to know to put it to rest."

"Just tell me about what you two were and weren't, so I stop worrying about it. She's obviously stunning—like, movie star stunning—and has money and I know she's a university graduate. Did you two date? Did your parents invite her for dinner? How long were you together? I just think if I know more, it'll help."

Sloan takes my hand and kisses my ring. "We never dated. We met up sporadically over four or five months. There were no dinners, no hanging out, no moments together where we shared anything other than our mutual dislike fer one another and physical attraction."

I'm not sure if the "nothing other than physical attraction" makes me feel better or worse.

Gah, why does she have to be so beautiful?

"It sounds horribly crude, but we were two people who barely tolerated one another having sex."

"Was it good sex?"

He scrubs a hand over his face and draws a deep breath. "Not really. There are no moments that stand out. There were no feelings. No connection. Nothing like what we have, Fi. I need ye to hear that and take it to heart."

My nose tingles with the threat of tears, but I refuse to let this get emotional. "Well, no. I know you never loved her and that you love me. Don't think I'm jealous or needy or anything. I just want to understand."

He brushes my hair behind my ear. "I don't think yer jealous or needy. I appreciate ye askin' before ye let it bother ye."

"Oh, it's too late for that. It definitely bothers me."

He chuckles. "All right then, before it bothers ye enough to come between us."

"I wouldn't let that happen... and I want to be excited for Emmet. I do. But this is *our* place. Is that selfish? This is the happiest of happy places for me. I don't know how I'll feel about her living here."

"Then we tackle that when ye find out. If it's upsetting fer ye, I'll buy the house across the road and move them there. Hell, I'll buy a house fer each of yer brothers if that's what it takes to make ye happy."

I laugh. "You don't need to buy up the entire street."

"I'd do it in a blink, *a ghra*. Property values in Toronto are a sound financial investment, but yer smile is an even better one."

"Okay, housing arrangements aside, I'm still not a fan. I love Kinu and spending time with her. I don't know if I can have that with Ciara. Even if I have nothing to feel threatened about, I still want to punch her stupidly beautiful face. It's catty, I know."

He chuckles. "Let me tell ye what *I* know. Two years ago, two druid heirs who no one valued beyond their outer packages hooked up a few dozen times. Neither had what the other needed, and the appeal soon soured, and they grew tired of one another."

"I like this story," I say, feeling a little better.

"Then, months and months later, a crazy, spirited, opinionated redhead left Canada in a huff and came crashing through Ireland. She was brash and overconfident and let no one define who she was."

"Okay, it's getting good now."

He chuckles. "The guy was at a loss, amazed, completely unprepared. He saw in the redhead everything he ever wanted—love, acceptance, loyalty, and unshakeable faith. He wanted that for himself—he wanted *her*."

"But she was much too busy having her life roto-tilled to fall for his suave charms."

"That's right, but he was patient. He watched from afar and learned about her world. He vowed to change his life and become the one she'd love forever. If he ever won her heart, he knew he would never let her go."

"He better not because it would crush her."

"Not a chance. Now, hurt and angry, the heir left behind lashed out and behaved badly. She wasn't a bad person, but she too needed time to change to become worthy of one of those crazy Canadians. Months went by, and she began to show promise. Then, when the goddess deemed her ready, she stepped in and bound them during a sacred ritual of love and new beginnings."

I smile. "I like the way you tell a story, hotness."

He leans forward on his stool and cups my chin "And they all lived happily ever after."

I draw a deep breath and exhale. "You bet your sexy brown ass they did. HEAs all around."

Standing, I shift forward and hug him. "Thank you for loving me. And just for the record, I wanted to grow and become the woman worthy of you too. I heart you hard, Mackenzie."

"I heart you right back, Cumhaill."

CHAPTER NINETEEN

Sloan and I polish off most of the pizza. Then he *poofs* us uptown to the driveway outside Garnet's Toronto home. The Grand Governor of the Lakeshore Guild of Empowered Ones is not only powerful within that frame, but he's also the Alpha of the Toronto Moon Called. In other words, he's the shit.

His official residence is in a swanky part of the city, but that's only his mundane, no magic address. His true residence is a sprawling bungalow compound in the middle of the African Savanna.

The two of us walk under the archway between his driveway and the house, and magic tingles over my skin. There's a momentary pressure and a subtle *pop* as we pass through the mirage and it transports us to Garnet's compound.

The sudden change in the sun's intensity and heat is like when you step off an airplane for a tropical vacation and climate shock slams you.

It was worse during the winter going from minus forty to plus ninety. Now that Toronto's winter season is over, it's not nearly as extreme.

Sloan and I follow the path into the compound and under the

shade of the covered verandah to access the main entrance. Imari is playing with her dollies on the outdoor couch and runs over to hug us.

"Hey, sweetie. How are you?"

"We were going to go to the bookstore today, but Mommy said we have to stay home. Daddy doesn't feel good."

"No, I know. That's why we came. I brought treats to make him feel better." I lift the bag of Tim Horton's cookies, and Sloan shows her the tray of drinks.

"That's a lot of treats. Are they all for him?"

I smile at her hopeful look. "Nope. I would never forget you and your mommy. Do you think we should take them inside?"

She shrugs. "Maybe not. His lion is very cranky."

Sloan nods. "I imagine he'll be back to his old self very soon. It's hard to be happy when you don't feel good."

"That's what Mommy said. I think I'll stay out here until then."

It's too cute that she's already avoiding her father when he's in a mood. Imagine how things will go when she starts dating. "Would you like some company? Maybe a bear to talk to?"

Her face lights up. "Can Bruin come out and play?"

"Only for a quick visit. We aren't staying long."

"Okay."

I release Bruin. When he materializes next to Imari, he lets out a menacing growl and shows his teeth. My heart jumps but Imari squeals with delight. "Oh, Bear, you're so funny."

Yeah, fricken hilarious.

Sloan looks at me, and I don't think I'm the only one who peed a little.

"Bear humor. I think you gotta be a bear to get it."

"I see," he says.

"All right, take your treat and enjoy it out here."

I fish her out a cookie and pull the real fruit slushie so she can take it back to her spot. "What about a cookie for Bruin? Bears get hungry, don't we, Bruin."

"Och, you know it, little cub."

I grab another one and dole it out. "Okay, you kids be good out here, and we'll visit again on the way out."

Imari's already sipping her drink, sharing with her dollies, and filling Bruin in on all her latest adventures.

I look through the glass door, and Myra waves us in. She's at the kitchen counter, and Garnet is in the adjoining living room on the phone with his back to us.

"I don't give two shits if he's gone to ground. You find the motherfucker and bring him to me." When he ends the call, Garnet roars louder and longer than I've ever heard him.

He must catch our scents in the air because he turns red-faced and scowls. "Knocking is considered polite."

"Now, stop." Myra comes to protect us. "Look, they brought refreshments."

Garnet growls and purses his lips.

"A thank you is considered polite too." Myra gives him a look.

"Thank you." Garnet chucks his phone onto the couch. "Please tell me you have some insight as to why Xavier blew us up and where the fuck he's hiding now that he failed to kill me?"

"Do you honestly think Xavier is behind the bomb?"

"You don't? He set the meeting. He missed the meeting. My men found vampires from his seethe hacked up in the rubble." That comment seems to calm him a little. "Please extend my appreciation and admiration to your bear. He has a lethal response I truly admire."

"I'll tell him." Walking over to the wide marble island, I set the cookies down and take the tray from Sloan. "Fruit slushies for the ladies and Iced Capps for the men. I figured you might need to cool down."

"Good call." Myra accepts her slushie and sips from the straw.

"My mate isn't the best patient. In fact, being patient isn't a strength of his either."

"Another thing we have in common." I smile and hand him a drink.

He sneers at the offering.

"It's manly, honest. Try it before you growl at me. You'll like it."

He glares at me, but I don't back down.

"Humor me. Your daughter is afraid to come in here because your lion is cranky. Simmer down and tell me where we are with things and what you need me to do."

Garnet looks outside at Imari playing with Bruin and exhales. "You're a pain in the ass."

"So you keep telling me. Yet still, you risked your life to save me. The least I could do was bring you a peanut butter cookie."

He accepts the iced coffee. "I do love peanut butter cookies."

"I know. I pay attention."

I grab the bag and hold it open to him. He selects one and takes a bite.

Myra grins. "And the Lady Druid performs the impossible task of taming the wild beast."

I chuckle. "I don't believe for a moment he's tamed. I'll settle for momentarily lulled into a non-murderous state."

Garnet arches an ebony brow. "I heard you had every intention of tracking Xavier down and collapsed on the floor of the clinic."

I shrug. "Collapse is probably an exaggeration. Momentarily lost the battle with gravity sounds better."

Myra sticks her hand into the cookie bag and snags one. "And laid there unresponsive while Nikon and I lost our minds for over a minute."

"Hush, meddlesome woman. Eat your cookie."

Myra laughs. "I'm glad you're feeling better. Sloan texted me this morning that you were still sleeping it off. I'm glad you took care of yourself."

"I don't get any credit for that. My body shut down without my permission."

"Because ye needed it."

I make a face at him, but he doesn't seem to care. "Fine. I needed it. And now I'm functioning at full capacity. So, Garnet, lay it on me. Where are we?"

Garnet updates me on Anyx's search efforts over the past day and a half. "No sign of Xavier. No sign of Galina. Four dead vampires chopped to undead bits in my demolished office."

"What about Martin?" I ask, thinking about the aftermath of the bomb.

"Dead. He got caught in the gunfire."

Crappers. I thought he seemed nice too. "You said the vampires were from Xavier's seethe?"

"They were."

"From his siring line or simply his nest?"

"His seethe but not his bloodline."

"Do vampires defect?"

Garnet pulls on his straw and swallows. "Defect? You think they set Xavier up as a show of faith while jumping ship?"

"Ye think Galina sent them?" Sloan asks.

I swallow a mouthful of mango chill. "Think about it. People within the seethe hear that Xavier is planning to pick up the serum at Garnet's office. Obvi, if they know that, Galina knows I bluffed when I said his bloodline was immune."

"Obvi," Garnet says, mocking me.

"On the street, Xavier has his guard up, but in your office, he's familiar there. He lets down his guard. They know when and where. They tell Galina, and she demands a blood initiation."

"You think she recruited vampires from his seethe to take him out?"

I shake my head. "No. Him *and* you. She knew who you were

at Copacabana and she wasn't impressed we'd taken an interest in her and her business. I got the feeling she didn't like the idea of the Lakeshore Guild policing her at all."

"It's a sound theory," Sloan says. "To prove their loyalty, Xavier's vampires need to take you both out."

"But Xavier doesn't show," I say. "Maybe he catches wind of something and drops off the map."

Garnet frowns. "You think he's gone to ground to stay out of Galina's sights?"

"Maybe while he regroups and plans his attack. I can't imagine him staying in hiding beyond that."

"No." Garnet stares off across the golden plains of the savanna. "If you're right, his revenge will be swift and violent."

"The worst part of this theory is that if Galina knows I lied about the serum, then she knows we haven't inoculated Xavier's bloodline, and they're still vulnerable."

"Ye think she'll use her lipstick to destroy him."

"As soon as possible, yeah."

Garnet takes another long pull on his Iced Capp. "All right. The first thing we need to do is get the serum completed. If I were her and knew my play at my enemy failed, I'd move fast to strike again before he has time to regroup."

Agreed. "We have to assume she found out the assassination failed when Xavier's vampires didn't return. She could've gone out last night and kissed any number of unsuspecting clubbers. We need to take Xavier's begotten off the playing field."

Garnet nods, hands Myra his half-eaten cookie, and strides into the back of the house. A few minutes later, he returns wearing his shoulder harness, his guns, and pulling on his suit jacket. "All right, Lady Druid. We have a place to start and a ticking clock. Let's go."

He kisses Myra goodbye and grabs his drink.

I chuckle and fall into step. "Told you that you'd like it."

During World War II, extensive renovations done on the stables outside of Casa Loma were a front for the construction of a secret military research facility built under the castle. It's widely believed that Station M, as it was known, was where they manufactured covert sonar devices used for U-Boat detection.

Fast forward more than seventy-five years and that secret facility, which officially never existed, is the perfect place to house creatures who technically don't exist.

The vampires.

"How quickly does the lab think the serum will take effect?" I ask as we park the car in the BlueBlood parking lot.

"They assure me it's immediate," Garnet says. "It acts as an impulse blocker and is triggered by adrenaline. The moment they're struck by *cântând sânge* their need to feed will kick their adrenaline into high gear and cancel the compulsion.'

"Smart. Then once it hits their system, they should be free from evil influence."

"In theory," Sloan says, frowning.

"In theory," Garnet agrees.

The three of us make our way out of the shadows where Garnet flashed us and take in the grounds of the castle sitting in the heart of Toronto's downtown core.

"Anyone know how to get to the super-secret vampire nest?"

Garnet tilts his head toward the carriage house and stables. "Follow me."

Assuming the demeanor of three tourists enjoying the historical significance of Casa Loma, we meander our way around the carriage house and into the stable section. Garnet strides toward the far end of the horse stalls and stops at the second from the end.

Nothing in this ten-by-twelve wooden stall screams entrance

to a super-secret vampire lair. In truth, nothing here even hints at it.

Which is likely how it remains super-secret.

Garnet grabs a wooden-handled hoof-cleaning tool hanging on the sidewall and sticks the metal point into a hole in the old, rusty box on the floor. With a twist, the top of the box unlatches, and Garnet puts his face in front of a security screen.

"Open up. The sooner I have my say, the sooner I'll leave you all in peace."

I'm not sure that's the way I'd go as far as an icebreaker, but it does the trick. There's a click beneath my feet, and Garnet waves his hand to shoo us toward the wall.

A center section of the straw-covered floor drops a few inches and slides back and out of the way, exposing a set of stairs.

Garnet leads the way. Instead of using the steel ladder attached to the inside of the wall, he steps off the edge and drops straight down.

I smile at Sloan and shrug. "I guess we follow his lead."

I step off the edge in a leap of faith and use *Slow Descent* to break my fall. I land on the balls of my feet and step out of the way for Sloan to join us. He lands as silently as a cat a moment later.

The moment the three of us have landed, the moveable section of the floor rumbles into motion twenty feet above our heads. When it locks into place, I realize it sealed us in an antechamber of some kind.

There isn't any visible doorway, so I'm not sure where we're supposed to go or what comes next.

Awesomesauce. We're stuck in a metal room at the mercy of a nest of vampires.

I call faery fire to my palm and hold it up to light the chamber. Metal floor, ceiling, and walls. No windows. No door. "Is it just me, or are you getting a *Star Wars* 'stuck in the garbage compactor' vibe here?"

The fact that Sloan and Garnet both arch an ebony brow at me in exactly the same way is too funny.

Before my imagination gets too far away from me, there's a mechanical rumble, and the far wall of the chamber swings open. The hollow *twang* reminds me of the hatch of a submarine opening. Except instead of water on the other side, there are vampires.

I release the faery fire from my palm and give my eyes a moment to adjust to the light beyond the door. The silhouette of the person in the doorway comes into focus, and my heart stops.

OMG.

CHAPTER TWENTY

"Laurel Mason?" I hug the pretty, pony-tailed girl in jeans as she opens the way for us and allows us entry.

"Ohmygod, Fiona? What are you doing here?"

"What are *you* doing here? I haven't seen you since... Oh, you're not dead, and you're blonde now."

Sloan laughs. "Oh, my luv. Yer the only one who would ever utter such a thing."

"What? What did I say?"

"Yer not dead, oh, and yer blonde."

Laurel makes a face. "Technically, she's right."

Garnet clears his throat, and Laurel stiffens and straightens. "My apologies, Governor Grant. If you're looking for Xavier, he's not—"

"I *am* looking for him, but I'm well aware he's gone to ground. I'm here anyway because I need to speak to the members of his bloodline."

She steps back and lets us pass. Not that she could've done much to stop Garnet if he was determined.

If my vamp-detector is working—she's not one.

Which means she's one of the feeder humans.

I need to adjust the way I think about them. Karuna was perfectly lovely and had good reasons to be loyal to Xavier. And Laurel...

"How did you end up a vampire companion?"

"The two of you know one another?" Garnet asks.

She closes the door and seals us in. "Yes. Fiona and I went to high school together."

"Yeah, Laurel was on the field hockey team with me but was killed in a tragic house fire. Or, at least, that was the story."

She shrugs. "There was a terrible fire. My dad got mixed up with some dodgy dealings with a loan shark. He took me as payment and burned our lives to the ground. Benjamin, my companion, offered me another option and I took it. I had no home and no family left, and honestly, it was the best decision I ever made."

We fall into step, and I wonder about her life down here as we walk. In my mind's eye, I envisioned the sheep trapped in a dark basement with coffins and men in velvet smoking jackets drinking blood out of expensive crystal goblets.

The reality is mind-warpingly normal.

The house's living areas are brightly lit, painted in cheerful shades of golds and creams, and filled with the rich scents of Italian cooking.

"Oh my goodness, is that lasagna?" My stomach growls at the scent of tomato sauce, garlic, and onions.

"It is. We were having lunch. Would you care to join us?"

"No—" Garnet says.

"Hells yeah," I say, interrupting him. "That would be awesome if you have enough to spare a piece."

"Of course. With a family as large as ours, we make sure there is always enough to feed unexpected additions to the table."

Laurel takes us into what was likely the commissary of the military facility when it was in use.

When we step into the room, the men rise from their seats and dip their chins in greeting.

"Everyone, this is Fiona and—"

"Sloan," I say, filling in the blank.

"And, of course, you all know Governor Grant," she finishes. By the looks Garnet gets, they might know him, but they don't like him.

"Govna." The man with the thick British accent is sitting to the left of the empty head of the table seat. "What can we do ya for? I'm sure Laurel told ya the boss ain't here."

Garnet nods. "She did. I'm sure you know why Xavier has gone to ground. There was an attack on me yesterday. Four members of your seethe thought bombing my office and shooting the lady druid and I full of bullets would be a good way to show their strength."

"Oh, no." Laurel grabs my arm. "Are you all right?"

I nod. "Now, but I can't say the same for the men who attacked us. They're all dead."

The shock on their faces is genuine. They might've had an inkling that their fellow vampires did something stupid, but they didn't know the outcome.

"Yes, unfortunately, they went the way of the hobgoblins after they attacked me. As interesting as all that is, that's not why we're here."

Laurel points at a couple of empty chairs at the table and cuts a piece of lasagna for me. I accept it with my thanks and sit. She takes a seat next to me. "Fi's a friend, you guys. We used to hang out together in my first life."

The vampires around me seem more shocked than offended, so I take that as a good sign.

I eye the food and smile at Laurel. "This is real lasagna, right? No secret vampire ingredients or anything?"

Laurel blinks. "Oh, no. Jesse makes it from his Nona's recipe."

Awesome.

"Did you want some, gentlemen?" she asks.

Sloan raises his hand and offers Laurel a polite smile. "Och, no thanks, Fi and I ate almost a whole pizza not an hour ago."

I nod, enjoying the lasagna more than a little. "In my defense, healing from bombs and gunfights gives a girl an appetite."

"Is there a point to this visit?" the British guy asks, getting impatient. "Are ya stayin' the night or can we look forward to the end of this social event?"

I swallow what's in my mouth and focus. "Sorry, I didn't get your name."

"That's because I didn't give it."

"Well, all righty then, I'll call you Oliver."

"My name is *not* Oliver."

I laugh. "Too late now, Oli. You had your chance."

I unfurl the cloth napkin Laurel set me up with and dab my mouth. "Oli has a good point. We should get to it. How much do you know about the student murders and how Galina Romanov can trigger any of the vampires in Xavier's siring line to lose control in a full state of *cântând sânge* madness?"

Cue the silent stares.

The vampires look annoyed. The ones I peg as human companions look a little afraid.

"All right, next question. Do you know we have the antidote so none of you needs to worry about succumbing to the thrall of her synthetic call?"

"We know ya *say* there's an antidote," Oliver-not-Oliver says.

I roll my eyes. "We're trying to save you and your bloodline from mass murder and destruction. There's nothing in the serum other than a block to the effects of Galina's call."

"Says the Guild official."

I laugh. "Don't be a dick, Oli."

He stands so fast, his chair shoots back behind him and hits the wall. It's a very impressive trick. "What did you call me?"

"Oli, it's short for Oliver. Geez, we've already gone over this. You're wasting time."

"Your posturing won't get you far, druid," another vampire says. "Do you think putting on a show will impress us?"

"Nope. This is me, boys and girls. No airs."

Laurel nods. "This is Fi. Speaker of truths, entertainer of students, and queen of after-school detention."

I bow my head. "A title I wore with pride."

"You might joke about the situation, Lady Druid, but our concerns are valid." I meet the cool gaze of a female vampire with vibrant, candy apple red hair. "Our species have been targeted in the past."

I go back to my lasagna and nod. "I'm sure you have, but that's not what's happening here. I'm a 'live and let live' kinda girl. I'm here solely because if Galina Romanov triggers you, there will be more dead human students. I don't want dead humans, and I don't want more of you sitting in Guild detention cells while we decide if we need to end you."

"Nothing like that will happen again," one of the older males at the far end of the table says. "We're staying secured down here."

"Which is better than nothing but how long will you be able to do that? Xavier has a business to run. You can't lock yourself away down here indefinitely while Galina takes over your territory and destroys everything Xavier and the rest of you have built."

That gets a round of male grunts and a few scowls.

"Seriously, if it makes you feel better, we'll give you the names of the two scientists who put together the serum. If something goes wrong, you can kill them."

Garnet's lion lets out a long growl. "What the fuck are you doing?"

"It's called negotiating. You know…give and take. We need

them to trust us quickly, and they have to get over themselves and realize we're trying to help."

Garnet rolls his eyes. "I'd rather not do that by offering up innocent men to be killed."

"The vampires won't kill them if they're innocent. See how that works? Win-win."

"You're such a pain in the ass."

Laurel laughs and scoops another forkful of lasagna into her mouth. "Same old Fiona."

I shrug. "Why change what isn't broken, amirite?"

It takes less than a half-hour to immunize the members of Xavier's bloodline who agree to trust me. Of the twenty-six of them, eighteen take the injection, and eight of them opt to wait.

Their thinking is that they can get back to business with the ones who agreed and if anything goes awry, there are plenty left to hunt us down and kill us.

I take that as an acceptable compromise.

"Now. I'm leaving twelve more doses," I say, patting the black medical kit we brought with us. "Once you see we're telling the truth, or before any of those of you not immunized go out, or if any of Xavier's direct line go bloodthirsty, administer them yourselves."

"What about Xavier?" the female with the bright red hair asks.

Sloan waves his injector in the air and zips it in the other case. "We still have enough for him and any others who weren't here."

"What about Jasper, Orion, and Gustov?" a thirty-something guy asks. He's one of the humans, and there's no mistaking his worry and heartache in the question. "There's no way any of them would've killed if Galina hadn't artificially enthralled them. They don't deserve to be destroyed."

Garnet nods. "I agree, but I can't make any promises. Their

fate will have to be a Guild vote. We must weigh in the human lives lost and risk of exposure."

"When will you vote?"

"Once Galina is caught and held accountable, and we know it's over."

Laurel sends me a pleading glance, and I understand what she's asking without her saying a word. "I'll speak on their behalf and argue for their release, I promise. I'll try to think of something other than them being dispatched to make up for the lives lost."

Laurel leans in and hugs me. "It was so good to see you. Now that you're part of the empowered community, maybe we can have lunch sometime."

"Absolutely." And that reminds me...

We say our goodbyes, and when Laurel walks us out, I lower my voice and hand her my card. "I know Xavier is gone all super-stealth and is likely planning on killing Galina before she kills him, but he seriously needs to be immunized. It looks bad for members of his seethe to kill, but if he's out there ripping up innocents, that's worse."

She shrugs. "I don't know what I can do to help."

"I'm betting you know how to get in touch with Karuna, right? Tell her everything that we talked about here, and maybe she can talk sense to Xavier. If not, tell her to call me if the *cântând sânge* triggers him and I'll try to stop him before things go horribly wrong."

Laurel's expression pinches. "Fi, you don't want to get between a vampire in blood lust and his prey."

"No, I don't, but I will if I have to."

The three of us exit the underground facility and my phone chimes with incoming notifications—a bunch of them. I pull out my phone, and there are six missed calls too. "Shit. Something's wrong."

I open the family chat and frown. My brothers have been blowing up my phone while I was out of range.

Dillan: Fi, where are you? Kinu's in trouble.
Emmet: 911 - We need Irish.
Calum: Is Nikon with you? He's not answering.
Dillan: Fuck, Fi. Aiden's losing his mind. Get home.
Nikon: I'm here! Taking them to Gran's.

"Shit. We need to go. Something's wrong with Kinu and the babies."

I send my thumbs flying over the keys and text back.

Sorry. Coming right now.

CHAPTER TWENTY-ONE

Sloan *poofs* us home, and I make a mad dash around the house. "You check next door. See if anyone got left behind. I'll check here, grab Dart, and meet you in the backyard in two minutes."

Sloan *poofs* out, and I race through the main floor and out the back door.

It's obvious people left in a scramble, but I try not to panic too much. Gran's with Kinu, and she'll call Wallace to help...

... but without Sloan there, Wallace is more than three hours away unless Gran can spare Nikon to get him.

Granda will call Tad...

... but who knows if Tad is picking up. He tends not to answer when he's got other things on his mind.

Dart trots out of the forest as I cross the lawn. As I expected, he's worried because I'm worried. "Hey, buddy. I'm good. We're going to take a quick trip to Gran's, okay? Would you like to visit Gran's?"

He snorts and pulls his head back, and I feel more than hear his objection.

"No. I'm not taking you back. You live here now. It's just a visit, I promise. We're partners. We're bonded. Nothing has changed."

He lowers his chin and seems content with that.

I reach around his jaw and snuggle him. "I love you, buddy. As soon as things settle down, we'll explore the city and truly make Toronto your home. You'll see. You'll love it."

Someone races into the driveway next door, and I cross the lawn to see who's coming through the gate. Kevin jogs in and turns to click his fob and lock up. "Sorry, I'm late. I was painting and had my headphones on. Then traffic was stupid."

"No worries. We just got the messages ourselves. Sloan's checking next door to make sure we're all accounted for. Then we're going."

Sloan *poofs* onto the back deck and jogs across the grass to join us. "No one there. No notes."

"Okay, then I think we're good to go."

Kevin raises a finger and runs toward the house. "Calum forgot Daisy's medication. He texted me not to forget it."

"Lock the back door on your way out."

"Yep. On it."

Once Kevin returns with their skunk companion's anti-seizure medication, I grab hold of Dart's wing on one side, Sloan grabs the other, and we both join hands with Kevin.

Sloan *poofs* us onto the back lawn of Gran's and Granda's place, and I release Bruin. "You guys have fun, and I'll see what's happening with Kinu and the babies." Da is sitting on the stone bench at the firepit, blowing bubbles with Meg and Jackson.

"Bubbles, fun. Play nice for Granda—he's old."

Da lifts his hand behind his head and flashes me a middle-finger salute. "Go inside and be of some use. And don't forget I'm out here."

"Yeah, of course."

We leave them to play and rush inside. I try to remind myself to take a beat to breathe.

Everything works out as it's supposed to. It has to. I toe off my sneakers and hustle toward the family room.

"Where the fuck have you two been?" Dillan snaps.

I don't take it to heart. Dillan gets cranky and mouthy when he's scared.

"Sorry. We were in Xavier's underground lair. No reception."

"Fucking vampires."

"Station M?" Emmet asks, brightening. "So, it's more than a conspiracy theory, then. It's real?"

"It's real. How's Kinu? What's happening?"

"Fuck if we know," Dillan snaps again. "No one's giving us updates. It's not like we matter or anything."

"Is Da here?" Sloan asks.

"He was." Calum shifts over on the couch to make room for Kevin to sit on the armrest. "When we got here, Tad had already brought him here to examine her."

"And he left?" Sloan asks.

"There was a massive accident near someplace called Kinvara. He and his team got called in to help."

"What kind of accident?"

"Human campers set a forest fire, and a community of forest elves tried to save their homes. It didn't end well." Tad is leaning against the trunk of the tree growing through the center of the house. "I took him back, grabbed his team, and dropped them off. It was bad. I don't know that he'll finish there anytime soon."

I close the distance and hug him. "Thanks for trying."

"Of course."

"All right. We'll head in and see if we can help Lara," Sloan says.

I reach for his extended hand and hurry toward the back of

the house. The muffled grunting and moaning seeping through the door makes my throat dry.

I swallow, but it doesn't help.

Please let everything be all right.

I stop with my hand on the doorknob of the spare room, afraid to go inside. "It's ironic," I whisper, "I don't think twice about facing off with homicidal fae and demonic entities, but I'm scared to face this. Part of me thinks if I don't go in, for this moment, right now, I can pretend everything is under control. Once we head inside, maybe it won't be."

Sloan squeezes my shoulders. "Whatever happens, yer family is strong. There's enough love to weather even the worst storm."

I swallow. "Haven't we had enough stormy weather this year? Don't we deserve some sunny skies and tropical waters?"

"Aye, ye do. Focus on that. Intention is everything."

I swallow and open the door. "Knock-knock."

Kinu is lying on the bed looking awfully pale, with Aiden sitting on the edge feeding her ice chips on one side and Gran laying hands on her belly on the other. As we step into the room fully, Kinu finishes groaning, and she brightens. "Hey guys, welcome to the party."

Aiden turns to nod hello, and my heart sinks. That is not the face of good news.

Sloan rounds the bed to the side Aiden's on and smiles. "So, what's happening? The boys said my father examined ye. What did he say?"

Gran meets his gaze, her smile locked in place. If it weren't for the lack of sparkle in her eyes, I might even believe her cheer. "It seems the wee buggers aren't content in there. We're tryin' to convince them to stay put a little longer, but it doesn't seem likely."

"Should Nikon flash her back home to the hospital?" I move in beside Gran and take Kinu's hand.

"We considered that," Aiden says, "but Wallace already gave

her the terbutaline that the hospital would to slow the arrival and the steroids to help the babies' lung development. Other than taking up a bed while strangers try to help her, we're not missing anything."

"Besides," Kinu says, groaning as she twists on the bed. "Here we get the added benefit of Gran and Sloan and Wallace."

"And that's quite a benefit, indeed." I rub her arm feeling helpless as her body tremors in a wave of shivering. "Are you cold, sweetie?"

"It's the medication," Gran says. "She's fine. Everything is fine."

No one who knows Gran would believe that, and it's plain to see by looking at her how tired she is.

"It's only been an hour or two since Wallace administered the drug. There's still time for it to take hold and stop this train from leaving the station, amirite?"

Aiden shakes his head. "No. It started first thing this morning, and Wallace administered it then."

Kinu shrugs. "We thought the drug would work and we wouldn't have to worry everyone."

Apparently not.

Sloan reaches forward and pauses over Kinu's belly. "Do ye mind me touchin' ye, Kinu?"

She groans and shakes her head, breathing in short bursts. "No. Whatever you need to do to fix this."

Sloan presses his hands over Kinu's nightie and closes his eyes. I watch him closely, trying to read his mind. Sadly, that isn't one of my powers. It seems like he's examining her forever, but when he opens his eyes, he winks and eases back.

"Well?" Aiden asks.

He looks at me, and I assume it's to gauge how much to get into. "We're lay it all out there people, hotness. Whatever it is, we'd rather know than not know."

Aiden meets his gaze. "Yeah. Just tell us what we're facing. Whatever it is, we'll rally."

He swallows. "Then I suppose we best have a family discussion because this is happenin'. And with the threat of Kinu's abruption, there will be risks to mitigate in order to end up with a happy ending fer all three."

Crap on a cracker.

"A happy ending for all three is the only option. Like you said, hotness. Intention is everything."

If there's one thing I admire most about my family, it's how we come through in a clutch. Tad and Nikon go outside to play with Meg and Jackson to relieve Da for the Cumhaill parley. Once Sloan's gone over the dangers and the real possibility of something going horribly wrong, the room seems to be frozen.

"All right," Da says. "There's nothin' to be done about it. This is where we are. Heads down and push through, yeah?"

"Yeah," we all agree.

Aiden agrees, but he looks shaky.

"This is how I see it playin' out," Sloan says. "Even with Da in Kinvara, Kinu has a better chance of survival at the clinic. Not to be too graphic, but when she starts bleedin' and the babies come, I'll need equipment and natural remedies on hand to act fast."

Da nods. "So we move to the clinic. What then?"

"Emmet, I'll need ye in the middle of it all to boost Lara and me. This has the makings of a long day. Yer not squeamish, are ye?"

Emmet shakes his head. "No. I'm there. Whatever you need."

He nods. "Where's Ciara? I'll need her too. With her gifts, she can monitor the babies and hopefully keep them calm and from goin' into distress. She can also calm Kinu if need be."

"She's waiting in the wings," Emmet says. "She didn't want to intrude."

Sloan nods. "Have Tad take ye to her place to pick her up and meet us at the clinic."

"On it." Emmet peels off and jogs to the front hall to get his shoes.

"Kevin and Nikon need to watch the kids because I'll need all the druid power I can get. I'm sorry I'm not the healer my father is, but—"

Da lays a hand on Sloan's back and leans into his line of sight. "There are no buts. Yer a gifted healer in yer own right. I have no doubt ye'll bring a win home for us, son. We believe in ye."

"Aye, we do," Granda says.

Sloan swallows. "All right. I think that's it for now. The rest will depend on how things go over the next couple of hours. Who knows, maybe by then Da will be back to help."

I hate to see Sloan so shaken. He's usually so cock-sure and confident. Worried and scrambling doesn't suit him. I understand why.

It's exactly why doctors aren't supposed to operate on family members. There's too much emotion involved when things go wrong.

"It's going to be fine." I slide my fingers into his. "We're going to rock this."

"In true Cumhaill style," Calum says, hugging Kev and handing him Daisy.

I breathe deep, and it's a struggle to fill my lungs. "We've got this. We have to."

When Sloan said this would be a long day, he wasn't wrong. It only takes twenty minutes for him and Tad to get us all *poofed* up to Stonecrest Castle and get her settled, but then the waiting begins.

I'm thankful Bruin and Dart opted to stay at Gran's with Kev,

Nikon, and the kids because as the hours roll by, we're all getting tired.

Da and Granda convince Gran to nap in a recovery room to refuel for the impending finale. She fights them at first but sees the logic.

We take the same argument to Aiden, but there's no chance he's stepping more than two feet away from Kinu while this is in motion. We compromise by getting him a pillow and him closing his eyes while bent over the delivery table holding Kinu's hand.

In the moments of quiet, we hug and stretch and curl up in chairs Dillan stole from the waiting room.

We've thoroughly invaded Wallace's space.

In one of the lulls, I make my way over to Tad. "You don't have to stick around if you've got other things happening."

He chuffs. "Other things like what? No. I'm good. At least here, I feel like I'm part of something."

"You are part of something." I squeeze his arm. "How are you?"

He quirks the side of his mouth up and lifts one shoulder. "I'm surviving. Not sure what to do with myself, honestly."

"Then it's the perfect time for a Toronto vacay. Dionysus just moved into town so the two of you can experience the city together. We have Beltane tomorrow night. And if the fates are kind to us, we'll have two new Cumhaills to welcome into our lives."

"Oh, speaking of Beltane." Emmet's sitting on a chair next to Ciara, holding her hand. "You should definitely come and celebrate with us. Ciara and I are tying the handfasting knot, and we'd be happy to have you witness our nuptials."

Tad laughs. "Yeah, all right."

When they simply look at him, waiting for him to clue in, he turns to me. "They're shitting me, right?"

I shake my head. "Nope. For reals. They're getting hitched, and Ciara's coming to try life as a Canadian."

Ciara smiles and lifts her fingers to count off a list. "So, if Emmet schooled me properly, I need to learn about hockey, eat maple syrup and poutine, say sorry endlessly and eh at the end of sentences, and wear a knit cap."

I chuckle. "That pretty much sums it up, but it's not just a knit cap. It's a toque. And you forgot about driving on the opposite side of the road. You don't want to forget that one."

She grins. "I think I'd be reminded quickly enough."

"True story."

Tad shakes his head. "So, ye are really doin' it?"

Ciara nods, and her face lights up as I've never seen before. "Aye, we are. If ye want to see history made, ye'll join us tomorrow night."

"Shannon and Da are getting hitched too," Em says.

"Yeah?" I search the room but don't see my dad around. "Wow, I'm out of the loop."

"I think between bombs and vampires and you sleeping around the clock, you missed the memo," Emmet says. "But yeah, Shannon got her dress today."

Tad looks thoroughly amazed. "Ye talked me into it. I wouldn't want to miss it."

Emmet grins and extends his knuckles for a bump. "Excellent. It's going to be a blast." He looks around and sobers. "Goddess willing."

It's close to midnight by the time the ground crumbles under our feet, and we're scrambling to help Kinu and the twins through this.

"Ciara, how are the wee ones?" Gran asks.

"Tired but good."

I'm worried about Sloan. He's taking full responsibility for the outcome of this delivery upon himself. As much as I want it to work out for Aiden and Kinu, I want it to work out as much for Sloan's sake.

It will slay him if someone dies here.

"How are you doing, hotness?"

"The same as the babes," he says, focusing on his hands. "Tired but good."

I bet he's tired. He's been drawing on healing energy for over an hour.

"Em? How are you holding up?" I ask.

He has one hand on Gran and one on Sloan and is too focused to answer. He simply nods.

The rest of us have our druid spell stones in our hands and are funneling as much healing strength into her girl parts as we can.

If the babies arrive while the placenta is intact, that will reduce the risk of oxygen loss and her bleeding too heavily.

Not that Sloan said anything, but I Googled it, so I knew what we're aiming for.

Gran is humming an enchanting tune and reaching into the drape zone. She's at the hoohaw end of the table with Aiden and Sloan, and as much as I admire the whole process, I'm happy to be up-drape. "The first one is comin' into the world now, luv. Yer almost there."

I press a hand on the amethyst amulet on her belly and give the healing spell surrounding her everything I've got. "You're doing amazing, Kinu. Remember the advantage to twins."

She lets out a guttural cry and winces. "Two for the size of one."

"That's it. Half the size, twice as easy, right?"

"It doesn't feel that way, Fi." Another contraction hits, and she cries out again.

I look across the bed at Dillan and Calum, and I'm pretty sure they'll both be having nightmares about birthing babies for years.

"You've got this, babe." Aiden's holding it together now that we're in the final stretches. I think if he didn't need to be strong for Kinu, he'd be a frazzled mess. "You're amazing. I love you so damned much."

"Stupid druid super-sperm…"

He barks a laugh with the rest of us. When Kinu found out it was twins, Aiden told her it was the power of the ambient magic during their visit to Ireland that gave his sperm the extra oomph for a twofer.

Magic laces Gran's humming, and I feel its effect coming through Kinu. Sloan says she has the strongest nature magic he's ever come across in the druid community. I believe it.

If I hadn't met Mother Nature last fall, I'd wonder if maybe she was the mighty mistress herself.

"Get ready, Aiden," Sloan says, watching Gran.

Aiden is gloved and gowned and ready to receive. When Gran sits back, she cleans the baby's nose and mouth and hands…her… to Aiden.

"Hello, Ireland," he says, staring at her. "This is your family."

He holds her up, and I have to blink fast to keep from tearing up. "Hello, monkey."

"Let me see her." Kinu cranes her neck to see.

Aiden lowers her so Kinu can see their new daughter. "One down. One to go."

"You've got this, sista," Dillan says. "You're kicking the snot out of this delivery."

"I hate to put a damper on the celebration," Ciara says, frowning, "but baby two is strugglin'. She needs out sooner rather than later."

Aiden hands Da baby Ireland to take to the warming bed to clean up and assess as planned. Granda has the APGAR chart out, and they're ready to roll.

"Kinu seems too chill to push out another one," Calum says. "How do you have a baby if the labor stops?"

"It didn't stop, luv," Gran says. "It just needs a little nudge to move things along. I'm sorry, Kinu. There's no rest for ye yet, I'm afraid."

Kinu sighs and we go again.

Seventeen minutes later, Gran's holding up another girl. "Another beauty. Take yer baby, Da."

Aiden accepts her and hugs her to his chest. "Hello, Carragh, welcome to Clan Cumhaill."

"Carragh," I say. "I thought you wanted Kerry?"

Aiden shrugs. "Kinu likes Carragh better."

"It's a beautiful name," Gran says. "Now, with the worst of things over, let's give the four of them a moment to bond while Sloan and I finish up, shall we? Out you go."

"I'd say so," Wallace says, stepping into the clinic looking haggard. "I got yer text and had Tad come get me at the first opportunity. I don't think we need the entire Cumhaill clan in here, do we?"

"Not anymore," I say, sending my appreciation out to the world. "Thankfully, the trouble has passed."

Wallace grabs a gown and strides over to the wash station. "Well, then, I guess ye don't need me then." He winks at Kinu.

"Och, no," Sloan says, "I happily turn over the reins, Da. I'm glad yer here."

I wait by the door as Sloan washes up, in no hurry to go out to the waiting room. "You were amazing." I reach up and cup his cheek, feeling the emotional dam about to break. "You handled everything, and it all worked out as it was supposed to. Yay you, Mackenzie."

Sloan bends forward and hugs me tight.

His entire body is shaking, and I'm not surprised when he lets out a heaving sob against my neck. "I've never been so scared in all my life, Fi. All I kept thinkin' was I couldn't let them die."

I rub his back. "You didn't. All three of them have you to thank for that."

It takes a few minutes, but once he's pulled himself back together, we head out to the waiting room. The moment we get through the door, my family gives him a standing ovation.

Sloan's pulled from one to the next to the next in chest-to-chest, back-slapping hugs.

Cue leaking eyes and sniffles all around.

"For you," Dillan says, presenting Sloan with an Oh! Henry bar. "For bravery and skill and dedication to our family that we can never repay. You have earned the Oh! Henry award of the highest order."

I wipe away my tears and laugh. "You bet your ass he did."

CHAPTER TWENTY-TWO

Sloan and I *poof* to the bookstore first thing in the morning and find Myra working at the back of the store, entering notes into her customer ledger. When we exit the aisle of books, she looks up and bows her laureled head. "Good morrow, fine friends. A blessed Beltane, to you both."

Sloan bows at the waist in a sweeping gesture and doesn't miss a beat. "Yer blessing is well-received and returned, milady. Blessed Beltane."

I blink at them both. "Did I take a header into a Renaissance Faire while I wasn't looking?"

Myra chuckles. "No, duck. Imari and I were reading about Beltane last night and decided to revive some of the old traditions. I hear from Garnet that we have two Beltane babies to celebrate."

"Yep. Fresh out of the oven just after midnight. Ireland and Carragh Cumhaill."

"I'm relieved. Garnet mentioned there was trouble."

I nod but don't want to get into it. Sloan and I are still a bit shaky about all of that. "There was, but all's well that ends well. Sloan's father kept them at the clinic for now, and Nikon will snap them home tonight for the celebration. I'm sure they won't stay for anything beyond the handfasting ceremony, but they will make a brief appearance."

"I look forward to welcoming them to the world. I'll make them a little something to commemorate their safe arrival."

"It looks like you've already been crafting," I say, pointing to the laurel atop her electric blue hair.

"As a child, my mother taught me the art of laurels and crowns. Now, with Imari eager to learn, I thought I better get back to it." She opens the top box of three and pulls out a tiara. "For you, Lady Druid."

She steps around the desk and slides the tiara onto my head. It's a pretty crown of sparkly crystals and blooming flowers and velvety-leafed vines. I shift around the old desk to look into the mirror behind.

The gems are raw-cut and unusual, and I feel an immediate connection to them. "I don't know these. What are they?"

"The turquoise one is amazonite, for breaking karmic patterns and replacing chaos with love and healing."

"That sounds nice."

"The rust one is aragonite and helps form a deeper connection to the Earth. It's also the one you need to ground and stabilize energies during times of stress."

"Lovely. And these are—these *aren't* emeralds are they?"

"Of course they are."

"They're huge."

Myra grins. "Emerald is your birthstone, duck, so you need it in your Beltane laurel. Emeralds are known as a symbol of truth, love, and hope as well as wisdom, intuition, and eternal life. While the ruby is the stone of passionate love, the emerald is the stone of faithful, deep, and mature love."

I wink at Sloan. "See, I'm mature."

"Yer ridiculous, but it's too late fer me. I'm a lost cause."

I grin and look at my Beltane crown. The vines and buds are

buzzing with energy and the green and copper crystals look amazing against the deep, russet red of my hair. "I love it, thank you."

Myra nods. "I figured with everything that happened yesterday that you might not be prepared for the Beltane celebration tonight."

"Prepared? I thought I was just showing up."

Myra arches a brow. "No, duck. Emmet has been pouring his heart and soul into the preparations of the rituals all week. You need to be truly present for him. Wearing the tiara for the day will help you get into the frame of mind."

"The whole day? Like when I'm running around town and searching for vampires and training with my dragon?"

She nods. "The whole day."

I frown at my reflection. I will feel odd out and about in the non-empowered world wearing a Beltane crown, but Myra asks little of me and does so much. I don't think I can say no. "All right. All day it is."

"Excellent." She taps her hand on what I thought were pie boxes. "There is one for Ciara and another for Shannon. I've written their names on the boxes. Please deliver them with my heartfelt congratulations for this evening."

"You're coming, aren't you?"

"I am, but these are to be worn all day by all of you. It's a tradition."

My only experiences with tiaras are wearing them at a buck and doe party or when I've been a birthday girl. Those were sharp and uncomfortable. This one feels quite lovely...too lovely, actually.

"Is this enchanted?"

Myra grins. "Maybe."

I arch a brow. "To what end? Enchanted to do what?"

Myra shakes her head. "Now, where would the fun be in that? If I simply tell you, it'll ruin the surprise."

I glance at Sloan, and he shrugs. "Don't look at me. I know nothing."

"All right. I trust you."

Myra nods. "As you should, duck. Now, take these, and off you go."

"Breakfast at Shannon's and Liam's place above the pub used to be a regular thing," I tell Sloan as we materialize in the back hall of the bar. "Somewhere along the line, that tradition fizzled out."

"Why do ye suppose that is?"

"I don't know. There was no event or reason. It was just one of those things that fades away gradually until you can't remember the last time you did it."

"Well, it's nice to revive the tradition."

I key the code into the door lock and let us into the staircase leading up to their loft apartment. "Yeah. It is."

When we get to the top of the stairs, I knock and walk and let ourselves in. "Hello, the house."

"In here!" Shannon calls from the kitchen.

I set the laurel boxes on the little stand by the door while we take off our shoes, then we head in and say our good mornings.

Da sets his coffee down and rounds the table to hug me. "Good morning, baby girl. How'd ye sleep?"

"Like a rock. After all the excitement and the power outlay, I think we were both drained."

He kisses my forehead and moves to Sloan. "I bet ye were." He pulls Sloan in tight, cups the back of his head, patting his back. "I was just tellin' Shannon how ye saved the day, son. We're so incredibly grateful to have ye in our lives."

The two ease apart and Sloan lifts a shoulder. "I appreciate that, I do, but honestly, I'm so feckin' relieved it turned out I can't even describe it."

"Niall submitted your name for sainthood," Liam says, joining us fresh from the shower. "We're waiting for the call back before we start planning the party."

Sloan chuckles and extends a hand to my bestie. "Och, I think there are more deserving candidates than me, but it's an honor to be nominated."

I laugh and hug Liam. "Hey, guy. I miss you."

He kisses the top of my head. "Miss you too. Tonight, eh? Big things happening. By tomorrow at this time, I guess we'll be family."

"We've always been family."

"Yeah, but now we'll be brother and sister."

I eye him up, and with all that we've shared and almost shared, that doesn't sit well. "Nah. Let's not look at it like that. That's icky."

"Right?"

We all get a chuckle out of that.

"Ye'll be what ye've always been," Da says. "Tonight is about Shannon and I acknowledgin' our commitment, not about changin' our family. Yer all grown, and we are and will be what we've always been."

"Wild and unruly," Liam says.

"Stubborn and mouthy," I add.

"Utterly ridiculous." Sloan smiles.

"Now you've got it, Irish," Dillan says, arriving with Calum and Kevin. "Jump in on those and add to the mayhem. I'm going with sexy and unyielding."

"Drunk and disorderly," Kevin says.

"Rough and ready," Calum adds.

Da chuffs. "Yer a bunch of eejits is what ye are."

Shannon laughs and heads back into the kitchen. "And you're wrong, Dillan. The last thing we need is more mayhem. It was always the boys in this patchwork family I worried about over the years. Fi was our peace-keeper. She was never the one to cause worry, but now she surpassed all of you and is trying for the record."

I shrug. "Maybe I bottled it up, and it burst free and is now biting you in the collective ass."

Da nods. "It is at that. Although, it eases my heart considerably to know Sloan's at yer side."

"Hear, hear!" Calum says.

"A keeper for sure," Kevin says.

"Meh, he's all right," Dillan adds, laughing and jumping out of the way as Da takes a swing at him.

"No. He's the perfect one for Fi." Liam winks at me and smiles. "Like you always say, everything works out how it's supposed to in the end."

Dillan snorts. "Can you say that about Emmet and Ciara tying the knot tonight?" He scans the expressions around the room and frowns. "I can't be the only one who thinks we're watching a slow-motion train wreck."

"Yer not." Da scowls. "But like all my kids, he's too feckin' stubborn to see it."

Since Emmet hasn't arrived yet with Ciara, I figure we better hash this out quickly.

"A year ago, I would've agreed with you, but now we deal with life and death every day. Emmet fell into the lake of fae prana—that could have killed him. He's been in a dozen battles without offensive powers—that could've killed him. He was thrown into a volcano by a tribe of cannibals—that could've killed him. With everything we went through last night, don't you think we should take a page out of Brenny's book and celebrate him seizing the day?"

"She has a point," Calum says. "Emmet has always led with his heart and embraced things without reserve. It works for him."

"He acknowledges his handfasting with Ciara is a leap of faith," I say. "He understands what's on the line and he's still sure. Why wait to celebrate life and love?"

Da lets out a long-suffering sigh. "You don't only live once... you only *die* once. If you're smart, you live every single minute of every single day."

With Brendan's life motto hanging in the air between us, the tide of negativity shifts.

"Come on, guys. Emmet needs us to support him. It's musketeer time."

Da nods. "All right, kids. Yer sister's right. All fer one..."

"And one for all."

"Good. To that end, Myra made the ladies ceremonial crowns for Beltane."

Dillan snorts. "I was wondering what was growing on your head. I thought it was a sloth thing and you have an algae and bug problem."

I stick out my tongue. "I don't have 'an algae and bug' problem. I have a 'my brother is an eejit' problem."

After breakfast, we discuss the plans for later tonight, and the apartment buzzes with family chatter. The building excitement for Beltane is taking hold of all of us. Shannon and Ciara both love their laurels, and both of them have the same sense of comfort and rightness wearing it that I do.

I have no idea what the enchantment is about. Seeing how Myra is an ash tree nymph, I'm fairly certain the magic behind the enchantment came from Dora.

Maybe we'll find out tonight.

Maybe it's something that will play out later.

My phone rings and I step into the hall to cut down the noise. That's not far enough, so I go out of the apartment and stand at the landing at the top of the stairs. "Hello?"

"Fiona?"

"Yes."

"This is Karuna. We met the other day at the medical building?"

"Of course. How are you? Is everything all right with Xavier?"

"Yes, everything is fine. Is it true what you told the family? You know it wasn't him who ordered the attack on Governor Grant?"

"It's what makes the most sense to us, yes. Unless we learn otherwise, that's our theory."

"You won't learn otherwise because he didn't do it."

"Then yes, he's in the clear as far as we're concerned."

Sloan opens the door and finds me on the phone. He flashes me a thumbs-up, and when I nod, he closes the door and leaves me to it.

"Where are you guys, Karuna? We really need to inject Xavier with the serum before something happens. Galina wants to take him down, and now that his siring line is free to resume their tasks in his business, we believe she'll come after him directly."

"I'm here, Lady Druid," Xavier says in the background. "I hope you understand my caution and accept my apology that those who I considered family caused you and Garnet harm. When I strike at a foe, I don't hide behind bombs and sneak attacks."

"No. I don't imagine you do. So, how about we get you the serum, then we can focus on taking down Galina instead of the danger your siring line poses to the innocents of the city."

"That is reasonable. I will accept your serum, but I am declaring a Vow of Vengeance against Galina Romanov. She came at me to ruin my family and me. I have the right to use excessive force to end this."

"Fine by me. You have my vote for the warrant. Just make sure the violence doesn't spill over onto any more innocents. We've already lost the three students and Garnet's PA."

"Martin?"

"Yeah, they killed him in the office attack."

"All the more reason to end this."

"Agreed. Send me the address where you are, and we'll come with the serum."

"Fine. In exchange, I want to know everything you do about Galina's operation and how she has managed to skirt detection. My men have searched every city block, and we're at a loss."

"I can help you there. First the serum, then the exchange of info that will give you what you need to track her down."

"You have my word, Lady Druid."

"And you have mine."

CHAPTER TWENTY-THREE

I call Garnet as soon as I hang up with Xavier and agree to meet him at the back of Shenanigans. "Goodbye, fam jam. I'll see you later. I have vampires to immunize and other vampires to help track down and expire."

"Since when did ye start makin' plans with vampires and smilin' about it?" Da snaps, narrowing his gaze on me. "What's changed?"

I shrug. "I don't know. It's been a crazy week. Maybe I'm warming up to Xavier."

I realize my mistake the moment his expression changes. "Warmin' up to him? Have ye lost yer head? Yer talkin' about the leader of the blood-suckin' undead. They have no regard fer the human race. They're the worst kind of criminals because they're lethal and don't give a flyin' fuck about the humans who get caught in the cross-fire."

I hold up a finger to slow his roll. "I appreciate your take on this, Da. I felt the same way too, until I got some education about Xavier and how he runs things."

"Oh? Are ye talkin' about how he runs his drug empire or his illegal gun sales? Enlighten me."

I draw a deep breath and try to remember he's my father, and he loves me, and this is his day because after more than fifteen years he's choosing his happiness over ours. "I hear your concern, and I acknowledge it. I'll be careful."

"Like ye were careful the night ye got kidnapped by the vampires and Liam took a bullet fer ye? Vampires are brutal murderers, Fi. Don't sugar coat it or ye'll get yerself killed."

"I'm not sugar coating anything."

"Yet yer warmin' up to the King of Vampires. Have ye developed some kind of schoolgirl infatuation? Is this another *Twilight* phase?"

Wow, okay. When Da gets riled, he's a pit bull with his jaws locked on a chew toy, shaking the shit out of it.

It sucks to be the chew toy in that scenario.

"I've grown a lot stronger and a great deal wiser since then, Da, and you know it."

He lowers his chin and pegs me with his anger. "If wisdom comes with age, ye'll never know more than me, baby girl. Accept that now."

I hold up my finger. "I am *not* fighting with you on your wedding day. Take Shannon and have a sexy soak in the hot spring in the grove or have Liam bake you CBD brownies or do whatever you need to do to chill out but you're not baiting me into a fight. Not today."

I take in the worried looks and wave their concern away. "Don't look at me like that. I'm not becoming besties with a vampire crime lord."

"You sure about that, Fi?" Emmet says. "Cause it kinda sounds like you are."

"No. I'm simply saying that despite the image we paint in our nightmares, not all villains are mustache-twisting psychopaths. Xavier is a criminal, yes, but he's more than that. It's my job as a Guild Governor to try to de-escalate violence in the empowered world, and it's my job as part of Team Trouble to de-escalate

AUBURN TEMPEST & MICHAEL ANDERLE

violence that endangers the innocents of our city. That's all I'm doing."

I sigh and head for the door. "Thank you for breakfast, Shannon. I'll see you all later... if I survive my school girl vampire infatuation. Go, Team Edward!"

I let out a throaty sigh as I exit the building and Garnet arches a brow. "Problems, Lady Druid?"

"Don't be a dick and underestimate Imari when she grows up. Seriously. At some point, let her stop being your little girl and trust her to be the woman she's destined to be."

Garnet smirks. "Niall and I don't agree on much, but I'm afraid I'll face the same pitfalls. My little girl will always be my little girl, and I will always be overbearing and protective of her."

I roll my eyes. "Awesome. Good talk."

Sloan joins us on the sidewalk outside and looks me over. "Are ye good?"

"Yeah. This is about more than me working with vampires. This is about Aiden almost losing Kinu and Emmet getting married *and* me working with vampires. I happened to be the lucky recipient of his meltdown."

"Shall I come with?"

I shake my head and kiss his cheek. "No. You do you. Attend your auction and spend a shit-ton of money on old, rusty trinkets. I'll meet you at home later to get ready for Beltane."

He meets gazes with Garnet, and some masculine passing of the torch occurs. I can almost hear them. Watch her. She needs a warning sign around her neck. I've got her. Don't worry. I'll return her in the same condition I'm borrowing her in.

Seriously?

Goddess save me from well-meaning men.

The address Karuna texted to me is an old, Georgian-styled mansion down by the lake. A long, rectangular stone building, it has lots of symmetrically placed windows, shutters, dormers, and columns.

It does not look like a vampire safe house.

As we step up the walk, I take a moment to close my eyes and focus on my shield.

All is quiet.

"You brought the serum kit?"

Garnet pats the left breast pocket of his suit jacket. "Of course. My motto is always be prepared. Didn't you know that?"

I snort. "That's the Boy Scouts of America, and you are no Boy Scout."

He flashes me a grin and bares his teeth. "No. I suppose that one is hard to swallow."

I'm still chuckling about that when he knocks, and the door opens. It's Karuna.

"Thank you for coming. We're in here."

We follow her through the main entrance and straight at a floor-to-ceiling portrait opposite the door. She steps to the side and swings the huge frame, exposing a metal door and a security pad.

"This is a safe house, I presume?"

She finishes keying in the security code, and the steel door unlatches. "That's one of its uses, yes. It's also my city home. If I want to have human girlfriends over or need time away from the family or want to swim in the pool or toil in the garden, this is where I come."

"Well, it's lovely," I say. "My boyfriend would love it. There is tons of character and architecture—"

My shield flares and I freeze in my tracks.

"Something's not right, Bear." I don't wait to release him. Heeding Da's warning I err on the side of caution and put him in play right away. He launches out of me and is off with gale force.

My shield rages into a fiery inferno on my back.

Collecting Karuna, I move her out of the open doorway to the downstairs passage, set her into the corner on our right, and call Birga.

Wind rushes past me, and I try to focus on the blur that caused it.

Vampires.

Garnet lets out a feral growl. "Karuna, take this."

He hands her a sizeable stake. "Center mass will immobilize them. All the strength you've got."

Karuna looks appalled as she grips the fine rope wrapped around the hilts of the stakes. "I won't stake—"

There's no sense arguing because he's already shifted to his lion form and is racing down the stairs.

There's a wild crash in the apartment below, and two more blurs of color burst through the front door.

Galina Romanov stops in a jarring jolt and strides forward as the other carries on.

The stunning European beauty is no more.

She's gone full vamp, from her leather slicker and thigh-high boots to her clawed fingers to her freaky red, glowing eyes. She opens her mouth, and her sharp and pointy incisors drop to cover her deep blue lips. "Step away from his whore, and I'll let you live, little girl."

"Why is that my moniker this morning?"

It could be the posies in yer hair, Red.

Oh, yeah, I guess it could be that.

In my limited experience fighting vampires, only one other time did their eyes go all hellfire freaky. That was crazy Mr. Denton in Ottawa, who stole the leviathan baby. It's terrifying, and at the same time, it makes it easier to reconcile ending her when I get the chance.

"If this is a safe house, you've got a vampire-proof panic room, right?"

"One on every floor," Karuna whispers behind me.

"Nice try," Galina says, pushing closer. "She won't make it ten feet."

"Karuna, when I say go, you run there and lock yourself down. Killer Clawbearer, you are her escort. Slaughter anyone who tries to stop you."

Bruin takes form between us and stands on his back feet. At over eight feet, even with the high ceilings, he's intimidating. And that's before he shows his incisors and bellows a ferocious snarl. "With pleasure."

Galina won't have understood him but still has the good sense to take pause.

"Karuna, go. My bear will protect you."

I give her credit. Karuna handles pressure well. She checks around the corner and then makes a straight run deeper into the house. Bruin rushes off in a swirl of air, and I shift to block the corridor.

No blurs of color or rushes of wind pass me.

Galina's lip curls up on one side. "You've only delayed her death. Make no mistake. She will die."

I hear the fury in her voice and see the betrayal in those freak show eyes...but there's something else there too —jealousy.

"You fell for Xavier, and he rebuffed you. He wouldn't feed from you. He honored his commitment to Karuna, and for that, you want her dead."

She scoffs. "Why would I want to be his food? No. I offered to be his partner—his equal."

It's all starting to make sense now.

Maxwell was right. This *is* personal.

"He wouldn't turn you. That's why you went after his siring line. He chose them but not you. That's why it wasn't enough simply to go after his business. It was personal. He rejected you on every front."

"Xavier is a fool. With my connections and business acumen, we could've built an empire."

The fight downstairs sounds like they've not only trashed the place, they are now in dumpster territory.

"When the hobgoblins almost killed you on New Year's Eve, you thought he came after you."

"Whether it was him or hobgoblins is irrelevant. If he had transitioned me, I never would've suffered the way I did. I was weak and vulnerable as a human. That was his doing."

The subtle shift in her footing promises the coming of an attack. I spin Birga in my palm.

Readying. Watching.

Two more vampires jolt to a stop in the foyer with us. I don't see a way out of this.

"That's it, little girl. It's beginning to sink in. You can't stop me. You're out of your depths here."

"Maybe. Or maybe your upstart seethe of criminals goes the way of the hobgoblins when Bruin and I put an end to you all."

My back hits the wall, my feet dangling toward the floor. My brain sloshes in my cranium as I struggle to figure out what just happened.

She was so fast.

I push against the hold on my shoulders, and Galina steps back, smiling and brushing her smeared blue lips.

"Let's see how much honor and control Xavier has now, shall we? I didn't get to watch with the others. This I'm going to enjoy."

I brush a touch over my mouth and stare at the waxy blue stain on my fingers. "You lipsticked me."

There's a momentary panic. Then my brain catches up with current events. "It's fine. It takes hours to initiate the call, and we've already immunized Xavier's siring line."

"His siring line maybe, but we were watching the house. You haven't immunized him."

"There's still time. And even if there wasn't, I'd lock myself down long before it takes effect."

An inhuman roar erupts from the basement, and Galina takes a couple of steps back. "Did I neglect to mention I tweaked the delivery system? Now, with the help of adrenaline the effect is almost instant."

Another roar and my shield flares hot.

"How much adrenaline do you think is coursing through Xavier's veins right now?"

Another tremendous crash has me turning toward the empty doorway. A hot wave of panic washes through me and catches in my throat. *Holy crapballs.*

Panic. I've got full panic. I need a panic room.

One on every floor.

"Bruin, I'm in trouble." My bear is back in a rush and takes form between the vampires and me. "Hold them back. I need to get upstairs."

Bruin rushes the three and I'm quick to move. I take the stairs at a run, two at a time, and cut the distance from me to the only place I can think of to hide from a deranged vampire. *"Detect Secret Space."*

I cast the spell and push it out with as much force as I can. Please make this easy for me. My Spidey-senses tingle like mad, and I follow my instincts to the end of the hall. In the bedroom on the left, I close the door and press my hand on the frame.

"Wood Wall." The wood of the door seals to a solid sheet, and the hinges and latch disappear.

I run to the closet and open the double doors. It's a walk-in, and I rush to the cedar panel on the sidewall. Gripping the edges, I fumble and feel along the seams and the top looking for a—

The latch clicks and I open the door. *Yes!*

No!

Cat crap on a cracker. The door is the same metal vault as the one downstairs, complete with a hand-scanner security pad.

"What kind of panic room screens panickers? That's rude."
Rushing out of the closet, I consider my options.

The crash to my right has me glancing at the door. Xavier has punched a fist-sized hole through the solid wood slab and is doing a Jack Nicholson impression from *The Shining* that will haunt my dreams forever.

His eyes are glowing scarlet and wild.

So much for his beliefs in proper decorum and Confucian principles. He sniffs the air and rips at the edges of the hole. Wood cracks and splinters, unable to withstand the incredible strength of a vampire.

I call my body armor and run for the window.

With no time to open it, I throw myself full-bodied through the mullioned panes of glass.

I'd like to say I tuck and roll in an elegant display of druid physical prowess, but that would totes be a lie.

I catch the sill with one of my feet and take a sideways tumble in the air. *"Slow Descent."*

I do slow, but I take a bad bounce when I hit the lawn and roll like a spastic ragdoll down a slope. When the ride comes to a full stop, I get my feet under me and—

The hit comes from behind and spins me like a top.

I barely get time to call Birga before I'm pinned to the ground gasping. My wrists are pinned to the ground, his strength too much to fight. *"Bestial Strength."*

The addition to my power is huge, but it's not enough to get out from under a vampire in the throes of *cântând sânge*.

Try as I might; there's no stopping him.

Xavier opens wide, lunges forward, and bites into the side of my neck.

The pain is excruciating and sharp—at first. Seconds later, the fight drains out of me, replaced by a lethargic fog. Everything is fine. S'all good. My mind drifts and I relax against the lush grass in a drugged haze. Being juice-boxed by the vampire king isn't the way I pictured myself going down for the final count.

Honestly, even worse than me dying on the day my nieces came into this world and my brother and father plan to tie the knot—or knots—I guess, is that Da has earned the ultimate I told you so.

Vampires are brutal murderers, Fi. Don't sugar coat it or ye'll get yerself killed.

You win, Da.

Not that he'll look at it that way…but it's true.

I close my eyes. This isn't all that terrible.

The suckling noises are kinda gross.

I try to focus on noises other than the slurping of my blood. In the distance, I hear the hum of my city: sirens, barking dogs, the horn of the island ferry crossing back and forth, the *whoosh-whoosh* of a fireplace bellows.

Weird. I'm on the back lawn of a mansion.

Whoosh-whoosh.

No. It's not a fireplace bellows.

I know that sound.

The angry shriek above me draws my fuzzy focus to the massive blue dragon descending over me. He grabs Xavier with his talons and flicks him to the side like a giant staple remover tossing an unwanted staple.

It makes me giggle.

Dart lands beside me and covers me with his wing. It's nice. He's so warm, and suddenly, I'm so cold.

There's a scuffle off to my right, but I don't have the energy to look. The roar of Garnet's lion is a comfort though. I worried about him battling in the basement for so long with so many vampires. I'm glad he's not hurt.

I'm glad for Myra and Imari too.

Dart lets out an anguished sound, and it breaks my heart. "I love you, baby boy." I stroke a patch of scales on his side. "You did well. Thanks for coming for me."

I don't want to think about the exposure issues it caused. It's mid-morning on a Friday, and the city is buzzing with activity. He's also still super-sized, so I'm sure he's visible by neighbors.

A wicked shiver takes me, and I can't stop my body from trembling.

Something shifts and Dart turns and blows fire. The heat of his flame warms my skin but doesn't touch the bone-deep chill I'm suffering from.

"Fi, we need Dartamont to stand down," Garnet says. "Xavier has regained control and needs to close the wound with his saliva. We need your help to talk your dragon down."

Uh-huh.

Garnet's words bounce around in my head, but I'm not sure what to do about them. Another shift and another shift and flame from Dart.

"Hey, buddy," Bruin says, brushing in beside me. "I need ye to shrink down and let Garnet and the vampire help her. Ye remember Garnet, aye? Ye met him the other day, and Fi said yer supposed to do what he says."

He grunts and looses a long guttural roar that says he isn't pleased with that.

"Please, Dragon," Garnet says. "I'm a friend, remember? Yours and Fi's." Garnet's voice is far away. It sounds like I'm underwater, drowning.

"She's bleeding out..."

I swallow. So, cold.

"We need to..."

CHAPTER TWENTY-FOUR

"Welcome back, Lady Druid." Garnet is standing over me looking more battered by life than usual. Blood and saline hang on the IV pole above me, flowing in more of a stream than a drip. "If it's your destiny to tempt death and escape close calls, it seems it's our destiny to worry on the sidelines."

The familiar brush of someone's touch across the pulse of my wrist brings my attention to Sloan standing on the other side of the medical exam table. "Howeyah, Cumhaill?"

"Sleepy but fine. No worries."

He chuffs. "Yer ridiculous. Of course. Why would I worry?"

I close my eyes and try to piece together what happened. I've got nothing. My hamster doesn't seem to have received the infusion of blood yet. "What happened?"

"Ye got drained almost dry by a vampire."

"I remember that. How'd I get here? Is Dart all right?"

Garnet arches a brow. "Your male is right. You are ridiculous. Yes, your dragon is fine. I had Anyx bring you here while I took him and your bear back to your grove. Bruin is staying with him to keep him calm."

"He should be okay now that I'm calm. He'll feel that in our bond and know the danger has passed."

"The two of you are truly linked that closely?"

I nod. "That's how he knew where I was and that I needed help. I'm told a dragon bond is a powerful link and it grows with time."

"The world has been without dragons for centuries. It'll be interesting to see how this all plays out."

I agree, and I'm happy to be around to witness it.

A med-tech reaches in and switches out an empty blood bag for a full one. "How long am I going to be here doing this?"

"Until ye have enough blood in ye that ye won't keel over the moment ye stand," Sloan snaps.

I make a face at him. "It was just a question. No need to get snippy."

He pegs me with a look. "If I thought fer a minute ye'd take it into yer head, I'd lay into ye about puttin' yerself in these kinds of situations."

"But?"

"I know yer too stubborn to take heed, and I'm also aware it's not all yer doin', so I'll save my breath."

"Did you tell Da?"

"No. He and Shannon have their day planned, and by the time I got here, ye were out of danger. I thought it best to let ye recover and see if yer well enough to make it to the Beltane celebration before I burst the bubble of the day's excitement."

I tap the side of my neck with my fingers and wince. "How bad is it?"

"Not as bad as it would've been if your armor wasn't activated," Garnet says. "The tensile force of a vampire lost to a feeding madness is incredible. Xavier managed to puncture your neck, but the armor saved you from him snapping your neck or tearing at your flesh."

"Yay me."

Sloan frowns. "Yay Dart."

I can't and won't argue that.

"What happened with Galina?"

"Bruin got her."

"I warned her that he's protective of me. She thought herself more dangerous than the Killer Clawbearer."

Sloan chuckles. "She was wrong."

"I thought you might like to know the Guild voted to release the three members of Xavier's siring line. Galina used them as a weapon in her vendetta. The Guild agreed that they shouldn't be held accountable for that. There will, however, need to be some kind of reparations for their actions. We have yet to hammer those out."

"Good. I think that's fair. What about Xavier?"

"He's distraught. He wanted to be here to tell you himself how sorry he is but didn't want to intrude on your recovery."

I shrug. "It's no different for him than it was for the others. He wasn't in control."

"No, but it was more personal with him. It was *you* he almost killed. He knows you weren't his biggest fan to begin with and now…well, no one can blame you for your opinion."

"I need time to recuperate and focus on our family plans this weekend. One night next week we can meet up. He can buy me dinner at BlueBlood and make it up to me. Karuna and Laurel can come too."

Garnet nods. "I'll let him know. I'm sure he'll be relieved to be allowed to make amends."

Whatevs. "If you don't mind, I'd like to lay in my bed at home. I'm sure Sloan can switch blood until I'm topped up. It takes hours, right?"

The med-tech nods. "Your blood volume was dangerously low when you arrived."

"My guy here is an amazing healer. He'll take good care of me, I promise. Can we get a to-go cooler or something?"

The tech looks at Garnet, and he nods. "It's fine. Gather what they'll need. Sloan can *poof* her back if he needs any assistance."

I sigh and close my eyes. "Thank you."

Eight hours later, I'm standing on the lush grass of our druid circle, staring at the transformation and wondering why we ever doubt Emmet. He may be a goof at times, say the most inappropriate things at the worst possible moments, and never seem to take life seriously, but when it's crunch time, he's the bomb.

Dressed to impress in black slacks, a mint green dress shirt, and with Doc wrapped around his neck and hanging like a living stole, he's as handsome as I've ever seen him and ten times happier. "You made it. I was beginning to worry. Is everything all right?"

"Of course. I ran into some trouble today, and it took longer than I expected to get sorted."

He's watching me as I speak and I know he's testing my sincerity. "As long as that's all it was."

I lean in and kiss his cheek. "I swear it. I'm on board, bro. We all are. This is an amazing moment for you."

He nods, his grin lighting up my heart. "What do you think of the ambiance?"

With the sun dropping low on the horizon, it washes the stones in a warm champagne hue. Candles lit atop each of the seventeen standing stones are flickering, their flames becoming more intense with each moment as dusk takes hold. In the center of the circle, the altar holds flowers and candles and boughs of evergreen prepared for the nuptials ahead.

"It's beautiful, Em. I'm only sorry you had to work so hard on your celebration. I let you down. I feel bad about that."

He waves that away. "You're here, you're with me, and you turned the tides of what everyone else thought too. Don't feel bad. Besides, having the day to put this all together with Ciara was amazing. We had a blast."

I find Ciara in the crowd and smile. She's wearing a smooth line, tight-fitting, champagne silk dress that flares at the knee and flows down to cover her shoes. It's modern and shows off the perfection of her slim, hourglass figure. "She's breathtaking, Em. You're a very lucky man."

"Damn straight." He lifts his hand toward Sloan and clasps palms with him. "Thanks for being the one for Fi and not Ciara. I truly believe we ended up where we belong. May we all live happily ever after."

"May the goddess be with you and bless you both."

"That's sweet of ye, Mackenzie," Ciara says, joining us. "It's a little awkward and odd, I know, but I hope ye both can be truly happy fer us."

Sloan leans forward and pecks her cheek. "We both wish ye nothing but a lifetime of happiness."

Ciara's gaze is both hopeful and guarded as she looks at me. "Is that true, Fi? I've not been sure."

I straighten and reach deep inside myself. "I had a few personal issues to work through getting here, but Sloan's right. Today is about new beginnings. From the twins to the handfastings to you moving to Toronto, these are exciting times."

The relief in her gaze boggles my mind.

How could Ciara Doyle, a stunningly beautiful, accomplished, and educated woman need my approval? "You look incredible, by the way—resplendent."

"Thanks, Fi. You don't know how much that means coming from you."

"From me? Why would you care?"

She chuckles and rolls her eyes. "Yer the heart of the family, Fi. They respect yer take on things. I made more than a few missteps with ye and worried we might not get yer blessin'."

"Well, as long as Emmet continues to smile like that, you'll have it."

She nods. "I plan on makin' sure he does."

The two of them stride off on a high, and I draw in a deep breath. It may not seem like much, but that took a lot out of me. "She's intimidated by me?" I whisper to Sloan.

He wraps his arm around my shoulder. "Ye don't realize the effect ye have on people, *a ghra*. Ye've got a way about ye that is hard to live up to."

I frown up at him. "That's crazy. I'm just me."

He squeezes my arm. "That ye are."

The two of us mill around with the other guests as night falls fully, and Dart, Bruin, Daisy, Doc, and Manx explore the forested areas around the standing stones. Gran and Granda spend a great deal of time with Da and Shannon. They've never met her, so I'm sure they're curious about the woman Da is about to marry.

Dillan, Calum, and Kevin are hanging with Dionysus for the ceremony and are in charge of keeping him out of trouble. Fingers crossed on that one.

Garnet and Myra seem a little dazzled to be having a drink with a Man o' Green, but Patty is a treasure and is putting them at ease.

"I'd like to say hello to Evan and Iris Doyle." Sloan points at where Ciara's parents are chatting with Wallace. "Will ye join me?"

"In a sec. Let me grab us a couple of drinks at the bar, and I'll meet you."

Sloan lifts his chin. "As long as ye promise yer not plannin' to run away with the bartender."

I scan Liam with an appraising gaze and shrug. "I don't know. You know how I crumble for a sharply dressed man. No promises."

He pats my ass and gives me an electrical charge.

I squeal and laugh as I head across the circle to Liam. "We just can't get you out from behind the bar."

He comes to the side of his portable stand and hugs me. "What can I say. Once the universe realizes your gift, your destiny is set."

I hear the subtext in the comment. It's more about me than him.

His gaze narrows, and he sobers. "What's wrong? What happened?"

"Nothing. I'm fine."

He shakes his head and chucks my chin. "Tell me."

I glance around to ensure no one will overhear, then I spill. "I had some trouble today with vampires. I got hurt, but I got patched up, and I don't want everyone to know and be freaking out when this is about celebrating."

"You're seriously patched up? For reals?"

I hold up my hand and raise my little finger. "Pinky swear."

He accepts the offer and links our fingers. "All right, I believe you. Please take care of yourself."

"Promise."

Stepping back, I round the bar to the customer side. "Barkeep, pour me some giggle juice."

He grins. "Coming up."

I watch him do his thing and smile. I've always loved to watch him work. All the girls love to watch him behind the bar. "Sorry you had to come to your mother's wedding stag. Is Kady mad?"

He winces. "That's one word for it, yeah. I made up some bullshit about it being last-minute and keeping it small and intimate, but the exclusion hurt her. She considers you guys friends if not extended family and doesn't know why I wouldn't be welcome to bring her."

"Kevin knows. I suppose if you feel she's around forever, you can tell her about the empowered world."

He shakes his head. "Nah. She's safer not knowing. It's hard being on the inside and yet still on the outside."

"I'm sorry about that."

He shrugs. "It is what it is, and it's better than a bullet to the chest."

I reach up and touch the pendant we made of the bullet Wallace removed when the vampires shot Liam. "I'm sorry about that too."

"Ancient history."

"Fi, you look yummy." Dionysus grapples me into his arms and plants a playful kiss on my cheek.

Huh, how very PG.

Not what I expected, but appreciated.

See, you *can* teach an old dog new tricks.

"Any chance you have an opening for going a-Maying later tonight?"

I laugh and shake my head. "Sorry. That position is full indefinitely."

"What does that mean?" Liam asks. "You going to an after-party later?"

"Of sorts," I say.

Dionysus waggles his brow. "Part of the druid Beltane celebration is going a-Maying, which means making love and sleeping outdoors."

Liam arches a brow. "All righty then. I'll be sure not to walk through the trees tonight. There are a lot of you druid folk here."

"True story."

"And I need a partner," Dionysus says.

His earnest pout makes me chuckle. "I'm flattered, as always, but I'm taken."

He runs a gentle finger over the tiara I'm wearing and sighs. "No harm in asking." He spins and takes in Liam next. "You're a good-looking guy. You busy after the festivities die down?"

Liam looks dazzled. "Dude, no. I'm into women and also spoken for."

"Disappointing. Fine. The search continues."

Liam laughs. "Should I point out, you're not a druid? You don't have to partake."

Dionysus makes a face. "Not partake? It's like you don't even know me." As Dionysus tromps off to seduce someone else, I scan the crowd and find Dillan chatting with Kevin.

I point at Dionysus. "Hey, dereliction of duty."

Dillan makes a face and hops back to it.

I laugh and take the drinks Liam prepared. "You gotta stay on your toes with him, or you'll wind up naked and mated to two swamp nymphs."

Liam laughs. "I'll take that under advisement."

By the time I meet up with Wallace and the Doyles, Sloan seems to have them wrapped around his finger. If they're not convinced that Emmet and Ciara are a lovely couple about to embark on an adventure worth getting behind, at least they're well on the way to seeing where it takes them.

"Life is wonderous," he says, winking as I hand him his drink, "and even more so when shared with an incredible woman."

He lifts his glass to Iris and winks.

"That's my guy. He's a charmer, for sure."

Dart is peeking between two stones close by, and I wave him forward. "Come here, buddy. It's fine. We're among friends tonight."

He trundles into the circle and presses his forehead into my chest. I'm a little worried about my dress, but don't let that stop me from handing my drink to Sloan and scrubbing Dart's horns. "There's my good boy. Is that all you wanted? A bit of love?"

He coos in contentment, and I chuckle at the looks of amazement on the Doyle's faces. "It's a crazy time of new experiences. Lots to look forward to."

"Aye," Evan says, "I suppose that's true."

"The babies are here," Shannon says. "Everyone come welcome the newest Cumhaills."

I kiss Dart and tilt my head over to the crowd of gathering family. "I'm going to say hello to the babies, buddy. Are you okay to go back to play with the companions?"

He gives me a rough-tongued lick and trots back to the land outside the stone circle.

The welcoming of Ireland and Carragh is quick, and everyone gives them their space. Still, it's lovely to see them if only for a moment. I'm looking forward to getting time with them after they have a chance to settle.

Kinu and Aiden both look happy but tired. I'm glad they were able to make it for the ceremony, though.

"Well then," Dora says, adjusting her green gown, "since everyone is here and currently content, let's begin the ceremony."

"Great idea." Da steps up to the altar stone and holds out his hand for Shannon. Emmet and Ciara join them. When Emmet looks back at us, he's beaming.

Dora moves to the far side of the altar, facing us, and begins. "As Beltane is the Great Wedding of the goddess and the god, it is a popular time for pagan handfastings, a traditional betrothal for 'a year and a day.' When sweet Emmet asked me to participate in his Beltane celebration, I was honored. His enthusiasm inspired me to embrace the old ways I haven't revered in centuries. I thank you for that, cookie."

He dips his chin in acknowledgment. "We're honored to have you no matter how rusty you are."

Our family chuckles. Wallace and the Doyles and even Dionysus look puzzled.

She flips back the lids of two wooden boxes. "It was my pleasure to not only prepare the ceremonial cords for tonight but to cleanse them and bless them for a future of happiness. Honestly, I've done what I can. The rest is up to you."

"We'll take it from here," Da says.

"Challenge accepted," Emmet says.

"Place the hand closest to your partner on the altar." Dora proceeds to wrap the red silk cord around the wrists of each couple in a figure-eight. "Tying the hands together symbolizes that the two have come together. Untying them later means they remain together of their own free will."

Sloan puts his arm around my hip, and I do the same. This is good. Da and Shannon deserve this.

"Now that I have you all trussed up, repeat after me. We swear by peace and love to stand heart-to-heart and hand-to-hand. Hark, O Spirit, and hear us now, confirming this our sacred vow."

The four of them repeat the vow, and voila, Emmet and Da are bound to their brides.

CHAPTER TWENTY-FIVE

After the joy of Beltane handfasting takes hold—or that might be the whiskey—the celebration gets underway. We all take a turn dancing around the maypole, but it mostly ends with one of us getting tangled hopelessly in the ribbons.

We do better at drinking around the bonfire.

"Congrats, you two." I hold up my glass as I toast Da and Shannon. "May your mornings bring joy and your evenings bring peace. May your troubles grow few as your blessings increase."

"Thank you, Fi." Shannon one-arm hugs me because her other hand remains tied to my father. "I have a feeling it won't be long until we reverse our roles. I half-expected you and Sloan to join us at the altar tonight."

"Och, don't give her any ideas," Da says. "She's young. Let her be young."

I shrug. "We talked about it, actually, but we're content to be exactly where we are in our lives. No need to change a thing."

Da *harrumphs*. "I'd like ye to change a few things, but I suppose I don't get a vote."

I hug him next. "You'll always get a vote, Da, but I hold the power of veto. Too bad, so sad."

"A head hard as rocks and as stubborn as a mule."

I laugh. "And where did I get that, huh?"

"Time fer the wish boxes," Ciara calls, pointing at a long table set up off to the side. "Emmet and I gathered everything ye need but feel free to add anything that speaks to ye. Write yer wish on one of the slips of paper while visualizing it coming to life and growing. Ye do this alone or with yer partner."

Sloan finds me in the crowd and tilts his head to meet him over at the table.

"Emmet and I prepared all the boxes with a triple moon, pentacle, or heart symbol," she says. "Choose the one that speaks to ye."

Emmet nods. "The holes in the lid and the soil, seeds, and acorns are there to help your wish to grow. Sprinkle them in, mix some rose petals and add the symbols you want to harness. We made cards with lists to help you choose."

I join Sloan at the table. Then everyone is there. He picks up the list and hands it to me.

Love & Marriage - gingerbread

Abundance - silver coin

Difficult Task - glove

Hearth & Home - thimble

Seeking the Truth - a sprig of rosemary

Health, Healing, Renewed Strength - blue & green ribbon entwined

Happiness, Good Luck - cinnamon stick

Seeking Knowledge - apple

To Find A Lost Item - feather

Protection - an old iron key

The two of us grab our slips of paper and cover them to keep the other from peeking. I fold mine up and slide it under the dirt and Sloan does the same.

"There aren't enough iron keys to keep yer sister from harm's way," Sloan says. "Sorry, folks, I need them all. And pass us some blue and green ribbons."

That gets a round of laughter.

"You're hilarious." I select a gingerbread penis and place it in my box. "Let me guess, Emmet was in charge of the gingerbread."

Ciara laughs. "How'd ye guess?"

We get our box set up the way we want it and wait for our instructions. Emmet points at the seventeen stones. "Ciara and I thought we could each pick a stone and bury our boxes at its base. Then it will kinda be our stone going forward."

Cooleroo.

"Which one is speakin' to ye, *a ghra?*"

Calum and Kevin are already kneeling in front of theirs, as are Da and Shannon, Gran and Granda, Evan and Iris, Dillon, and Aiden. He took Kinu and the babies home right after the handfasting but returned with Kinu's insistence.

"How about this one?" I ask.

Sloan nods. "It's as good as any. Would ye like to do the honors?"

"Yes, thanks." After handing him our wish box, I hike my dress up over my knees and kneel on the grass. Pressing my palms to the ground, I connect with the soil beneath my palms. *"Move Earth."*

The process reminds me of Morgana's grimoire buried deep in the ground in the cemetery behind our house. I need to figure out a better long-term spot for it, especially with the Culling coming.

That's a problem for another day.

Once our wish box is planted and ready to grow, I replace the earth and Sloan helps me up. "What did you wish for, hotness?"

He grins. "Och, if I tell ye, it won't come true."

"Fine then, I'm not telling you mine either."

He nods. "Fair is fair."

We finish that and join the rest of the gang in the center. Emmet's grinning and holding a clipboard. "That concludes our

Beltane celebration except for those of us embracing the going a-Maying part of the evening. If you are, please stay after class for your glamping assignments."

"We have assigned spots?" Calum asks.

"Of course. I set up lovely outdoor tents with gossamer drapes and memory foam mattresses. Sightlines have been checked and double-checked, and no one is to drift out of their allotted areas or risk the grossness of stumbling on a family member *in flagrante delicto*."

I laugh. Only Emmet.

"For everyone leaving, we thank you for coming to the first-ever Cumhaill Beltane celebration. We hope you had a blast. We love you all. Safe home."

There's a round of hugs and well-wishing as everyone prepares to depart.

Emmet holds up his hand. "One last thing. It's tradition to close the Beltane celebration with song, and since this is Ciara's special night, I left it to her to choose our closing song."

She bows her head, her crystal laurel catching the light of the fire. "The choice practically made itself. This will forever be our song because it's impossible to hear it without thinking of Emmet."

Ciara raises her hand, and I start to giggle. I think I know what's coming. When the redneck lyrics of a country song blare at top volume, I burst out laughing. The fiddle picks up in the clearing, and a strobe of disco lights starts flashing up into the night sky.

"Ye didn't," Da groans. "Must we do this again?"

I snort and grab Sloan's arm, pulling him into the clearing to dance. "Oh, we *must*."

"Hells yeah," Emmet says, grabbing Ciara and swinging her on his arm.

Cotton Eye Joe blares through the air, and the sound-activated strobe machine picks up on the frenetic beat. Colored lights explode into the sky and bounce off the stone monoliths.

It's perfect.

No matter what chaos gets thrown at us, no matter what we're put through, at the end of the night, when our family and friends are around—life is good.

Thank you for reading – *A Fated Bond.*

While the story is fresh in your mind, and as a favor to Michael and me, click <u>HERE</u> and tell other readers what you thought.

A star rating and/or even one sentence can mean so much to readers deciding whether or not to try out a book or new author.

And if you loved it, continue with the Chronicles of an Urban Druid and claim your copy of book ten:
A Dragon's Dare

NEXT IN SERIES

The story continues with *A Dragon's Dare*, available at Amazon and Kindle Unlimited.

Claim your copy today!

AUTHOR NOTES - AUBURN TEMPEST

WRITTEN JULY 11, 2021

Here we are again, wrapping up another adventure with Fiona and the fam jam. What a ride it's been. Michael and I have been so thankful for the popularity of the series and how you have embraced Fiona and her crazy cast of characters into your lives.

What you may not know is that Fi is modeled after my zany niece Emily. Many of the quips and sayings I use in the book I've written down as Em breezes through the room or a rant. She's hilarious, and honest to a fault, and says whatever comes to her mind without filtering.

She is my Fiona—and yes, she talks like that.

She once told me she was so full she could fart a shrimp. She uses words like totes and sack out with your rack out and a million other crazy things in her everyday vernacular. That's one of the things we love most about her.

She's odd and pure joy and a disaster waiting to happen.

She once tracked dog shit through a sacred synagog on a school trip. She put Purell in her eyes in public school when her friend got pink eye... She is genuinely, uniquely herself.

I've had a few reviewers on a rant about the way Fi talks and relates to the world asking me to please stop and make her talk like a regular, normal, adult. My answer to that is... how boring. If Fi talked and acted like everyone else, she wouldn't be Fi. She's not a regular adult, she's a twenty-three-year-old, kind-hearted, oddball.

And look where that brought me—here to you.

Blessed be,
Auburn Tempest

AUTHOR NOTES - MICHAEL ANDERLE

WRITTEN JULY 9, 2021

Thank you for both reading this story and these author notes in the back!

A little behind-the-scenes.

So, in order to publish the quantity of well-edited stories LMBPN puts out *it takes a village.* Ok, I perhaps expanded the total to make it seem HUUGE and completely swiped it from a book.

So honestly, it's a handful of people located around the world.

The ringmaster of the editing crew is Lynne Stiegler whom I have spoken about (in glowing terms, I assure you) in books before. However, this time I'm going to drop her here front and center into these author notes to give you a peek into the backend of managing the editorial crew.

Here's Lynne!

<Lynne starts babbling>

I have no idea why Michael Anderle thinks an editor can write, but here goes.

When I first joined the team in May 2017, I had little idea about what I was getting into. Over the next four years, this place grew to consume my life (in a very good way).

At first, it was me, Michael, and the ever-amazing Steve Campbell, the Ops manager, aka ZenMaster Walking®. Then Michael had the brainchild of publishing four hundred (400) books in 2019, and I had to up my game (to be fair, he gave us four months' warning). The others were on their own. What to do? I located some other editors, two who didn't work out and one who did—in spades.

That is the incredible Judah Raine, editor extraordinaire, who lives and work in Durban, South Africa. She has been with me through thick and thin over the past three years, and she is an amazing addition to the team!

She and I were editing over a million words a month each during LMBPN's most prolific periods (most I ever personally did was 1.5 million), working seven days a week almost twenty-four/seven. After some months of that, we got sensible and added another editor to the team, the inimitable Tracey Byrnes.

Tracey, who lives in the US, joined us at the height of the pandemic in 2020, and she has been invaluable ever since. She bravely hops in wherever we need her, and she did her own almost million words in June of this year.

We also have Nat Roberts, amazing author and all-around wonderful person, who does editing for us from time to time. She lives in England. Fortunately, Tracey and I are night owls, so the whole team is on almost the same schedule, global time zones notwithstanding.

I am the luckiest person in the world to have this team!

Also, those who don't know Michael might not be aware of his kind and giving spirit, which manifests whenever someone is in need. In fact, even most who know him are not, but he is incredible, and he does it all with such grace. He's also endlessly creative, which will ensure that y'all have books for years to come.

He has created a major work of art and a home for many at LMBPN, and I for one will be forever grateful.

I appreciate Lynne suggesting she can help with the author notes as I enjoy both allowing readers to see behind the scenes and bringing out many of the unsung heroes that accomplish amazing results to bring you, the readers, our stories week in and week out.

Ad Aeternitatem,

Michael Anderle

ABOUT AUBURN TEMPEST

Auburn Tempest is a multi-genre novelist giving life to Urban Fantasy, Paranormal, and Sci-Fi adventures. Under the pen name, JL Madore, she writes in the same genres but in full romance, sexy-steamy novels. Whether Romance or not, she loves to twist Alpha heroes and kick-ass heroines into chaotic, hilarious, fast-paced, magical situations and make them really work for their happy endings.

Auburn Tempest lives in the Greater Toronto Area, Canada with her dear, wonderful hubby of 30 years and a menagerie of family, friends, and animals.

BOOKS BY AUBURN TEMPEST

Auburn Tempest - Urban Fantasy Action/Adventure

Chronicles of an Urban Druid

Book 1 – A Gilded Cage

Book 2 – A Sacred Grove

Book 3 – A Family Oath

Book 4 – A Witch's Revenge

Book 5 – A Broken Vow

Book 6 – A Druid Hexed

Book 7 – An Immortal's Pain

Book 8 – A Shaman's Power

Book 9 – A Fated Bond

Book 10 - *A Dragon's Dare*

Misty's Magick and Mayhem Series – Written by Carolina Mac/Contributed to by Auburn Tempest

Book 1 – School for Reluctant Witches

Book 2 – School for Saucy Sorceresses

Book 3 – School for Unwitting Wiccans

Book 4 – Nine St. Gillian Street

Book 5 – The Ghost of Pirate's Alley

Book 6 – Jinxing Jackson Square

Book 7 – Flame

Book 8 – Frost

Book 9 – Nocturne

Book 10 – Luna

Book 11 – Swamp Magic

Exemplar Hall – Co-written with Ruby Night
Prequel – Death of a Magi Knight
Book 1 – Drafted by the Magi
Book 2 – Jesse and the Magi Vault
Book 3 – The Makings of a Magi

If you enjoy my writing and read sexy/steamy romance, my pen name for the books I write in Paranormal and Fantasy Romance is JL Madore. You can find me on Amazon HERE.

CONNECT WITH THE AUTHORS

Connect with Auburn

Amazon, Facebook, Newsletter

Web page – www.jlmadore.com

Email – AuburnTempestWrites@gmail.com

Connect with Michael Anderle and sign up for his email list here:

Website: http://lmbpn.com

Email List: http://lmbpn.com/email/

Social Media:

https://www.facebook.com/LMBPNPublishing

https://twitter.com/MichaelAnderle

https://www.instagram.com/lmbpn_publishing/

https://www.bookbub.com/authors/michael-anderle

OTHER LMBPN PUBLISHING BOOKS

Sign up for the LMBPN email list to be notified of new releases and special deals!

https://lmbpn.com/email/

For a complete list of books published by LMBPN please visit the following page:

https://lmbpn.com/books-by-lmbpn-publishing/